PRAIS SHADOWS

"Michael Kelly's Shadows and Tall Trees is a smart, illuminating investigation of the many forms and tactics available to those writers involved in one of our moment's most interesting and necessary projects, that of opening up horror literature to every sort of formal interrogation. It is a beautiful and courageous journal."

—Peter Straub, Best-Selling Author of *Ghost Story*, and
A Dark Matter

". . . elegant digest-sized format and consistently good supernatural, ghost, and weird fiction...This looks to be the perfect magazine for aficionados of low-key horror. Bravo!"

—Ellen Datlow, *The Best Horror of the Year 3*

"Like mist creeping though a northern forest, this journal of the ghostly and ghastly will have you starting at sudden noises, and recoiling from half-glimpsed faces in the shadows on the wall."

—Laird Barron, Author of *The Croning*, and *Occultation*

"Shadows and Tall Trees comes on like the wendigo, or a will-o'-the-wisp, consistently quiet and ominous and delicious and very welcome indeed."

—Glen Hirshberg, Author of *The Book of Bunk*, and
Motherless Child

"Shadows & Tall Trees is a really strong collection of stories, a high quality product with high quality writing. I thoroughly recommend it."

—Anthony Watson, Dark Musings

"Shadows and Tall Trees appears to have a bright future and may well become one of the places to go to find new weird fiction."

—*Speculative Fiction Junkie*

"Just received a copy of the latest issue of this superb little publication from Undertow Books. The editor, Michael Kelly, is creating something quite special here, I feel. Expertly produced and presented, an example of what a horror publication of this type should 'feel' like when you pull it out of the envelope. Another great selection of tight, quiet horror stories in this issue, stories that unsettle and cause the reader to think beyond the parameters of the ordinary. Issue 2 contained a story 'Back Amongst the Shy Trees' by Steve Rasnic Tem that any writer of horror ought to aspire to.
—Danny Rhodes, *The Crow's Nest II*

"Editor/publisher Michael Kelly's aim, is, professedly, to offer good quality short fiction in the horror genre. I can testify that he's doing a great job and the third issue of Shadows & Tall Trees provides further evidence of his continuous success in that difficult task. The journal (which actually has the format and the layout of a short story anthology) manages once again to recruit excellent writers at the top of their game. I guarantee it's worth your money."
—Mario Guslandi, *Horror World*

"Kelly is doing a wonderful job collecting and publishing authors who really have significant literary talents."
—Benjamin Uminsky, Goodreads

Shadows &
TALL TREES

ISSUE 6
Spring 2014

EDITOR | Michael Kelly

COPY EDITOR / PROOFREADER | Courtney Kelly

An Imprint of

ChiZine Publications

First Edition

Shadows & Tall Trees 6, edited by Michael Kelly
Cover artwork © 2014 Santiago Caruso
Cover design © 2014 John Oakey
Interior design, typesetting, layout © 2014 Samantha Beiko

Distributed in Canada by
HarperCollins Canada Ltd.
1995 Markham Road
Scarborough, ON M1B 5M8
Toll Free: 1-800-387-0117
e-mail: hcorder@harpercollins.com

Distributed in the U.S. by
Diamond Book Distributors
1966 Greenspring Drive
Timonium, MD 21093
Phone: 1-410-560-7100 x826
books@diamondbookdistributors.com

ISBN 978-0-9813177-3-1

Undertow Publications
Pickering, ON Canada
www.undertowbooks.com
undertowbooks@gmail.com

Printed in Canada

Dedicated to
the memory of Joel Lane
(1963 – 2013)

Shadows & Tall Trees is an annual anthology, in print and eBook format, of strange and weird tales. Many of our stories have been selected for reprint in various "Best Of" and "Year's Best" anthologies. We publish stories of exceptional literary merit.

Submissions of exceptional literary merit, up to 7500 words, are welcome and are assumed to be original and previously unpublished. Please do not query about reprints. Unsolicited manuscripts accepted for publication are paid at 1-cent-per-word to a maximum of $50. Contributors will also receive 2 copies of the journal.

All correspondence, including submissions, should be sent to: undertowbooks@gmail.com

For detailed guidelines, please visit the website:

www.undertowbooks.com/submissions

TABLE OF CONTENTS

EDITOR'S NOTE

Welcome to volume 6 of Shadows & Tall Trees. If you've read any of the previous issues you'll notice we've moved away from our journal format to a yearly trade paperback and eBook anthology. We've doubled our size, bringing you twice the amount of fiction, all, we trust, to our usually high standards.

Alas, I had planned on running some non-fiction but did not receive any suitable submissions.

The other big news is that Undertow Publications, home to *Shadows & Tall Trees*, and the *Year's Best Weird Fiction*, is now an imprint of ChiZine Publications, and will be available worldwide through ChiZine's established distribution channels. If all goes well, you may see more titles from Undertow Publications.

Anthologies are a hard sell. I love short stories. I love the way they whisk you away to another place. I love how compact short stories are. You can experience so much in 5 minutes, 20 minutes, what have you. I love their language, their diversity, and the way they convey so much in so little words. They are magic. They are, to me, the perfect art form. I will always champion the short story. It's a lot of work to put together an anthology. But it's worth it.

Here's to many more years of magic.

Michael Kelly
April, 2013

To Assume the Writer's Crown: Notes on the Craft
Eric Schaller

Introduction

Bookcases proliferate in my home. I could write *house* rather than *home* but, to me—and I think you and I may be alike in this regard—books define my *home*. One of my bookcases is a magnificent construction of bird's-eye maple. Another is of oak: warm wood with swinging glassed doors. These represent my Platonic ideal of book collecting. Most of my bookcases, sadly enough, are of the *requires-some-assembly* variety and, as soon as one bookcase is filled, I assemble another. There is never enough space. Books pile on their shelves, on my couch, on the floor. My cats knock over the books and piss on them.

I'll let you in on a secret. Although I call myself a writer of fictions—my publications confirm this assessment—much of my library consists of non-fiction. The first book I bought, at the innocuous age of six, was a biography of Cortez. Cortez the Killer, as Mr. Neil Young would have it. One of my most influential books was *Two Little Savages*, which under the guise of a children's tale has much to instruct on wilderness lore. Reading that book, I painted my face with blue clay, deciphered and followed animal tracks, and devised snares to trap pigeons. The following Christmas, my parents gifted me with a wonderful book on knot tying. I still own all three of these books.

To Assume the Writer's Crown

But it is not to discuss my facility with knots that I began this essay; rather it is on the craft of writing itself. The secret within the secret I now confess is that my bookshelves contain as many books on writing as they do writings themselves. I exaggerate, but the truth is that I have always loved the non-fiction that proliferates around fiction as much, if not more, than the fiction itself. In this essay, I will share with you some highlights of what I have learned over the years. Relax. Pour yourself a drink. The next few minutes are ours and ours alone. Writing is not all fun and games, but let's pretend for the moment that it is.

First Things First

In my estimation there are but two classes of writers: those who write and those who don't. "But how can anyone be a writer if they don't write?" you of the first contingent assuredly exclaim. By their own proclamation is my answer. Moreover, I believe this second contingent is in the majority. They are the jealous fools, who upon hearing you have written a story or two, perhaps a dozen, in my case over a hundred, none of which they have read, will declare themselves writers of equal merit, if only... These two words ("If only...") are the key to their thwarted ambition. If only they had not been engaged in more lucrative enterprises. If only they had not raised a family. If only they had found the time to set their words to paper.

If only...

These wasters have assumed the writer's crown without any more exertion than the flapping of their puerile lips. Run, I say, should you meet such a *writer*, run with all alacrity and hide. Above all, do not show them this essay, for they will claim the ideas for their own and, never recognizing the contradiction, scoff that you should sympathize with it.

The Cage of Words

The key to successful fiction, its heart, its soul, is in the character. Some imbeciles will state that a genre, like science fiction, is more about the idea than the character. But an idea without a character is a bodiless brain. Even the most idea-driven science fiction employs characters to carry the reader through the story.

How then to best capture a person in words?

There is the obvious possibility of describing the character's physical features. For instance, a woman—blonde hair, blue eyes, tanned—so close to a cliché that you could be arrested for artistic delinquency. Instead, how about: hair a sun-bleached blonde, eyes the silvery-blue of beach holly, skin a deep natural tan. This description suggests something of the woman's history but at the expense of a truckload of adjectives. All the reader now knows is that the character spends a carcinogenic amount of time in the sun. Let me give you the scientific name for that variety of cancer: *longinquus*. That's Latin for *boring*.

Physical description is wasted unless it is freighted with emotion. David Morrell, in *Lessons from a Lifetime of Writing*, advises writers to emphasize "the *effect* that a character's appearance has on others." To revisit our example: the woman, her blonde hair disheveled, her skin slick with sweat, turned at my approach, her eyes hunted...

Hunted? Haunted, I meant.

The Pathetic Fallacy

This phrase, coined by John Ruskin, was intended as a pejorative against attributing human emotions to nature, of having the universe sentimentally reflect the state of your characters. In my opinion, Ruskin's concern points to the effectiveness of this technique, none having employed it to more success than Edgar Allan Poe ("The Fall of the House of Usher"). Let's give it a shot with our female character. Note how I use this technique to capture her essence:

Mary—for so I shall call my female character—has gone for a run on a blustery October afternoon. She always runs when she's troubled. What has happened? She's thinking about her boyfriend and the gossip that he was seen at the movies with another girl that looked a lot like her. Mary feels a raindrop on her cheek and glancing up sees clouds clotting darkly above the rooftops. How could he cheat on her? How could he touch another girl? The wind gusts, her flesh prickles, and she wishes she'd worn sweats instead of shorts. There's not far to go, just a shortcut through a wooded lot. She gulps air. Smells evergreen. A bird trills, and for the briefest of moments she smiles, a toothy smile at this wonderful inconsequential song in the face of the coming storm. Where is that bird? Why the hell did he do what he did with that girl? Why did he fondle her secret places? There's a slippery movement beneath the pines and then a tug at Mary's shoulder. Mary lashes out. She stumbles. Her hand tears at leaves. Wet fragments stick to her fingers. She's on her knees. Thunder cracks and she's dragged forward. Her cheek smacks metal. Her nose, erupting blood, is engulfed in a carpet that reeks of mildew and cat piss. She screams. Too late. The door of the van slams. Trapped.

THE BARE NECESSITIES

Frank O'Connor wrote, "There are three necessary elements in a story—exposition, development, and drama. Exposition we may illustrate as 'John Fortescue was a solicitor in the little town of X'; development as 'One day Mrs. Fortescue told him she was about to leave him for another man'; and drama as 'You will do nothing of the kind,' he said."

This is, in fact, the universal struggle of the author with the written word, with his or her characters. Consider the following:

"The author lived in an oppressively large farmhouse at the end of gravel road.

"One day he decided to write a story.

"'You'll do nothing of the kind,' Mary said."

THE WORST ADVICE

David Morrell describes how he once heard a teacher, intending to simplify the writing process, exhort his students to imagine their stories as movies and to then write what they saw. A fool teaching fools! The limitation of this advice is that it only engages the sense of sight. Writing grants you the supernatural ability to spy inside a character's mind, revealing thoughts and experiences, and engage *all* the senses. Let's return to my character, *our* character, and bring this sensory information into play.

AN EXERCISE

There is just one rule for this exercise: you may not use the sense of sight for your description. Imagine yourself in a darkened room, a basement. I recommend that you try this for real. You descend the stairs, running your hand along the wall to maintain balance. Feel the texture. Describe it. Do the stairs creak? What is the smell of the basement? How is it floored: poured concrete, gravel, barren earth? This is called "Setting the Scene."

Now, to introduce some drama: stepping out onto the basement floor, you turn. What was the sound you heard? A moan. A distinctively feminine moan, in fact. Does this excite you? You come across the body of a woman. Is she naked? You have only your non-visual senses to inform this decision. Her feet, which you encounter first, are certainly bare.

What's this twined around her ankles? Something hard, serpentine: the plastic-coated metal of a bicycle chain. The woman is bound to a chair. What kind of chair? You can determine this through your senses of touch, smell, and yes, even taste.

The woman is cold, as one must expect of a body without the comforting benefit of clothes, but just as assuredly alive. Her skin prickles at your touch. Her calf muscles tighten yet she does not struggle. Her breaths come short and shallow like submerged hiccups. The skin on her legs tastes of salt as if she had been swimming, or running. Her knees are skinned. Her pubic thatch, to your surprise, is shaved, scented, as if in preparation for a boyfriend.

For you?

You avoid her breasts. You don't want her to get that idea. Nevertheless when your hand trails past her shoulder, brushing her neck for the barest instant, she moans again. You can't tell whether from fear or desire. Her cheek shivers.

To Assume the Writer's Crown

Note the texture of her skin: the fine hair (the cliché of peach fuzz comes to mind), the puffiness, the *fleshiness,* all ending abruptly at the bony lower orbit of her eye. She has, you discover, clenched her eye lids shut. Even though it is dark. Even though she cannot see you. She has not, in fact, ever knowingly observed you.

Mary is not entirely naked as it turns out. She wears a misshapen hat: a bird made of felt fastened to her head with a stretchy band that runs under her chin. The hat was probably once a cat's toy but has been re-purposed. It smells of cat pee, that's for certain.

Write What You Know

One of the most limiting writing recommendations ever set to paper, if interpreted literally. Do you want to produce nothing but thinly disguised autobiographies? Consider a re-interpretation: write from the emotions that you know. Write, as so many books on my shelves implore, from what you care about.

For me, it always returns to a woman, a girl from my high school. Her name was Mary (not her real name) and she had the most gorgeous smile. I think she needed braces, but braces would have ruined that smile. Her smile appeared without preamble in response to the school heaters burping in winter, the rhymes of children jumping rope, the crackle of the PA system. It could light up the room, as they say. Part of me loved her, but I had never pursued a woman before. I sat two seats behind and across the aisle from her on the school bus. Sometimes she wore a red sweater. On those days she rhythmically pressed her thighs together, revealed only by the tension in her legs. I imagined myself as her. I imagined how the cloaked space between her legs felt in response to those rhythms.

Then I dreamed of Mary. Initially she was how I knew her: sweet, innocent, smiling. But she changed. She devolved. Have you ever seen the Bugs Bunny cartoon in which skinny, wise-cracking Bugs devolves into a burly Paleolithic version of himself? Something similar happened with Mary. In my dream, she became coarse and broad, hairy and hulking.

Bigger than me. After that, I could never look at Mary the same way again.

In every story since then, I've tried to infuse my female characters with that initial element of desire I felt for Mary, and I've tried to avoid the subsequent revulsion. On the first score I've had some success. On the second, perhaps less.

DIALOGUE I

Character: Why are you doing this to me?
Author: (no answer)

THE NARRATOR

Who to choose as the narrator for your tale? The girl? She may scream from blind fear until she is hoarse. She doesn't know that she is locked in a basement far from town and the chances she will be heard are slim to none (and slim has already left town). This dawning realization can be communicated from her point of view. But how much more damning if the narrator should be someone else, unnamed, who can describe the same scene from a contrasting viewpoint. Black humour can be effective here, especially when the victim is of limited perception, a girl whose ideas of horror are blinkered by some appallingly bad movies. "Is the key to the lock behind my eye?" she asks. There is of course no answer, and the reader is left wondering if the girl will, in fact, gouge herself blind on the chance that this will illuminate the basis for her captivity.

A remark about Oedipus would be apropos, but would be lost on our character. Hence the silence of the narrator with regards to the victim. But not in regards to you, the reader, who one hopes will understand (relish?) the reference.

One of my favourite stories is by Kipling, the most black-humoured piece I have ever read, and one of the most instructive. The story is called "The Record of Badalia Herodsfoot." It is not frequently reprinted, but it does appear in *The Oxford Book of Short Stories* (1981 edition), as chosen by V. S. Pritchett. "Her husband after two years took to himself another woman, and passed out of Badalia's life, over Badalia's senseless body; for he stifled protest with blows." After that it goes from bad to worse for Badalia, ending in the tragedy of her death. Readers—it's a fact—do not like weak-willed characters that are buffeted by events like tissues in a purse. However, under the guise of humour, any crime may be committed with impunity.

REVISION

The sad fact of writing is that nothing will match your initial vision. Our character Mary may seem perfection itself. But try this experiment—I certainly have—leave her alone in the basement for a few days, a week, a month, and then return. Formerly an angel, she will now be dirty, rank as onions, a clawing creature of the pit. With revision, she may once again approach that original ideal. Below, I suggest several strategies for revision.

The Kingectomy: Even Stephen King, one of the most prolific writers of our age, in his book *On Writing*, describes how he excises 10% of a story to achieve final form. Perhaps your character could use a *diet*, her excess ten percent whittled away symmetrically. But don't feel so constrained. How about amputating a leg just below the knee? A one-legged runner has narrative possibilities.

The Straubing: In Peter Straub's short story, "Blue Rose," there is a description of how the narrator inserts a thick needle into the arm of his hypnotized brother. This scene, running for pages, captures the obsession with which an author focuses on a particular scene in need of revision. The author might, for example, flay a finger tip, then deciding this is not sufficient, retract the skin to the second knuckle. Blood dribbles. Something is still not right. The author extracts strands of muscle with a pen point, exposing pink nubs of bone. The author licks and tastes the tainted calcium, then gnaws at it to reveal the divine white bone of memory.

The Flauberation: Gustave Flaubert is quoted as saying, "I spent the morning putting in a comma and the afternoon removing it." Do you remember Mary's silvery blue eyes? She has only one now, having lost the other in a misguided attempt for freedom. But didn't she function better with binocular vision? Editing is sometimes harder than even Flaubert could imagine.

DIALOGUE II

Author: I'm doing this for your own good.
Character: (no answer)

THE WILLING SUSPENSION OF DISBELIEF

First coined by Samuel Coleridge, this is one of the most cumbersome phrases to make its way into common parlance. Yet...

ESCAPISM

I thought I had my character trussed up tighter than a Thanksgiving turkey. I did mention my facility with knots, did I not? I used a good granny knot—not the most elegant choice, but a damn sight better than a square knot.

A knot?

Wasn't it a bicycle chain ("hard and serpentine")? A fumbling inconsistency. So easy to overlook. But, just like that, Mary is

going

going

gone.

Really and truly gone. Not a stray hair remaining. Not a whiff of her sweet salty skin. Only this: that strange felt hat with its stretchy band. A felt bird. Yes, it's true. My character has gone and given me the bird.

ON SYMBOLS

In spite of what your English teacher may have told you, there are no hidden meanings in stories. That doesn't mean items in a story can't take on a significance greater than themselves: an idiosyncratic felt hat, for instance.

To Assume the Writer's Crown

The Lonely Voice

How often is an author abandoned by their main character? Far too often, I'm afraid. But on those occasions of true and honest success, when every rope is knotted, every door locked, and your character left no recourse for escape, on those occasions one can spin tresses into gold, guts into glory. Consider Ursula K. Le Guin's finest story, the Hugo-award winning "The Ones Who Walk Away from Omelas." Here we have the earnest depiction of a utopia made real in its last pages by the description of the abused child held captive in the dark basement of the city. It is on the frail shoulders of that child that the whole edifice stands. Yet, for all Le Guin's willingness to exhume that child as a symbol of the horrors that create wonder, I have a feeling that should Le Guin ever read my own small contribution to the literary arts, should she ever meet me in person, she would abhor me. Abhor is not too strong a word for it.

Frank O'Connor titled his influential book on the writing of the short story, *The Lonely Voice*. We are all lonely voices. Remember this. I won't say it again, but it almost owes repeating. Abandoned by our characters, despised by those we love, the author is the lonely ghost haunting the story, refusing to relinquish it.

The Second Person

I'm all out of advice. All out of jokes, too. My main character is gone, lost due to a momentary lapse, a failure in editing, a rupture in your "willing suspension of disbelief." What is left?

Why you, my dear friend, my diligent reader. You who have followed this narrative since its inception, who wonder of wonders are still with me. It was only with your willing participation that I was able to create a character. *Our* character. I wrote the words, but you gave Mary life. You explored her, edited her. You lived with her, breathed the perfume of her flesh, and, dare I say, loved her. This narrative would not exist without you.

What is left? (I repeat myself.)

You and I. Alone, together.

Pablo Neruda, commenting on his great friend Federico Lorca, told of how Lorca would pick up prospective lovers with the line, "Let us be alone, together."

In short stories, any number of texts will warn you against the use of the second person in a narrative. Use of the second person causes a rupture in the uninterrupted dream that is, according to these texts, the ultimate goal for any true short story writer.

However, you and I are not in a short story. We stand outside the story, living our own circumspect lives — different jobs in different cities, maybe different countries, continents — knowing nothing of each other until we meet within the confines of these pages. How did this piece come into your hands? I have no idea, yet here we enter into a collusion. Ours is the faith of long-time friends. Together, we build a grand artifice. Together, we clothe our dreams in flesh. New worlds blossom in the cold, dark reaches of space. Glass cities erupt from the desert sands. A populace dances, loves, fights, and screams in the glittering streets. Together, we create and live the story of their lives.

Who is the writer and who is the reader? Neither? Both? We are all creators. We are all writers. We are alone, you and I, together.

THE GIFT

I have something for you.

A thank-you gift for having been my accomplice in this enterprise.

It's nothing much, but I want you to have it. A hat. Again, nothing much, but once upon a time it was quite fine: created by a true mad hatter. The hat is of felt. Bird-shaped. Feel how soft it is. Perhaps not so much any more. It was quite fine once but — confession time — the cats got at it. To be frank, it still smells of cat piss on occasion. Only when wet, though. Otherwise it can be quite dandyish. So I've been told. Some might call it a crown.

I trust you'll wear it.

I'm afraid I've nothing more to offer.

Onanon
Michael Wehunt

He'd missed Christmas and her last two birthdays. His mother looked the same, a husk that never seemed to age. They sat at a short oval table, her walker standing sentry on its hollow aluminum legs. Adam laid four white pages beside her. A nurse passed by the open door, humming something he almost recognized. He repeated "Mom" in a soft cadence until her face lifted and found him.

"I remember Dad telling me once," he said, "not long before his heart attack, that you were born in Norway. He said Amanda wasn't your birth name, but you never told him what it was."

She focused in on him. He had a hard time looking at her in these rare moments because she never blinked. Her eyes would dry out as she stared.

"Is that right, Mom?" He reached over and picked up the cold bones of her hand and held them. "What was your name?"

She was still. Her pupils dilated and the hazel darkened. Her thin greyed hair reached past the rails of her collarbones. He tried to remember the woman she once was, but a distance had been in place from his earliest memories. She'd spent far more time staring out her bedroom window than with her only child. He was still a boy the last time he'd gotten anything more than her sad parting sentiment. But now her mouth opened wide as though tasting the air and she said,

"Some say it is Dronning." He was amazed as ever at the crisp enunciation in her voice, despite the loss of all her teeth more than twenty years earlier.

"Dronning." Adam watched their twined hands and took a shaky breath. "I think you were mentioned in a story a girl I know wrote. Does the name Meli Gramia ring a bell?"

He thought she smiled then but she would say nothing else. Her face was directed back into her other world now. Every visit he asked her pointlessly where she'd gone when he was a boy, but today he didn't. Instead he waited in her silence a while longer before hugging her goodbye.

"You will be my son," he heard as he turned to close the door behind him. But she always said that.

You lay in the dark and heard the wet parting of my mouth. Warmth dripped onto your face from above the bed, where I clung in a corner of the room.

You closed your eyes against the scuttle of fingernails across the ceiling. When I was gone the room hung in quiet. You threw the sheets away from yourself and went to the window and twisted the blinds open. Below, figures on all fours skulked behind parked cars. Another watched you among the low bones of dogwood trees. The line of them stretching to the right, their petals gone.

In the fog of your breath you wrote MOTHER on the glass. You wrote DRONNING, and I had never filled your heart more.

He'd never thought Meli was the girl's name, even when she murmured it against his neck the night they'd met at a reading in September. She was the earthy type he'd pick out of a room first, twenty-ish, hovering at the fringe of the bookstore. Milk skin with grease spot freckles, high rounded cheekbones and dense black hair. A girl who wore scarves in late summer, more like a Jennifer or a Karen, something that buried the truth of her under a soft screen.

Afterward she'd quoted one of Adam's old stories and

complimented the rhythm of his sentences. They both agreed he was better than the guy they'd listened to. Her praise and the way her body moved and he was half in love. In bed she asked a lot of questions about his childhood and he gave answers that even he thought were foggy. She was insatiable and let him do everything but stick his tongue in her mouth.

He'd woken alone in the early morning and found the sheets speckled with flowers of her blood.

Though Meli had softly demurred when he asked about her own work, she left a manuscript beside his laptop. A surreal story about a woman who believes she has become a great queen and explains her new status to her son. It was titled "Amanda," the same as his mother and his stalled novel. From the first sentence the hours fell away and a vague despair built up around him.

Her prose read like it burned in her blood and spattered out of her. But she also wrote as if she had the time to pick up every seashell on some prehistoric beach, examine the sound inside each one until she found that inimitable tone.

He spent the day curled up staring at those twenty-nine pages, flipping back and forth to find so many passages beating with raw life. He felt sick with envy of a gift that was lifetimes beyond his own.

A few nights ago they'd run into each other—or she'd found him—at a release party for a poetry chapbook. Incestuous little circles of writers. They steeped themselves in drink and weed. Same as before, she wouldn't talk about her work, and sometime in the night she left him. He woke tangled in sheets sprinkled with more bloodstains and heavy with her scent. A new manuscript lay on the floor beside the bed. It was titled "Dronning," with the byline "from a novel by Adam Storen."

His head throbbed at the seams. He wadded the bedding up into the trash chute. Dripped whiskey in his coffee and crawled back onto the stripped mattress with the story.

It was more scene than plot, twelve hundred words that cut off with a face in the window of a mountain cabin. The strange and singing prose was still there but had diminished over some dark threshold. The words felt ill, somehow, concerned as they were with some implied creature on the periphery of the page.

Yet something in the writing opened its jaws and he could almost hear them creak as he placed his head inside.

When he got back from questioning his mother, he booted his laptop and opened the bloated file of his novel. It sagged there half-written in its window, the cursor blinking at him. *Amanda.* She was so murky to him that he couldn't even fictionalize her. His own words rode together as neat and hemmed as cars in traffic. Tuneless things. Dry as his mother's eyes. He'd been plugging square blocks into the round holes in his childhood.

Eleven months out of work for the Great American Novel. He'd cashed in the paltry 401k and it would be fumes by spring. Edging into his thirties and this was what he'd slopped his soul into. He skimmed the first chapter but couldn't make it through. He started drinking instead.

Meli's stories sat on the desk. He lifted them and let the pages flutter. He sat and wished he could have her again, bed sheets be damned. Stronger still was a sort of hatred for her and the resonance of her words. He opened the trash bin icon at the bottom of the screen. Dragged the novel into it and clicked EMPTY and a thousand hours were gone.

The nights grew into things rimmed with glare, like days with their bulbs just clicked off and afterimages burned into his eyes. He stood at his fourth floor window and watched the parked cars below. Thought he saw a face peering from the black beneath his old VW Rabbit. The bare dogwoods shivered along the street. A sense of standing within the girl's story draped over him. He heard a sound outside his door and pressed an ear to the wood, his glass clinking ice in a hand he couldn't still.

In the sleepless dark he stared at the ceiling above his bed. The threads of a memory brushed him, a boy looking up and waiting for a shape to fill the corner, until the room turned from black to grey.

According to Google, *dronning* was Norwegian for "queen." The word, the thought of it, gave him a vague panic.

He spent hours searching for Meli Gramia online. He trawled bars and readings. Chased her like a legend but she seemed less than a ghost. In the end he thought to use the words in "Dronning" to find her. Certain descriptions were a little too detailed, as though she'd spelled things out for him. Drawn him a map in prose.

So he left the city for the rust of nature. It struck him as a thing many lost and grasping writers did. He brought a fresh journal in the event she was leading him on a wild goose chase. He'd find a place to stay and take a break instead. Now that the novel was gone he meant to recapture the art of the short, which had made what faint name he'd enjoyed back in the days when people whispered about his potential.

Following the route in Meli's story trimmed a good chunk off the drive and soon he passed through the creases between mountains. The Rabbit wasn't happy as the land rose up but it made the trip without shuddering apart. He parked in the V of two low hills. The cabin was situated there in the way she'd written, "curled in the elbow of a dead giant." Beyond it the Appalachians began their long course north. He stood in the dooryard and the shallow air, holding the better part of his recent life in a cardboard box. The place was a comforting trope with its uneven, knotted planks and thin chimney jutting from the end of the roof like a straw in a cup. It was half porch. It was perfect.

He stepped through the unlocked door and breathed the dust. Put the box down on the scarred table next to the wood stove. An ancient beehive the length of his forearm hung from the ceiling. Someone had tied a yellow ribbon just above the top of it. On the narrow bed was a sheaf of papers with "Onanon" crouching in the center of the top page. Beneath it in a leaning scrawl were the words "read

& remember." He didn't move for some time. He stared at the pages and listened to a sort of quiet he'd never heard. Through the three windows dusk dropped quick and finally he went to the box and opened one of the bottles of whiskey he'd let himself bring.

In "Dronning" the writer had texted the girl. He found the story in the box and skimmed it. The number was right there on page three. Phone reception was spotty but outside he had one bar and a wavering second. Halfway through the bottle he left a voicemail letting her know he'd made it to the cabin and was about to crack open her latest opus in the lonesome bunched wilderness. He told her if that didn't get her up here he'd eat her words.

He sat at the edge of the porch in a splintered rocking chair. The sky spread and wide stars punched through to glimmer down at him. Trees gathered in the dark. Already the cold was deep, the first of November crawling down the mountainsides. He got up and slipped a hooded sweatshirt over his head and sat back down. His phone lay mute against his thigh.

My love, I hunched on the roof. The whisper of my hands rasping above on the shingles. Splinters in my palms. Beyond the streaks of the windows mountains sharpened toward you in the starred black. The world leaned in to see.

I had to leave you those years ago. I sought my home. My husbands and at last my sleep. But I woke old as earth with you in my nostrils. I woke in a new and ready season. You spoke my name and I had never filled your heart more.

"Dronning," you said, and the sound was ripe, your chin wet with drool and blood. You listened to the vacuum as I took the split moon into my mouth and the stars tipped in behind it and the sun struggled up above the peaks. You slept and the windows filled and opened.

You will be my son. Remember the nights in your child-bed.

Onanon

Late morning he set off into the wild blur of color. Spruces and pines and oaks. He thought of the girl not calling back. The journal was in one back pocket, her latest pages folded into the other. He searched for a first sentence of his own but kept circling back to the opening words of "Onanon." *I put my tongue inside you, Adam.* He bent over waiting to vomit. The sun beat almost summer-hot through the foliage. He sat down in the dead leaves and tried to read the first paragraph over and over. The words swam away and sank into his stomach where they soured. It was hours before he looked up and saw the humps of the mountains were cutting the light.

His phone buzzed on the table when he came back. A text from Meli, "did u read it." He smiled though he didn't want to and thumbed out "I'm trying. Where are you?"

The whiskey bottle cast sweetened light onto the table. He watched it shifting then went out on the porch instead. Opened the journal and licked the tip of his pencil like some old grizzled novelist and stared at the lined page.

An hour and he'd written, *Honeybees coated the hill.* He tapped the words with the pencil. He stood up and went inside and came back out with four fingers of whiskey in a plastic cup. Dark swallowed the cabin. He sat on the warped boards of the porch and listened to the crackle of movement in the trees.

After fitful sleep Adam woke to another "did u read it" on the screen of the phone. His head felt like shards rubbing against one another. He got up and noticed a photograph pinned to the floor under the night table. A shot of the cabin, framed so that the trees all reached toward it, giving the scene almost the effect of a fisheye lens. The image was washed out with a smudge of black on the roof. He rubbed at it with his thumb but it was part of the picture.

He tossed it onto the bed and found some aspirin in the cardboard box. Eggs wouldn't stay down but he wished he had them anyway. He chewed on a granola bar and texted Meli back. Circled the cabin and sat on the porch with the journal open on his lap. Noon came and the mountains felt redder than yesterday. He hadn't added a thing to the four lousy words about the bees.

He snapped the pencil in two. Left the journal behind and took "Onanon" into the woods. Against the scabbed trunk of a pine he nodded off then lurched awake to the sound of leaves breaking deeper in the trees. He heard someone laugh in a high voice. A bird strangled a cry in the distance and quiet rippled out from it.

I coupled behind stars, the first page began. At least he thought that was what he read. Earlier it had been something different but he couldn't be sure. "Dronning" was simple enough; it was strange but it was made of words. This new one made his eyes ache. Like reading worms instead. The things on the page wouldn't stay still.

On the second page he managed to read a paragraph about the mother burying her teeth in the dirt beneath a cabin before returning to her family. To ready her son and herself. Looping migraine phrases. He found himself weeping and the sun halved the sky and the letters on the page changed. *A hive swarmed and you opened your mouth. When you were a boy I folded myself into your bed and suckled you. Sowing your blood and murmuring songs of home. The time to leave was nearing. Mountains mossed red yellow gold called from their roots over the horizons. I paused, humming, and fed my saliva between your lips.*

He lay down in the leaves and watched the cloudless sky through the trees.

A second photo, creased with time, waited on the night table. A young Adam sleeping, posters on the wall of his first bedroom, the blood leached from his face in the slight overexposure. He had to squint to be certain but there was

Onanon

an insect spreading its wings beneath one eye and another bridging his lips. The vantage point looked down from a high angle above the head of the bed. His arms were tucked at his sides under the blanket and a shadow draped across his chest, trailing out from something tubelike just reaching into the left side of the frame.

He crumpled the photo and let it fall. A few minutes of furtive searching turned up nothing creepy or crawly in the eaves or along the edges of the walls. The old hive hung full of dust above the stove.

Two days up here and he was moving in circles. He took a fresh bottle of Bushmill's out into the falling cold and saw three more photographs taped to the porch posts.

In the first he was a boy again, even younger than the picture back in the cabin, cradled in his bed by a mass of black. He saw vague arms holding him, a dark blur reaching toward his mouth, but whatever it was hadn't translated through the lens.

He tore the second photo down and saw his father lying tangled in sheets and the limbs of a woman. A film of sudden sweat made him shiver. It was Meli. She should have been a child when his dad was alive, but right there was the same too-pretty face, the same spill of black hair, the same blood spotted on the sheets. Her arm lifted toward Adam, holding the camera in a lovers' self-portrait.

He peered at the last photo, his nose almost smudging it. After a moment what he was seeing clicked. Bees covered a figure seated in a wooden chair. There was enough in the frame to recognize his mother's room in the nursing home. The figure's face, openmouthed and entirely coated in the bees, was turned to a closed window.

Beyond the porch the trees gave up nothing as he scanned them, listening for the rustle of footsteps. Silence clustered and he thought of shouting Meli's name into it.

Instead he sat and wrote about his mother and father. This time he didn't embellish. He wrote of a boyhood that had always felt like a grey smear. No family portraits, the three of them smiling off toward the photographer's hand. No beach trips. Just school years and few friends and always being tired. He remembered a telescope he still felt guilty about seldom using. He chewed on a new pencil but couldn't dredge up anything so disturbing from before the day his mother climbed out her bedroom window and disappeared.

She was gone for seventeen months. He'd watched his father give up hope, not quite understanding the hope himself. His parents had done little more than live in the same house. He was thirteen when she returned one night, her clothes stained and hanging off her as she stood swaying beside his bed. She'd lost all her teeth. Two days later she was taken to the home.

A half hour drained along with the late afternoon light as he sat and tried to remember why she'd been sent away. For her own good, Dad had said. So she could feel better.

Memory became hazier still then. He remembered a woman, or women, haunting his home at night, faces reluctant to swim to his recall. Now Meli's face plugged itself in. His father had receded from him, greyed and shriveled until the week after Adam graduated high school, when he succumbed to heart failure in his sleep. Adam had spent a few more months in the house before selling it and moving to the city. He'd started writing. After only a few years his stories began to appear in journals, culminating with *Harper's* in '05 and *The New Yorker* the following year. Inevitably, he published a collection that many admired but nobody read.

He scratched this all in the journal. Even the rehashing of his lost glories eased him. But nothing both specific and profane in his memory bobbed to the surface.

He hugged himself and wished he'd brought a jacket against the chill. Meli's words were making him sick. That had to be it. They were in his sinuses and tingling in his fingers like pine needles. He went inside and found a lighter in the cardboard box. He pulled "Onanon" from his pocket and sat on the porch steps. The million trees whispered around him now.

He scraped the wheel of the lighter and held it to a corner of the pages. The words or worms twitched on the paper. *Sleep in the dirt under the floor. Dream and remember. Hear the sound of your mother loping over roads and creeks and up into the mountains. From my dry and waiting mouth the proboscis emerges.*

Onanon

The fire ate it all and in the last corner he read, *Stars swell in their bed. You reach over the mountains for them as a child for Mother's jewels. A moth or a magpie. I am come and you will be my son.*

Heat reached his fingers and he dropped the pages. Charring bits swirled into the yard and winked out. The skin on his fingertips blistered. He put his head in his hands and bit his tongue. Dark fell at last and he burned "Amanda" and "Dronning." He pulled the battery from his phone and lay in the bed and stared up into the corner.

Honeybees coated ~~the hill~~ ~~the tired leaves~~ *the new earth*

A heavy thump out on the porch woke him and he looked at the windows. Each seemed as though a face had just pulled away. He went outside into the muddled stillness and walked around the cabin twice. The stars were sprayed everywhere. The place had no foundation and he dug his way beneath it in a moment. There was a crawlspace of sorts and he wriggled inside and lay down. Black as absence. He felt something curl up beside him and he slept in its warmth, grateful.

A finger jabbed him in the ribs. The girl lay pressed against him, her face an inch from his. She licked his mouth with something too stiff to be a tongue.

He tried to scoot away and knocked his head against the underside of the cabin floor. Sunlight pried in nearly all the way around. He watched as Meli pawed at the dirt and plucked things out of it. "Hey," she said, her face streaked with filth, "open your hand."

"What do you want?"

"Just do it, open your hand."

He held his palm out and she poured a stream of small objects onto it. Human teeth. He wasn't about to count them but he thought there could be thirty or more. A full set.

"What the hell are these?" he said. "Why did you want me up here?" He tried to look away but couldn't. His mouth watered at the smell of her.

Meli smiled and he saw she had no teeth of her own. "You don't get it, do you?" she said, and laughed. Her speech was as strong and clear as his mother's. "What do you think you've been reading? Come on, you're a writer, we reached out to you in your own language. And in case you're a visual learner, I hoped those pictures I took would help you along a little quicker. I had to come up here just because you're so slow."

"Are these yours?" He shook the teeth in his hand.

"Look, I know you had trouble with the stories." She paused and inched toward him. Pushed her hand into his crotch. "Her style is a bit abstract, I guess. You do get that they were from Amanda, right? Dronning? Your mother is ready to make you in her image. Those are her teeth, remember? This is where she lived when she was a girl fresh across the ocean. She buried them here later. When she stopped needing them."

"You don't know me. That's what I remember." It was difficult not to push her down and climb onto her.

"Haven't you ever wondered about your mom? I would've thought up a hundred stories in all these years. Did you know she got out of the home last night? They're looking for her right now. If you put your battery back in you can listen to the voicemail."

"My mom's practically catatonic. She gave up on herself a long time ago and now she can hardly walk or string together a sentence." He reached to slap away her hand but she started kneading him through his jeans.

"Call it sleeping, what she's been doing all this time. It's what the Queen does until the petals open. Where'd she go when you were a kid? It's in the stories, dummy. Home to the old country, where she found her true husbands, her drones, and they fucked in fjords and fields beneath mountains different from these. She'd yearned for so long. Maybe that's when she gave up on life and took on something else."

Yearned, yes. Her fingers squeezed and everything he thought to say turned to vapour. A door slammed shut and the floor overhead gave a long stuttering creak.

"And maybe she came back with me in tow, her sprouting little girl. We purebreds have a quick gestation. A couple of years and I was menstruating. So I was able to watch you grow up. You don't remember me keeping your dad company while Mother had gone inside herself to wait. The nights I slept over or the night I had a little too much to drink and his heart stopped beating for me."

She slipped his belt open and unzipped him. He was moaning already, trying to tell her to stop it, wanting to claw his way out from under the cabin, get to the car and drive anywhere that was away. "Maybe now is our time," she said. "Onanon, without an end, and I mean you, too," and she took him into her burning mouth and he lay in the fading light and shuddered.

She climbed from under the cabin and left him still spurting into the dirt. He barely had the strength to tug his pants back up. When he emerged, the yard was empty and the sun had fallen behind the mountains. A bulging moon lifted. The teeth were still clenched in his hand. Biting his palm. He dropped them into a pocket and fastened his belt.

He took a step toward the cabin and stopped. His mother peered out at him from a grimy window. The pane lifted up and a long pale tube slipped beneath it where her mouth should have been. It tapered and petaled. The rest of her face followed, eyes opening wide into wet holes.

"Mom?" A liquid hum came from her as she wormed through the window. It took on a melody. He recalled the nurse outside her door and something stirred further back in his mind. "Mom?"

She folded down onto all fours and scrabbled across the porch. Adam ran to his car. He was behind the wheel when he realized the keys were in the cabin. His mother dropped onto the hood and placed her hands against the windshield. Long blackened fingers splayed on the glass.

He fell from the car and fled into the trees. The hum grew.

Something vast pulled at the air. His mother, he thought, singing the sky dark. Songs of home. He ran through limbs and the rising sound of birds screaming as they escaped with him.

Before long the land steepened and he came to the crook of the two hills, the cabin behind him and the far slope dipping down to the feet of the looming mountains. He saw bees dotting the ground at his feet. They had no wings. The sky was a blind expanse stretching from end to end of the earth. He gazed up at it and the stars were gone, whitish blurs in their place. As if they had been rubbed with pencil erasers.

Leaves crunched behind him as he watched the heavens flicker to violet, to orange, to the brown of rich soil. The moon broke open like a fruit and the sun was already coloring the jagged horizon again. Hands slipped around his waist and up under his shirt, barbed fingers tracing patterns on the skin of his belly. He struggled and the arms locked him in place.

Meli stepped up beside him. "Think of it as pollination," she said, "instead of trying to wrap your head around the old human evolution bit. Every hive starts with one Queen. There will be many of us. You'll get the hang of it when you feed. Look around you, the world is in bloom." He watched her tongue slip from her mouth but it kept coming, a hollow, curved thing hanging past her chin and sucking at the air. Her eyes went black and he looked away, down to the ground covered with red and yellow and gold leaves and the sluggish bees trundling over and between them.

He felt his mother's proboscis push into the base of his neck. Her humming song vibrated there and a sweet numbness spread. She caressed him and at last he was able to remember the nights she tucked him into her arms against her breast, until he fell into his childish dreams and God knew what she had done then.

"Mom," he said, his tongue hardening against the roof of his mouth.

Now she was drinking him. Three of his teeth loosened and fell from the gums. He swallowed them. A groan slipped out and his mother turned him around to her and passed his

Onanon

fluids back into his mouth blended with her own. He again tilted his head to the sky. He looked everywhere for its stars but saw only a great paling lens. A jar lowering, a world going on and on.

IT FLOWS FROM THE MOUTH
ROBERT SHEARMAN

I'd been flattered when asked to be the godfather of little Ian Wheeler, of course, but I'd had certain misgivings. When I'd met up with Max in the pub, something we liked to do regularly back then, I'd tried to explain at least part of the problem. "Oh, don't worry about the whole spiritual adviser nonsense," said Max. "Lisa's no more religious than I am; this is just to keep her parents happy." So I caved in, and went along to the christening, and watched Ian get dipped into a font, and afterwards posed for photographs in which I must admit I passed myself off quite successfully as someone just as proud and doting as the actual father and mother.

But my real concern had nothing to do with any religious aspect, and more with the discomfort of shackling myself for life to a person I had no reason to believe I would ever necessarily like. I'd had enough problems when Max started dating Lisa—Max and I had been inseparable since school, and now suddenly I was supposed to welcome Lisa into the gang, and want to spend time with her, and chat to her, and buy lager and lime for her—and it wasn't that I *disliked* Lisa, not as such, though she was a bit dull and she wore too much perfume and I had nothing to talk to her about and she had a face as dozy as a stupefied cow. It was more that she had barged her way into a special friendship, with full expectation that I'd not only tolerate the intrusion but welcome it. She never asked if I minded. She never apologized.

It Flows From the Mouth

And so it was with little Ian. I'm not saying he was a bad child. It was simply that he was a child at all. I'd never been wild about children, not even when I had been one, and I had always been under the impression that Max had felt the same, and I'd felt rather surprised that he wanted one. Surprised and, yes, disappointed. But then, Max had done lots of things that had surprised me since he'd met Lisa. And my worst fears came to be realized. On the few occasions I went to visit, I would be presented before Ian, as if he were a prince, and every little new thing about him was pointed out to me as if I should be entranced—that he had teeth, or that he could walk, that he'd grown an inch taller—sometimes I was under the impression I was supposed to give the kid a round of applause, as if these weren't all things that I myself had mastered with greater skill years ago! I just couldn't warm to my godson. It seemed to me that he was constantly demanding attention, and I could put up with that if it was only his mother he was bothering, but all too often he'd pull the same stunts on Max. Still, I tried to be dutiful, and at Christmas and on birthdays I would send Ian a present. But is it any wonder he made me uncomfortable?—this infant who had crept into my life, though his birth was none of my doing, though his existence wasn't my fault. With his strangely fat face and his cheeks always puffed out as if he were getting ready to cry. I played godfather the best I could, but I felt a fraud.

When Ian was killed at the age of three, knocked down by a car (and safely within the speed limit, so the driver could hardly be blamed), I was, of course, horrified. The death of a child is a terrible thing, and I'm not a monster. But if a child was going to have to die, then I'm glad it was Ian.

Max and I had always been rather unlikely friends, or so I was told: at school he was more popular than I was, more sporty, more outgoing. I suspect people thought he was good for me, that's what my mother said, and I resented that—I'd point out that, in spite of appearances, he was the one who had sought me out, who wanted to sit next to me in class, who waited to walk home with me. I'd been there for him when he failed his French O-levels, when he got dumped by the cricket first XI, when he first smoked, drank, snogged.

I'd been best man at his wedding to Lisa, and I'd arranged a very nice stag night in a Greek restaurant, and given at the reception a speech that made everybody laugh. And I tried to be there for Max when Ian died. We'd meet up at the pub, at first it was just like the good old days! And I'd get in a round. How was he feeling? "Not so good, matey," he'd say, and stare into the bottom of his pint. "Not so good."

We drifted apart. And I'm sorry. I would have been a good friend if he had wanted me to be. But he didn't want me to be.

Max and Lisa sold their house and moved up north. We exchanged Christmas cards for a couple of years. In the last one, Max told me they were moving again, this time overseas. He promised he would write to me with his new address. He didn't.

One evening I was at home reading in my study when there was a phone call. "Hello? Is that you, John?" The number was withheld, and so I'm afraid I gave a rather stiff affirmation. "It's Max. You remember, your old friend Max? Don't you recognize me?"

And I did recognize him then, of course; he sounded like the old Max, the one who'd call me every evening and ask for help with his homework, the one who always had a trace of laughter in his voice.

He told me he was down in the city for a 'work thing,' and the firm had given him a hotel for the night. "Would you like to meet up on Thursday?" he said. "We could go to the pub. No problem if it's too short notice. But we could go to the pub."

It was rather short notice, to be fair, but I didn't want to let Max down.

The pub was heaving with businessmen—it was just after the banks had shut, and the pub Max had chosen was right in the financial district. And I felt a sudden stab of discomfort—what if I couldn't remember what Max looked like? What if I couldn't tell him apart from all these other smart suits? (What if he couldn't remember me?) But he'd arrived first, and he was guarding a small table in the corner, and I knew him at once, he really hadn't changed a bit. He was standing up, and laughing, and gesticulating wildly to

It Flows From the Mouth

catch my attention. No, I was wrong—he *had* changed—a bit, just a bit, actually, as I got closer I could see he'd put on some weight, and his hair was grey. But I'm sure just the same could be said of me, I'm sure that's true, I'm not as young as I was, though I try to keep myself trim, you know? I stuck out my hand for him to shake, and he laughed at that, he was laughing at everything. And he pulled me into a hug, and that was nice.

"What are you drinking?" was the first thing he said. "My round, I'll get the drinks."

We stayed rather late that night, and we had a lot of beer, and I suppose we got quite drunk. But that was all right. For a while we had to shout over the crowd to make ourselves heard, and that was a bit awkward, but pretty soon all the bankers began to go home to their wives and left us in peace. He asked me what I was up to these days, and I explained it the best I could, and my answers seemed to delight him and he laughed even more. I asked him how long he would be in England.

"Oh, we've moved back now," he said. "Mum's dying, I wanted to be close. Well, not too close. But the same country is good. Back over last year, sorry, should have been in touch."

I told him that it didn't matter, he was home now, he'd found me now—and I expressed some sympathy for his mother, I remember quite liking her, when I went to Max's house she'd give me biscuits.

"We've got this lovely house in the countryside," Max said. "A mansion, really. Almost a mansion. And the garden's fantastic. Lisa has been designing that, but of course, no surprises there!" I wondered why it was no surprise, I wondered whether Lisa was famous for designing gardens, I supposed she might have been. It was the first time he'd mentioned Lisa, and I said I was glad they were still married.

We shared anecdotes about our schooldays, some of the ones Max told me I had no memory of whatsoever, so they were quite fresh and exciting. I asked him how Lisa was, and he said she was well. I didn't bring up Ian at all, and I felt a bit bad about that—but then, Max didn't bring up Ian either, and the evening was mercifully free of dead children.

I said I'd walk him back to his hotel.

"You should come and stay," he said to me as we walked the streets. He hung on to my arm. It was raining, and Max didn't seem to notice, and I didn't care. "Come and stay this weekend. It'd be lovely to see you properly. And I know Lisa would just love to have you." Before I knew it he was all over me with practical details—the best train I could catch, that they'd pick me up from the station. I said I wasn't available the next weekend, I was too busy—I wasn't as it happens, but I still didn't want him to think he could just swan his way back into my life and be instantly forgiven. I promised to come up the weekend after.

Now, I am aware that I don't come out of the following story too well. I can't pretend I understand more than a fraction of what happened when I visited Max, so I'll just tell it the best I can, warts and all. And I think you'll accept that the circumstances were very strange, and perhaps, to an extent, extenuating.

Max met me at the station in his car. I asked if it were a new car, and he smiled, and said it was. Then we drove to his house through the rolling countryside, and he talked about his new car all the way. He'd said that he lived somewhere conveniently situated for occasional commutes into London, but I'm glad I hadn't got a taxi, as the drive was half an hour at least.

Lisa was standing in the driveway to welcome us. I wondered how long she had been standing there. I had been concerned she might remember that I had often shown her a very slight resentment, but she gave no indication of it. She smiled widely enough when I got out of the car, she opened her arms a little in what might have been the beginnings of a hug. I didn't risk it, I offered her my hand. She accepted the hand, laid hers in mine like it was a delicacy, gave a little curtsey, tittered. I still didn't like her very much.

I had to admit, she looked better than I'd expected. Some women grow into their faces, do you know what I mean?

It Flows From the Mouth

They just age well, their eyes take on a certain wisdom, maybe, they just look a bit more dignified. (Whereas I have never known that to be true of men—we just get older: flabbier or bonier, it's never better.) I had always likened Lisa to a cow, and it wasn't as if she had totally thrown that bovine quality off, but the fleshier parts of her face that I had once dismissed as pure farmyard now had a certain lustre. She was beautiful. There was a beauty to her. That's what it was, and I was surprised to see it.

At first I couldn't see why Max had referred to his house as a mansion. It wasn't especially grand at all—bigger than my house in the city, of course, but you'd expect that in the sticks. They showed me their kitchen, and the stone AGA that took up half of the space. They showed me the lounge, the too—big dining table, the too—big fireplace. I made the right sort of approving noises, and Max beamed with pride as if I were his favourite schoolmaster giving him a good report card.

"Let me show John the garden!" said Lisa. "Quickly, before the light fades!" And she was excited, impatient.

And now I understood why Max had used the word 'mansion.' Because though the house was unremarkable, the gardens at the back were huge. "It's just shy of two acres," boasted Max, and I could well believe it, it seemed to stretch off into the distance, I couldn't see an end to it. But it wasn't merely the size that was impressive—on its own, the size was an anomaly, a vast tract of land that had no business attaching itself to a house so small, like tiny Britain owning the whole of India. What struck me was the design of the thing, that it was truly *designed*, there was honest to God method in the placing of all those shrubs and hedges, the garden was laid out before us like a fully composed work of art. Even in the winter, the flowers not yet in bloom and the grass looking somewhat sorry for itself, the sight still took my breath away.

"I did all the landscaping myself," said Lisa. "It was a hobby." We walked on pebbled paths underneath archways of green fern. One day the paths would lead to big beds of flowers. "I've planted three thousand bulbs of grape hyacinth," Lisa told me, "and, behind that, three thousand of species tulip—so, in the spring, there'll be this sea of blue crashing on to a shore of yellows, and reds, and greens! You'll have to come back in the spring." And every archway opened out to another little garden, different flowers seeded, but placed in ever winding patterns; there was topiary, there was even a faux maze: the design was intricate enough, I could see, but the hedges were still four feet tall, only a little child could have got lost in there.

And then, through another archway, and Lisa and Max led me to a pond. There was no water in the pond yet, this was still a work in progress. And, standing in the middle of the pond, raised high on a plinth, a statue of an angel—grey, stone, a fountain spout sticking out of its open mouth.

The wings were furled, somewhat apologetically even, as if the angel wasn't sure how to use them. Its face was of a young cherub, and I stared at it, trying to identify it—it seemed familiar, and I wondered what painting I'd seen that had inspired it, was it Raphael, maybe, or Michelangelo?

"It's Ian," said Max helpfully. And I had a bit of a shock at that. But now I could see it, of course—the infant hands, body, feet; the strangely fat face; those puffed out cheeks he had always had, now puffed out in anticipation he'd be gushing forth a jet of water.

"We gave a photograph of him to a sculptor," said Lisa. "Local man. Charming man. Excellent craftsman. Can you see the detail in that?"

"This way," said Max, "it's like Ian is always here, watching over us."

I said I could see the effect they were aiming for. And I couldn't help it, I actually laughed, just for a moment—I remembered that nasty, sulky godson of mine, and thought how unlikely an angel he would have made. If there's an afterlife, and I have no reason to believe in one, God wouldn't have made Ian Wheeler an angel, he wouldn't have wasted the feathers on him. And I thought too of how, had he lived, he'd be a teenager, or nearly a teenager?—if he were still about by now he'd be even nastier and sulkier. Instead here he was, preserved as a three year old, forever in stone, with wings sprouting from under his armpits.

I apologized for laughing. "No, no," said Lisa. "The

fountain of remembrance is supposed to make you happy."

We went back to the house. Lisa had prepared us a stew. "Only peasant stock, I'm afraid!" she said. The meat was excellent, and I complimented her on it. She told me it was venison. We opened the bottle of wine I had brought, and disposed of it quickly; then Max got up and fetched another bottle that was, I have to admit, rather better.

After we had eaten we settled ourselves comfortably in the lounge. Max took the armchair, which left me and Lisa rubbing arms together on the sofa. Max smiled, stretched lazily. "I like being the lord of the manor!" he said.

"It suits you very well!" said Lisa, and I agreed.

They placed another log on the fire, and we felt safely protected from the winter outside. But I thought there was still not much warmth to the room. It felt impersonal somehow, as if it were the waiting room for an expensive doctor, or the lobby of a hotel. It was neat and ordered, but there were no knick-knacks to suggest anyone actually lived there. No photographs on the mantelpiece.

There were more anecdotes of our childhood, and Lisa listened politely, and sometimes even managed to insinuate herself into them as if she had been part of our story all along. The wine was making me drowsy, so I didn't mind too much.

I said how happy I was they were back in England.

"Oh, so are we!" said Max, quite fervently. "Australia was all well and good, you know, but it's not like home. You can only run away from your past for so long." It was the only time Max had ever suggested he had run away at all, and Lisa frowned at him; he noticed, and winked, quite benignly, and the subject was changed.

"It's a lovely community," said Lisa. "There are village shops only ten minutes' walk from here, they have everything you really need. The church is just over the hill. And the local people are so kind, and so very like-minded."

At length Max did his lord of the manor stretch again, and smiled, and said that he had to go to bed soon. "Church tomorrow," he said, "got to be up nice and early."

"Max does the readings," said Lisa. "He's very good. He has such a lovely reading voice. What is it tomorrow, darling?"

"Ephesians."

"I like the way you do Ephesians."

I expressed some surprise that Max had found religion.

"Oh, all things lead to God," said Max. "It was hard, but I found my way back to His care."

"Maybe you could come with us in the morning, John?" said Lisa. "You don't have to believe or anything, but it's a nice service, and the church is fourteenth-century."

"And my Ephesians is second to none," added Max, and laughed.

I said that would be very nice, I was sure.

"I'll show you upstairs," said Max. "Darling, can you tidy up down here? I'll show John to bed."

"Of course," said Lisa.

I thanked Lisa once again for a lovely meal, and she nodded. "A proper peasant breakfast in the morning, too!" she promised. "You wait!"

"We've put you in Ian's room," said Max. "I hope you enjoy it."

I must admit, the sound of that sobered me up a little bit. And as Max led me up the stairs, I wondered what Ian's room could be—would it still have his toys in, teddy bears and games and little soldiers? Would it still have that sort of manic wallpaper always inflicted upon infants? And then I remembered that Ian had never lived in this house at all, he'd died years ago—so was this something kept in memorial of him? And I had a sudden dread as we stood outside the door, as Max was turning the handle and smiling and laughing and ushering me in, I didn't want to go in there, I wanted nothing more to do with his dead son.

But I did go in, of course. And it was a perfectly ordinary room—there was nothing of Ian in there at all as far as I could see. Empty cupboards, an empty wardrobe, a little washbasin in the corner. Large bay windows opened out on to the garden, and there was an appealing double bed. My suitcase was already lying upon it, it had been opened for me in preparation, and I couldn't remember when Lisa or Max had left me alone long enough to take it upstairs.

"It makes us happy to have you here," said Max. "I can't

begin to tell you." His eyes watered with the sentiment of it all, and he opened his arms for another hug, and I gave him one. "Sleep well," he said. "And enjoy yourself." And he was gone.

I went to draw the curtains, and I saw, perhaps, why this was Ian's room. I looked out directly upon the garden. And from the angle the room offered I could see that all the random charm of it was not so random at all—that all the winding paths, the flowerbeds, the aches, all of them pointed towards a centrepiece, and that centrepiece was the pond, and in the centre of that, the fountain. Ian stared out in the cold, naked with only bare feathers to protect him, his mouth fixed open in that silly round 'o'.

I pulled the curtains on him, got into my pyjamas, brushed my teeth, got into bed. I read for a little while, and then I turned off the light.

I felt very warm and comfortable beneath the sheets. My thoughts began to drift. The distant sound of running water was pleasantly soporific.

I vaguely wondered whether it were raining, but the water was too regular for that. And then I remembered the fountain in the garden, and that reassured me. I listened to it for a while, I felt that it was singing me to sleep.

I opened my eyes only when I remembered that the pond was dry, that the fountain wasn't on.

Even now I don't want to give the impression that I was alarmed. It wasn't alarm. I didn't feel threatened by the sound of the water, anything but that. But it was a puzzle, and my brain doggedly tried to solve it, and its vain attempts to make sense of what it could hear but what it knew couldn't be there started to wake me up. I don't like to sleep at night without all things put into regular order; I like to start each day as a blank new slate with nothing unresolved from the day before. And I recommend that to you all, as the best way to keep your mind healthy and your purpose resolute.

Had Max or Lisa left a bath running? Could that be it?

I turned on my bedside lamp, huffed, got out of bed. I stood in the middle of the room, stock still, as if this would make it easier to identify where the sound was coming from. It was outside the house. Definitely outside.

I pulled open the curtains, looked back on to the garden.

And, of course, all was as it should have been. There were a few flakes of snow falling, but nothing that could account for that sound of flowing water. And poor dead Ian still stood steadfast in the pond, cold I'm sure, but dry as a bone.

I was fully prepared to give up on the mystery altogether. It didn't matter. It wouldn't keep me awake—far from it, now that I focused on it, the sound seemed even more relaxing. And I turned around to pull closed the curtain, and go back to bed.

If I had turned the other way, I know I would have missed it.

The window was made up of eight square panes of glass. I had been looking at the garden, naturally enough, through one of the central panes. But as I turned, I glanced outside through another pane, the pane at the far bottom left, and something caught my eye.

There was a certain brightness coming from it, that was all. A trick of the light. But it seemed as if the moon was reflecting off the pebbles on the path—but not the whole path, it was illuminating the most direct way from the house to the memorial pond. The pebbles winked and glowed like cat's eyes caught in the headlamps of a motor vehicle.

And there, at the end of that trail of light, at the very centre of the garden, there was the fountain. And now the fountain was on. Water was gushing out of Ian's stone mouth, thick and steady; I could see now how his posture had been so designed, with his little hands bunched up, and pressed tight against his chest, to suggest that he was *forcing* out the water, as if his insides were a water balloon and he was trying to squeeze out every single last drop.

There was nothing even now so very untoward about that. If the fountain was on, so it was on. But I changed the direction of my gaze, I looked out at the garden through the central pane again—and there the fountain was dry once more, the garden still, the pathways impossible to discern in the dark.

I'm afraid I must have stayed there for a few minutes, moving my head back and forth, looking through one pane and then through another. Trying to work out what the trick was. How one piece of the window could show one view, the other, something else. I'm afraid I must have looked rather like an idiot.

And I tried to open the window. I wanted to see the garden without the prism of the glass to distract me, I wanted to know what was real and what was not. The catch wouldn't give. It seemed to freeze beneath my fingers.

Then there was a knock at my door.

It brought me back to myself; rather, it wasn't until then that I realized it, that I was on the verge of hysteria, or panic at the very least. I don't know whether I had cried out. I thought I had been silent all this while, but perhaps I had cried out. I had woken the house. I was ashamed. I forced myself to turn from the window, and as I did so, with it at my back, I felt like myself again. I smoothed down my pyjamas. I went to open the door. I prepared to apologize.

Lisa was outside in a white night dress. She came in without my inviting her to do so, smiled, sat upon my bed.

"Hello, John," she whispered.

I said hello back at her.

"Did you never want children of your own? I'm curious."

She began unbuttoning her night dress then. I decided I really shouldn't look at what she was doing, but I didn't want to look through the window again either, so I settled on a compromise, I stared at a wholly inoffensive wardrobe door. I said something about not really liking children, and that the opportunity to discover otherwise was never much likely to present itself. I was aware, too, that something was very odd about her arrival and the ensuing conversation, but you must understand, it still seemed like a welcome respite from the absurdities I had glimpsed through my bedroom window.

She seemed to accept my answer, and then said, "Would you help me, please?" Her head disappeared into the neck of the night dress, its now loose arms were flailing. I gave it a tug and pulled the dress off over her head. "Thank you," she said. She smiled, turned, pointed these two bare breasts straight at me.

"What do you think?" she asked. "Are they better than

you were expecting?" I endeavoured to explain that I had had no expectations of her breasts at all. She tittered at that, just as she had when she'd curtseyed to me in the driveway; it was a silly sound. "They're new," she said, and I supposed that made sense, they seemed too mirror perfect to be real, they seemed *sculpted*. And they didn't yet match the colour of her chest, they were white and pristine.

I wanted to ask her about the view through the window, but it seemed suddenly rather impolite to change the subject. What I did ask, though, was whether she was quite sure she had the right bedroom? Didn't she want the one with her husband in it? And at this her face fell.

"Max hasn't told you, has he?"

I said that he hadn't, no.

"Oh God," she said. "Bloody Max. This is what we... This is why. God. He's supposed to tell. Why else do you think he brought you here?"

I said that we were old friends, and at that she screwed up her face in contempt, and it made her rather ugly. I suggested that maybe he wanted to show me the house and the garden.

"Max hates the fucking house and garden," said Lisa. "He'd leave it all tomorrow if he could." She grabbed at her night dress, struggled with it. "Bloody Max. I'm very sorry. We have an agreement. I don't know what he's playing at. This is the way *I* cope." She couldn't get her arms in the right holes, she began to cry.

I said I was sorry. I asked her whether she could hear running water anywhere, was it just me?

"I've always liked you, John," she said. "Can't you like me just a little bit?"

I said I did like her, a little bit. More than, even.

"Can't you like me for one night?"

I tried asking her about Max, but she just shook her head, and now she was smiling through the tears. "This is the way we cope. Can't you help me out?" I said, yes. I said I could help her out. I said I was puzzled by the fountain outside, but by this stage the night dress was back over her head again, maybe she couldn't hear.

She said, "Now, don't you worry. I'm not going to do

anything you won't like." Then she climbed on top of me and gripped me hard between her thighs. She let her long hair fall across my face, then she whispered in my ear. I expected her to say something romantic. She said, "I won't get pregnant, I've been thoroughly sterilized."

I hadn't touched a woman in years. Not since I was at school, not since Max had discovered girls, and had started touching them, and I had touched them too so he wouldn't leave me out.

But even accepting my unfamiliarity with the whole enterprise, I don't think I did an especially good job. To be honest, I let Lisa do all of the work, the most I contributed was a couple of hands on her back so that she wouldn't fall off and sprain herself. And I listened to the sound of the fountain outside; sometimes the mechanical grunts of Lisa would drown it out, and I'd think maybe it was over, but then she'd have to pause for breath, or she'd be gnawing at my neck with her lips, or she'd be sitting tall and gritting her teeth hard and screwing her eyes tight and being ever so quiet, and I could hear the fountain just as before.

At length she rolled off, and thanked me, and kissed me on the mouth. The kiss was nice. I grant you that, the kiss was nice. She curled up beside me and went to sleep. Then she turned away from me altogether and I was alone, so alone.

The curtains were still open, but there was no light spilling into the room, it was just black and bleak out there. And from my position I couldn't crane my head to see whether there was any light coming through the pane on the bottom left.

I didn't want to wake Lisa. I got out of bed very gently. It was cold. My pyjama trousers had got lost somewhere. I'd have had to turn on the bedside lamp to find them. I wasn't going to turn on the bedside lamp.

I went straight to the pane. I looked out.

As before, the pathway to the centre was lit by sparkling pebbles. But this time the snow was falling in droves, big clumps of it, and every flake seemed to catch the moon, and each one of them was like a little lamp lighting up the whole garden. The flowers were in bloom. It was ridiculous, but the flowers were in bloom—the blanket of red and white roses was thick and warm, and the snow fell upon it, and the roses didn't care, the roses knew they could melt that snow, they had nothing to fear from it. I looked out at where Lisa had planted the hyacinths and the tulips—it was, as she'd said, like a wave of blue breaking upon a brightly coloured shore.

And at the fountain itself. Ian was throwing up all the water he had inside him, and he had so *much* water, he was never going to run out, was he? But I would have thought his face would have been distressed—it was not distressed. The worst you could say about the expression he wore was that it was resigned. Ian Wheeler had a job to do, and he was going to do it. It wasn't a pleasant job, but he wasn't one to complain, he'd just do the very best he could. And the flowers were growing around him too, and vines were twisting up his body and tightening around his neck.

Over the sound of the fountain I heard another noise now. Less regular. The sound of something dragging over loose stone. Something heavy, but determined—it seemed that every lurch across the stone was done with great weariness, but it wasn't going to stop, it might be *slow*, but it wasn't going to stop. And I can't tell you why, but I suddenly felt a cold terror icing down my body, so cold that it froze my body still and I could do nothing but watch.

And into view at last shuffled Max. He was naked. And the snow was falling all around him, and I could see that it was falling fast and drenching him when it melted against his skin, but he didn't notice, he was like the roses, he didn't care, he didn't stop. Forcing himself forward, but calmly, so deliberately, each step an effort but an effort he was equal to. Further up the path, following the trail of sparkling pebbles to the fountain. Following the yellow brick road.

I tried looking through the other panes. Nothing but darkness, and the snow falling so much more gently. I only wanted to look at that garden, at that reality. But I could hear the sound from the other garden so much more clearly, I couldn't *not* hear it, the agonized heave of Max's body up the path. The flow of running water, the way it gushed and spilled, all that noise, all of it, it was pulling him along. I had to look. I did.

Once in a while the bends of the path would turn Max

It Flows From the Mouth

around so that he was facing me. And I could see that dead face—no, not dead, not vacant even, it was filled with purpose, but it wasn't a purpose I understood and it had nothing to do with the Max I had loved for so many years. I could see his skin turning blue with the cold. I could see his penis had shrunk away almost to nothing.

And now, too soon—he had reached the statue of his dead son. At last he stopped, as if to contemplate it. As if to study the workmanship!—his head tilted to one side. And maybe his son contemplated him in return, but if he did, he still never stopped spewing forth all that water, all the water there was in the world. Then—Max was moving again, he was using his last reserves of energy, he was stepping into the freezing pond, he was wading over to the stone angel, raising an arm, then both arms, he was reaching out to it. And I thought I could hear him howling. He was, he was howling.

I battered at the window. I tried again to open it. The catch wouldn't lift, the catch was so cold it hurt.

But Max had his son in his arms now, wrapping his arms about him tightly, he was hugging him for dear life, and he was crying out—he was screaming with such love and such despair. And then, then, he fell silent, and that was more terrible still—and he put his mouth to his son's, he opened his mouth wide and pressed it against those stone lips, and the water splashed against his face and against his chest, and yet he kissed his son closer, he plugged the flow of water, he took it all inside and swallowed it down.

The window gave. The rush of cold air winded me. I called out. "Max!" I shouted. "Max!" But there was nothing to be seen now the window was open, nothing but dead space, dead air, blackness.

"Darling," said Lisa.

I turned around. She was awake.

"Darling," she said. "Darling, close the window. Come back to bed." She patted the mattress beside her in a manner I assumed was enticing.

I closed the window. I looked through the pane once more, I looked through every pane, and there was nothing to make out, the moon was behind the clouds, the darkness was full and unyielding. I went back to bed. I did as I was told.

I had fully intended to go to church the next morning. I had made a promise, and I keep my promises. But when I woke up the house was empty. Max and Lisa had gone without me. I made myself a cup of tea, and waited for them to come back. Eventually, of course, they did. All smiles, both looking so smart, Max in particular was very handsome in his suit. "Sorry, matey," said Max. "I popped my head around your door, but you looked like you needed the extra sleep! Hope you don't mind!" And Lisa just smiled.

Neither of them said a word about the adventures of the night before, and neither treated me any differently. Lisa had told me she'd cook a big peasant's breakfast, and she was as good as her word—bacon, eggs, and sausages she said were from pigs freshly slaughtered by a farmer friend she'd made. Then we settled down in the lounge, and shared the Sunday newspaper, each reading different sections then swapping when we were done. It was nice.

Some time early afternoon, though, Max looked at the clock, and said, "Best you get back home, John! I've things that need doing!" And I hugged Lisa goodbye, and Max drove me to the railway station, and we hugged too, and I thanked him for the weekend.

We drifted apart. I don't know who drifted from whom, I doubt it was anything as deliberate as that. No, wait, I sent them a Christmas card, and they didn't respond. So they're the ones who drifted. They drifted, and I stayed where I was, exactly the same.

That would be the end of the story. I had heard from an old school friend that a couple of years later Max and Lisa had separated. It was just gossip, and I don't know whether it was true or not, and I felt sorry for them just the same.

That was maybe six months ago. Recently I received a letter.

It Flows From the Mouth

Dear John,

You may have heard that Max and I have gone our different ways! It was quite sad at the time, but it was very amicable, and I'm sure one day we will be good friends.

But sometimes when something has died, you just have to accept it, and move on.

I still have the house. Max was very generous, to be fair. All he wanted was half of the money, and the fountain from the garden. We had to dig it up, and I'm afraid it has made the garden a bit of an eyesore! I tried to tell Max it won't work, it was specially designed to fit with all our underground piping, but as you know, there's no talking to Max!

I'm going to rethink the garden. I'm sure I can make it even better.

All the locals have been very nice, and they're attentive as ever in their own way. But I don't know. I think perhaps they liked Max more than they ever liked me.

If you would like to stay again, that would make me very happy.

Maybe I shouldn't say this. But that night we spent together was very special. It was a special night. And I think of you often. Sometimes I think you're the one who could save me. Sometimes I think you could give me meaning.

But regardless. Thank you for always being such a good friend to me and Max, and for being best man at the wedding, and any other duties you took on.

Best regards,
Lisa Howell (once Briggs).

I haven't written back yet. I might.

Hidden in the Alphabet
Charles Wilkinson

The auteur has been tripped up on the pavement outside the Acme Hotel. He's just come through the revolving doors, down the marble steps and turned in the direction of the main thoroughfare. It was not the tip of the sole of his right shoe (chestnut gleam of leather on the upper) catching an uneven paving-stone. And no, it has nothing to do with an occasional weakness of the knees, allowable in a man of seventy years, or even a failure to adjust to his new bifocal spectacles, which lie broken (spider-cracks in both lenses, the frames askew) six inches away from his outstretched right arm (hand marked with chalky grazes, a droplet-chain of blood). It is as if someone's curled a foot, or the curved handle of an umbrella, around his ankle and jerked his leg violently upwards.

Later, he will tell himself that he lost consciousness for several seconds, although now as he levers himself upright, blood dripping from the side of his chin, he is not aware of having done so. But this will be his only explanation for the fact no one is anywhere near him on the street.

The pigeon (iridescence of wing-glaze, white mark on the throat) perched on the roof of a derelict warehouse is not an adequate witness to what happened, though it knows the south side well: has flown many times through the open windows of buildings that glass has forgotten; alighted on chimney tops tufted with wild grass; hopped under bus shelters to inspect abandoned Chinese takeaways; examined crisps wrappers with a critical eye. It has an excellent view of the Acme Hotel: the marble steps, washed every day; the brass glint of the revolving doors; the shafts and arrowheads of black railings; the orange-red brick of the façade; the Gothic windows in all storeys but the sixth, from which you can see the gleaming towers of the second city's centre, though not the ring road that ropes them in.

The pigeon may have noticed the auteur, his silver hair and white linen jacket bright in the sunshine of a waning summer, when he pushed the revolving door, walked down the marble steps and into the street (just as a blue van was passing, too quickly for the driver to witness what happened next) and he could have observed a man or the shadow of a man or a shadow from a nest of English shadows, slipping out from an abandoned factory, or a shop with shuttered windows, where no one has been served for thirty years, and coming up swiftly behind a man leaving a hotel on his way to a meeting with the son, his only child, that he has not seen for a quarter of a century.

As the man brushes himself down (an action he immediately regrets as a streak of blood appears on the right pocket of his linen jacket) and hobbles back to the Acme Hotel, the pigeon flies off in the direction of a café, where there will be the crumbs of croissants and sesame seeds, left over from *de luxe* burger buns.

Cotton wool, commiserations, antiseptic cream and directions to the nearest optician have been provided by the staff at the Acme Hotel. The auteur has phoned his niece and asked her to postpone the meeting. He must not appear in the restaurant (expensive, central, overlooking a canal) with sticking plaster on his hands and chin. As he will be unable to see further than his own table, the other diners will be indistinct blobs of colour, the details on the menu squashed insects on a white background. It is most important that he should meet with his son. There are questions he must ask. He will need to observe his reactions closely.

It is a hot day. The domed mosque with a minaret, the greengrocers selling unfamiliar fruit, the women in *niqabs*, the men with their long beards and traditional dress - all surprise him. Only the red brick of the shop frontages and the scarlet pillar boxes are familiar. He has not visited his native city for many years; it pains him that on his return he is no longer a wealthy man.

The optician's shop is in a side street and as he walks past a row of semi-detached Victorian villas (bow-windows, trimmed box hedges, neat front gardens) he feels a faint longing for his childhood. Opposite is a low white building with a flat roof that consists of three shops. There is a florist and the optician, but the middle unit is empty. A yellow skip sits next to a pile of salmon-pink bricks. The auteur is slightly early for his appointment. He peers through the window. The reception area is not welcoming. No one is behind the desk, and only one rack, which is attached to the wall, has any frames for sale. A free-standing display unit is just shining skeletal bars, somehow sinister, as if it has been expertly boned. In one corner, there are two uncomfortably upright chairs and a low table. Just as he takes the decision to kill time in the florist's, a door at the back opens and a man in an open-necked white shirt steps out. As he is standing in front of an oblong of yellow light from the treatment room, the auteur cannot see his face, but there is no mistaking the gesture signalling him to come in. A bell rings, a tiny ecclesiastical note; for a second, the auteur thinks he can smell incense. Then the dust coats the back of his throat and he coughs.

Instead of waiting for him, the optician has gone back into his room, but the door is open. The auteur knocks once and then enters without waiting for an answer.

The optician, who has his back to him, is bowed over a work space. His elbows are moving very slightly as if he is carrying out some delicate operation.

"Please sit down. I won't be long."

Hidden in the Alphabet

"I'm sorry to be slightly early."

"Don't worry. I assure you that will not be a problem."

The treatment chair reminds him of the dentist (a sharp psychosomatic stab in a back molar) but he takes his seat. As the optician materializes behind him and swiftly positions the chin and head rests, the auteur thinks of a film he once made: the head of a knight encased in a helmet.

"I just need you to sit very still, eyes wide open, look this way."

He grasps the horizontal bars. A puff of air in each eye. The beam of a torch and then the test card appears in the wall mirror. One lens is exchanged for another until the letters start to clarify. He reads the top two lines only. A change, much sharper now, AXO TVH and then—quite clearly—SEX.

The woman who gets off the bus dresses with an eloquent simplicity unusual for the area. Her skirt and blouse are a vibrant blue. In the midst of shoppers in shades of milk chocolate, grey and mouse-brown she has the electric plumage of an American jay in a garden of house sparrows. She was seen in the lobbies of Parisian hotels. If it were not for her tinted glasses, we might recognize the eyes that once stared at us from the back covers of magazines (*Vogue*, *Tatler*). Her blonde hair touches her shoulders and is cut straight across her forehead. And she wears a loose silk scarf (perhaps Jaeger or Hermes) with a blue and yellow pattern. Her shoulder bag has the sheen of soft Italian leather bought in Milan.

She walks quickly, ignoring the outstretched hand of the beggar in khaki trousers (army surplus) squatting on a rug outside the supermarket. At first she appears to be heading past the pawnbrokers, the snooker hall and the curry house towards the *patisserie* on the corner, with its display of baked bread in the window, its coffee shop and small courtyard garden: the one place redolent of France in a suburb of chain shops, *halal* butchers, convenience stores, moneylenders, estate agents and one laundrette that smells of hot metal, washing powder and Saharan-dry heat. But without pausing to look at the baskets filled with almond croissants and *pain-au-chocolat*, she makes her way past the chairs on the pavement. One man looks up from his newspaper and knows in an instant the damage done to the perfectly symmetrical features: the hairline cracks beneath the repaired porcelain skin, the brittle lips that threaten breakdown and grief. And then she turns down a side street.

Now that she is away from the crowds, her pace slows, and once she halts and rummages in her shoulder bag. Beneath her dress is a slim white body that appeared naked in a film made in Paris. An art house movie directed by her uncle. Every night and every morning when she steps into the shower, she returns to a scene in the film when she showered with a camera on her side of the curtain. But now she is thinking of a building with a flat roof and three shops, a florist's that sells red flowers only on Tuesdays, an empty room that was formerly filled with brochures for holidays abroad, and an optician's. She knows that if she maintains her pace she will reach her destination in under two minutes. As she is moving more slowly, it is easier to see the streaks of silver in her blonde hair. But there is no one else in the street to observe this. In spite of the heat, the thick green foliage of the trees lining the pavement suggests the dampness of the winter months has yet to be entirely dissipated. The refuse is to be collected today and the front gate of every house has at least one squat black sentry with a topknot on guard next to a wheelie-bin.

She catches sight of the yellow skip and the pile of pink bricks ahead of her and knows there's not much further to go; and indeed it is not long before she opens the door of the optician's (the bell gives its priestly tinkle) and walks over to the reception desk. Although there is no one there, a spectacle case, with a rubber band wrapped around it, is waiting for her. This she slips into her shoulder bag and turns to leave. But before she reaches the front door she hears the sound of someone moving around heavily in the treatment room. She looks at the skeletal frames on display in the racks, the uncomfortable straight-backed chair and the side-table that has no magazines on it. Perhaps she should tell someone that she has collected the glasses. The noise in the treatment room stops. Which would be worse, she wonders: opening the door and seeing no one or finding somebody there?

Even objects he knows to be hard-edged are indistinct. The hotel staff, from Poland, Lithuania and the Tamil-speaking tip of southern India, hover as they walk, their white-sleeved arms blurred like the wings of hummingbirds. The auteur can't read his newspaper, which lies folded on his lap. He is waiting in a fudge-coloured leather armchair in the residents' lounge. His niece has agreed to fetch his glasses (he is shaky, a delayed reaction to his fall) from the optician's and then meet him for lunch. What troubles him most is that he remembers neither the second half of his eye examination nor choosing his frames—or his return to the Acme Hotel. His first recollection is waking in the middle of the night and knowing he has been dreaming about the alphabet: black letters, like those on the treatment chart, swirling in a space as white as snow.

At first light, he wakes up, with a sentence half-formed on his tongue.

A message has been left at the reception desk. His new glasses are ready for collection. Has he already paid the optician? He cannot remember having done so. But now the swing doors of the residents' lounge open and a figure in a blue dress advances (even in the soft world there is a familiarity about her flowing movements) towards him.

He rises and they kiss. (A perfume he doesn't recognize).

"Have you got my..."

"Yes, they are here."

He takes his spectacles and puts them on. The residents' lounge takes a pace sideways. He sees the silvery wires in his niece's blonde hair, scuffed leather on the arms of the sofa; the pattern on the carpet sets in sharply delineated surroundings.

"Do I owe you anything?"

"I don't think so. There was no one there to pay, but since there wasn't a bill I assume you must have paid already. Can't you remember?"

"I've told you—it's all a bit hazy."

As they walk towards the dining room, he remembers the scene in the waterfall: his eighteen-year-old son naked with his niece, the patches of glistening light on their slippery flesh, the sun picking out streaks of lemon and ash in their hair. Their dancing steps in the brilliant white water foaming about their feet. That was the first of his films to be shot in colour. It had something of the freedom of the times, he thought. But later, when his reputation declined, the critics claimed there were scenes that marked his transition from film-maker to pornographer. Such snobs! Why was it that black-and-white had this curious kudos? And as for those people who couldn't distinguish simplicity of vision and candour from pornography…

The *maitre d'* fussing with the chairs. Two enormous menus and a wine list. Would they like bread and jug of iced water? Olives, perhaps?

"And so he's refusing to meet up tomorrow?" the auteur asks.

"I wouldn't put like that. It's simply not possible. He has other engagements."

"Ah, I see he's punishing me for not turning up yesterday. Didn't you explain to him how badly I was shaken? Since I've come all the way from Paris to meet him, I want to be on reasonable form."

"He's not trying to punish anyone. And he's had to fly from America."

The auteur remembers the ten-year-old who lurked outside his study when he was trying write. Always a creak of the floorboards or a tentative knock at the door just when the words had begun to flow. Of course, it was understandable. So much time had to be spent away, on location or talking to potential backers. And of course, the boy loathed his boarding school.

"Well, tell him it's absolutely necessary that we meet as soon as possible. I've urgent business in France, but it's unthinkable that I should leave without seeing him.

Hidden in the Alphabet

Especially as he won't even agree to speak on the phone."

"He's every bit as keen to meet up as you are. He wants an explanation."

A summer afternoon years ago. And a creeping about on the landing outside the study. A deadline for a script and no ideas. What did the child want now? He was a good-looking boy in a slightly pale way. Delicate features and enormous blue eyes, but with a sort of shivery sensitivity that was irritating, like a pedigree dog that had been badly inbred. The auteur gave up and they went to the shops and bought comics (*Beano*, *The Dandy*) and ice creams.

They were in the garage when it happened. The boy had both feet on the floor and one arm trailing slightly behind him when the auteur slammed the door shut. A scream, the fine lines of a face crumpling, jets of tears. The auteur opened the door, took the boy's hand in his: a half moon of hanging flesh, the beginning of the blood grin on a middle finger that would have to be ice-packed and bandaged.

Even now the auteur is not sure whether he did it deliberately.

"An explanation for what? In the circumstances, I'd say that we are the ones who are owed explanations, don't you think?"

"Have you chosen?"

He lifts up the menu, but it's a blur. The glasses aren't bifocals.

The lunch and the wine have made her drowsy. She is not used to being the object of hospitality in the middle of the day. And now it is well past four o'clock and none of the small tasks (the payment of a bill, the visit to the dry cleaners) she set herself have been accomplished. She knows that if she were to change out of her blue dress and shower, or even make herself a cup of tea (fragrant, lemony), she would revive, but she is listless, heavy with the inertia of late afternoon. There are four more days left before she is due to return to the office. Although spending her holiday in the city where she works has had the virtue of economy, she regrets the loss of the two weeks on a Greek island that she had planned.

There is a small patio with plants in terracotta pots and garden furniture bleached by the sun. She pours herself a glass of iced water from the fridge and goes outside.

If she takes her shoes off, she knows the warmth of the flagstones will remind her of the summer she was an actress. The year she was in a film written and directed by her uncle. She remembers the scene, shot from behind, in which she and her cousin are standing on the fringe of the beach: dunes and marram grass beside them, and beyond the full length of the bay at low tide. The sugar-sparkle of white sand. The sheen darkest where the tide last reached. They wriggled out of their clothes. Her cousin was naked first and for a moment he stood beside her. The viewer knew from the angle of his head that he was looking down at her. Waiting for the moment when she too was naked and they would run off together, their footprints the first of the day, the dents almost invisible at first, then slowly darkening until the first wave came dazzling across the breadth of the beach.

What the film will never remember was how fine the sand was, silkily running through her toes. The first shock of the wave, unexpectedly cold on such a hot day. And later the taste of salt on her cousin's skin.

They were often mistaken for brother and sister. To be close seemed natural.

She sips the water. The sunlight falls on the bench opposite her and the dark shadows of the slats paint the flagstones. At the western edge of the city the evening is gathering melancholy light.

She was just that much older than him, and so it was that she went to his room. The moonlight shone through the blinds, striping his blanket with silver. Then she was with him, skin to skin, both loving as if untarnished. Later they were told, after the anger, shame and embarrassment subsided, that the children of such close unions are frequently, and quite naturally, stillborn.

Hidden in the Alphabet

At dusk there is a hint of pink in the red brick of the Victorian villas. The trees in the front garden darken and hover, as if about to float towards nightfall. There is no traffic and the auteur is conscious of how his every step rings clearly in the street. Yellow-gold light drenches the lace curtains in front windows. A small wooden summer house is mysterious as a shrine. Then, sooner than expected, he is there. At twilight, the white building looks almost nautical. He would not be surprised to see a funnel appear on the flat roof. Although the florist has closed, the shutters have not been drawn. The auteur can see white flowers pressing against the window pane as if they are the trapped ghosts of seabirds longing for flight.

His appointment with the optician is inconvenient, but tomorrow he is due to fly back to Paris for a meeting on *La Rive Gauche* after he has had lunch with his son. Now that he is no longer rich he can't afford to turn down the optician's offer to replace the lenses without further charge. Contacting him to make this arrangement has not been easy. He'd phoned repeatedly from the Acme Hotel and had no answer. It was late afternoon (past 5 o'clock) before he finally managed to speak to the optician's assistant (her voice distant, muffled, possibly foreign) and he'd had to ask her to repeat what she said several times. But when at last he'd explained his predicament in sufficient detail, she told him that since the optician was working late she would find him an appointment, provided he was prepared to come after eight o'clock.

He is one minute early. Although the front of the shop is in darkness, a cord of light is visible, shining from under the door of the treatment room. He presses a button and waits, but there's no sign anyone is prepared to come out to greet him, although he can hear a ringing. He turns the handle and slips inside: the sound of the bell (a memory of kneeling to pray). At once the door of the treatment room swings open, as if its release has been triggered by his action.

An empty chair held in a cone of light.

"Please go in and take a seat. I'll join you in a minute."

The voice comes from right behind him. Yet this is hardly possible since the auteur has taken no more than a couple of steps into the room. Either the man must have been pressing himself against the inside wall or he has followed him in soundlessly. The auteur begins to turns round and then stops. What if there is no one there? The front door shuts with a sharp click.

"Thank you for agreeing to see me at this late hour," says the auteur, making his way towards the chair.'

"Not at all, not at all." The voice is soft, difficult to place.

And now he's in the chair, hands from behind him move the head and chin rests into place. Something is being attached to the top of his skull. He can't remember this happening before.

"What's that?"

"Just a metal cap. Something of my own devising. I use it when I want to make absolutely sure that the head stays completely still. Look upwards and left. And now you'll just feel a puff of air…"

"Are we going to go through the whole thing again? Surely you must have most of the information already."

"Unfortunately my colleague did not keep the notes from your last appointment. No doubt he thought that because you live abroad they would not be needed again."

"And so you're not the optician I saw last time?"

The man laughs lightly, as if acknowledging a whimsical remark made by a small child.

"I assure you I will accept no fee for this appointment."

A test card appears in the mirror; the letters are twigs blurred beneath ice. Lenses change in quick succession until the top two rows sharpen. And then quite plainly, on the third line from the bottom … L O V E.

"Love! It said 'sex' the other day. That's not usual, is it? I mean the letters don't normally spell anything?"

"I'll change the card."

Once again, the auteur begins to read from the top. Everything is much clearer now. He is even able to make out the second to last line without too much difficulty:

"D….A….no, E…A …T…*Sex, Love & Death* . That's the title

of one of my films! What's going on here?"

The test card vanishes. He can hear a faint rustling as the optician comes round to the front of the chair. The auteur tries to raise his head so he can see the man's face, but even the slightest movement is impossible. A white shirt and the bottom of a tie come into view.

"I hope my glasses will be ready by tomorrow. Half-past eleven at the latest. I have an urgent meeting with my son before I fly back to Paris. At six in the evening."

How pressing is an engagement with a son who has been dead for thirty years? A son, briefly famous as the co-star of *Desir, l'amour et la mort,* who was supposed have taken his life in the state of Illinois nine months after he had made it plain that he would never speak to his father again. The auteur still has the private detective's report in the bottom drawer of an *escritoire* in Paris. But now his niece has been saying that this was all lies: his son had bribed the detective.

"You can be quite sure that everything will be arranged. Now can you see my middle finger?"

"Yes."

"Tell me what you notice as I move it slowly towards you."

"There's no nail facing me and the remaining three fingers and the thumb have been tucked into the palm of..."

A silver crescent in the flesh, an old wound's emblem. "I think I'll leave now, if you don't mind."

"If you could stay for a little longer, I'd be grateful. There are a few things I may need to attend to."

The man has moved round to the back of the chair. A cabinet rolling open followed by the reassuringly professional rustle of paper. The auteur sighs and tries to relax. To panic would be unbecoming. Even at the most difficult times on set, he always remained utterly unruffled. The scar could be anybody's scar. As a writer he should know how the alert mind is always ready to find hidden words, however the alphabet is presented. And anyway his film had a French title.

But now there is no sound from behind him. Although he has not heard the creak of the door, he knows the man is no longer in the room. Indeed, he can hear noises coming from the reception area. Furniture is being shifted. He is quite sure the display stands and the uncomfortable chairs are being manoeuvred onto the street. Voices; bottles are being opened. The murmur sounds civilized. Like the opening of an exhibition or a book launch. Then, very faintly, there's a series of gentle chinks. At first he thinks it's merely celebratory: glass glancing convivial glass. But soon the chink changes to a clink and a scrape. Then another clink and scrape. Something is being built. He remembers the bricks and the skip outside. He begins to struggle, and shout and scream, but he is being held fast in the treatment chair. He has never heard himself beg before.

A bright light in the mirror; the test card reappears. For a moment, every vowel and consonant is quite still and he half expects a voice from behind asking him to read, but then the letters whirl and swirl around before finally reassembling themselves: *Desir, l'amour et la mort*. The screen is too narrow for his film, his greatest attempt to fix the permanence of his longings. There will be no images: it is his script. The opening scene is scrolling down. He can no longer see anything in the room except the mirror and its message. Only language moves in the dark. He will fade, walled in with his words.

DEATH'S DOOR CAFÉ
KAARON WARREN

Theo thought of the pain in his veins as the clawing of bats, the smell in his nose their guano, the rawness of his throat torn by their smoke. It was this, the pain in breathing, that made him climb out of his car at last and walk a block to the Dusseldorf Café.

The large purple door had a suburban brass knocker and a spy hole. A plaque beside the door read *The Soldier*. In larger text: b1922, d1946

Up close he could see dark stains in the wood. He touched his fingers to the marks, feeling the door's thick grain, wondering if he'd get a sense of 'ending', an understanding of the death it had once concealed.

He knocked.

When the waiter opened the door, Theo jumped back. He turned away, wanting to run, knowing he wasn't able. Once, he could have been around the corner before the waiter even raised a hand. Now...he had no choice. Even walking one block from the car had sapped his strength.

"Table for one?" said the waiter. "Did you have a booking?"

Theo shook his head. The café wasn't in the phonebook or online; he'd only found it by walking up and down the street.

"That'll be okay, we can squeeze you in. A cancellation, aren't you lucky?"

Theo stepped inside. The waiter led Theo across the room, saying, "There's a great table over here in the corner. Right next to the magazines." Theo stood close to him.

"Who was The Soldier? If that's not a rude question."

"It's always the first thing people want to know: Who died behind the door?" The waiter's face shifted, became serious. "The Soldier was back from war a year, and he was listening to some gloomy music, some sad sort of song, they say, when there was a knock on that door." The waiter rapped loudly on the table and Theo jumped.

The waiter handed him the menu.

Theo hadn't eaten solid food for more than a week. Even glancing at the Chef's Specialities list, with its 'South-Coast Swordfish' and its 'Hazelnut Chocolate Soufflé', made him feel ill.

"The super special today is a lamb tagine with blood plums. The chef tells me it's very good," the waiter said. "So the soldier opens the door, that very door you came through, and who is standing there but his old sergeant? And the sergeant says, 'You've brought shame to an entire division,' and he reaches in and slashes the soldier's throat. The soldier bleeds to death so fast he's gone by the time the killer reaches the front gate. They say the music was still playing two days later when the body was found. As if that poor dead soldier kept hitting replay." The waiter shrugged. "So, what'll it be?"

Theo felt sick. "Could I just have a green salad?" he said. The waiter smiled.

"We sell a lot of green salads. Chef does a very good one. Anything else for now? Some nice toast? We sell a lot of toast, too."

Theo nodded. Smiled. His dry lips cracked. He didn't know what to say, how to ask for what he wanted.

"Drinks?"

Theo shook his head. "I'm not really drinking. I'm…" He hadn't told anyone yet and he didn't know what words to use. "I'm not well."

"Oh, you poor thing. How about I bring you one of our fabulous Virgin Marys? We leave out the vodka for sick people." The waiter smiled. "We get a lot of your type in here."

Death's Door Café

The café was full, but remarkably quiet. Gentle music played, something with pan pipes and an ethereal female voice. The chair was comfortable; high-backed, soft-seated. Theo shifted back to give himself more room and there was no scraping sound, as if the legs were muffled. The walls were painted all around with a mural he took to depict Dusseldorf and the River Rhine. Along the banks, stylish people strolled, perfectly groomed, laughing, small dogs at their feet.

There was nothing dark, no hint of death beyond the door he had walked through.

Theo couldn't eat his green salad when it arrived, but he drank his tomato juice. He watched to see what people did. He wanted a clue, didn't want to mess up, miss out.

An emaciated woman held a bread stick. She was dressed in hot pink as if to draw attention away from her pale face. Her companion, a red-cheeked woman with a high, far-reaching voice, did all the talking, frivolous stuff. She barely took a breath. Theo thought she was frightened the sick woman would speak. He understood this kind of avoidance.

He had good hearing (Batboy, his mother called him, because he picked up everything) and didn't have to strain to listen in.

"They've got it in green, blue, brown, orange and red," the healthy woman said. "But they don't have all the sizes, you'd have to try them on to see. But first you'd decide if you wanted green, blue, brown, orange or red. I, me, I'd choose red or orange though I wouldn't mind brown..." without a break, desperately filling each space.

Finally the sick woman reached out a finger and touched the loud woman's wrist. The loud woman stopped instantly.

The sick woman nodded.

"Waiter! Waiter. We're ready to see Jason now," the loud woman said, waving the menu.

Theo opened his menu. The owner's name was there, in large, ornate type. "Your host, Jason Davies," it said.

Jason Davies came and sat at the table with the women. He was young, black hair, pale blue eyes. Theo saw the patrons in the room all watching him. Nobody spoke or moved; all focused on him.

He talked with the sick woman for a while (*"How did you*

hear about us? And is this a friend? A relative?" "I've answered all this," she said. *"I've told you."*) then led her through a door at the back of the café. She walked slowly, relying heavily on a cane.

Theo swallowed. Winced.

The friend stood by their table, clutching her handbag. She started towards the back door, but the waiter gently led her to walk towards the front.

"Leave it with us, now."

"I need to give her a lift home. She can't manage."

He smiled. "She'll be fine."

He moved over to Theo. "Can we help you with anything else today, or just the bill?"

"Could I see the owner? Jason? Can I talk to Jason?" he asked, wondering if he was being reckless, ruining his chances. The waiter stood by the table and looked at him.

"Come back tomorrow."

"I can't. I haven't got the time," and that meant a different thing to someone with cancer.

"I'll ask him," the waiter said. "You may have to wait. What's your name?"

It was fifteen minutes before the waiter said, "He can't see you today. Maybe next time."

"How many visits until you're considered worthy?" Theo asked. He hoped he didn't sound sarcastic. He meant the question.

"It's not so much worthiness. Often it's persistence."

"How many times did that woman visit?"

"I'm not sure. Many. Many times. Some of our regulars come for months."

"But I may not have months."

The waiter looked at him.

"Jason will know."

Theo felt a ticking in his ears, sign that waves of pain were on their way. He paid. The waiter said, "Come back soon. Tomorrow's special is French Onion Soup. It's fantastic. If I had to choose a last meal, that would be it."

His direct gaze told Theo, *I'm not joking and I'm not being cruel.*

He handed Theo a sheet of paper. *Questionnaire,* it said.

"Bring it with you next time," the waiter said, ushering Theo out. "Be as honest as you can. That's what Jason always says."

In the car, Theo swallowed pain killers and waited for the nausea to pass before driving. His doctor had told him he shouldn't be on the road, but that was advice he would ignore for as long as possible.

He looked at the 20 page questionnaire. *What do you fear, what do you love, what to do you miss most about childhood, where do you think you are going to, do you believe in God? Are you ever tongue-tied or lost for words? What will you do with the rest of your life?* He laughed; he hadn't answered such personal questions since a long-ago girlfriend had wanted to know everything about him before making a real commitment.

That hadn't worked out so well.

Before he was five pages in, he was tired. He listened to podcasts: stuff about good eating habits, slow cooking, a bat cave near Denpasar Town, Bali where the bats are known to keep bad things at bay, and children's theatre. He watched people come and go from the café, so many of them clearly ill. He liked watching them.

Two hours passed.

He had nowhere to go.

Three hours.

Then he saw the woman all in pink. She must have left via the back door. She seemed taller and she had no cane. She put out her hand for a taxi, then lowered her arm and walked to a bus stop. As Theo watched, she counted the money she held. Shook her head. Laughed.

He started the car, drove alongside her and offered her a lift. "I was in the café," he said. "Death's Door Café."

"You were? I'm sorry. I noticed very little."

In the café, she had looked over fifty. Now, she seemed to be in her mid thirties. Her face glowed and she bounced on her feet as if full of energy.

She leant into his car. Looked at him. Then climbed in.

"Where do you want me to drop you?'

She seemed a bit stunned by this. Lost for words. "To your friend's house?"

"No! No. To the airport. I'm, ahhh…"

"Holiday?"

"Holiday." She looked at the money in her hand again.

"You need money."

She shook her head. Then nodded. She laughed. "I'm not sure, actually."

Theo smiled. "I can buy you a ticket. Easy. Money's just burning a hole in my pocket."

"What would you want in return?"

"Nothing, really. Just to talk."

"I can't tell you anything,"

"You look fantastic."

"I do, don't I? And I feel better than I have in maybe two decades."

"So what happened in there?"

"I can't say. I really can't. Not even for a plane ticket."

"I'm going to buy you that anyway," he said. It really did mean nothing to him. Even ten thousand dollars wouldn't make a dent. "But...how do I get in? How do I get Jason to talk to me?"

They approached the airport.

He said, "Do you want me to give a message to your friend?"

She stared at him for a moment. "Oh. No. No. Best not. Look, if you want to get in? Keep going back. And be honest. As honest as you can force yourself to be. And good luck."

She kissed his cheek, her lips warm, soft, alive.

"Keep going back," she said.

Theo was not the only regular.

Some had a constant companion, like the little boy and his mother. She carried him in, set him up with pillows. Ordered milkshake, chocolate cake, but that made the boy cry with frustration. He took a sip, but Theo could see that it rose straight away back into his mouth.

They were invited through the door on the day the boy didn't stir as the mother walked in with him.

Some were always alone. These, like Theo, carried a book or magazine to read, or concentrated on phones, not wanting to look lonely or needy. They exchanged glances, sometimes sat together, but they didn't talk. Theo wondered if amongst them were potential friends, or long-term partners. The mother of his child. But all they really had in common was illness.

Some came in with a new companion every time, paid nurses. An elderly man who walked with a cane always had his nurse bring gifts; he owned a series of stores, Theo discovered. He never said anything, just smiled as the nurse handed out pens, notebooks, chocolates.

A sort of camaraderie built amongst them. There were light cheers any time one was allowed through to the back.

Jason Davies sometimes nodded at them. Sometimes he'd smile. The regulars would exchange looks when one of them was so blessed.

Day after day, Theo drank carrot and ginger juice, ate dried yam chips. At times, the nausea would be too much and he would push through the beaded doorway, (*Mountain Walker*, the plaque beside it said, b1933, d1972), walk along the increasingly chilly hallway, open the dented back door (*Teen Singer* b1985, d2001), stumble every time over the rock which sat too close to the path, and enter the toilet, (*Three Year Old* b1998, d2001) which shared space with a laundry tub and what appeared to be rejected artwork from a teenage girl's bedroom.

He pretended to work at a variety of tables, taking his laptop in, using his phone. He spoke if spoken to, like the day when the elderly man sat at the next table with his eyes closed, humming softly. His nurse fussed over him, smiled around the room, stayed connected.

"You're a busy, busy man," she said to Theo. She was in her twenties and smelt faintly of cigarette smoke and breath mints. "What is it you do, busy all the time?"

"I've got a sonar equipment company." He handed her his business card.

"Love the bat," she said. Theo had drawn it himself; he had drawn bats from the age of five. "I love bats."

Theo was called Batman at school, because of the cave on his property. He didn't mind at all; he'd take kids there in groups, let them throw bat poo at each other, tell them things they didn't know.

After all the bats were killed, though, he couldn't bear to hear the name spoken. Each time was like a punch to the heart. He knew he deserved it, every hard hit, for not stopping the slaughter.

He didn't tell the nurse any of this. He might, he thought, if something happened between them. If she really loved bats, he could show her the cave, they could see it together and she'd cry with him, maybe.

But she didn't come again. Next time, the nurse was a man, bright faced and cheery, who made them all laugh.

One morning, Jason appeared. There was silence as always. He surveyed the room. "Can you stay for a while, Theo? It would be good to have a chat."

Theo nodded.

"Excellent," Jason said. He walked over to the elderly man, placed his hand on the back of the chair, and leaned over to whisper in his ear.

The elderly man gave a little shudder. "Me?" Theo heard him say.

Jason led the elderly man though the door. The waiter (there were three of them, Theo knew, all kind, efficient, professional) said to the nurse, "You're all done now. You'll be paid for the month. And thanks."

The other regulars congratulated Theo. He still didn't know what he was lucky about. No one discussed it. But it was a cure; they'd seen it. They knew it worked. Theo himself had seen six people go through the door and never return to the café. He'd seen three of them later, walking down the street, transformed. Flowers appeared in the café, with notes saying THANK YOU. Like flowers sent to nurses in hospital.

There was no follow-up because he knew no names, but still, even to have one day feeling that way would make it worthwhile. Even if it was just that one day.

Theo ordered herbal coffee and cheese but could swallow nothing. Sometimes he felt so exhausted, so suddenly and completely drained, he wanted to lay his head on the table and sleep. Sometimes he did nod off, wake to find himself still there, his coffee cold in front of him.

Theo was grateful for the pile of magazines, so he could withdraw into himself, not engage. Many were tourist magazines from Dusseldorf and he flicked through these, looking for things to talk about

When Jason sat down an hour later, Theo said, "How long did you live in Dusseldorf?" thinking it a safe, intelligent question.

"Never even been. I just like the sound of the name. Don't you?"

"Except people don't call your cafe that, do they?"

"Don't they?"

"They call it Death's Door Café."

"Because of the doors."

He pointed at the huge wooden door where the ill people entered. The door Theo wanted to enter.

"We call that Gladiator. We dunno how many died behind it. But plenty. You can see sweat marks from their hands as they stood leaning against it. Some came through okay. But plenty died."

"I'm...curious to know what's behind that door." Theo wished he had a script, but everyone spoke to Jason differently. "You've taken a lot of people through."

"I have. When I get to know someone well, sometimes I'll let them through."

"I'd like that. I need that."

"People do."

"But I've been given..." Theo couldn't say the words aloud. He'd told no one the timing, barely acknowledged to himself that his life could be counted in months.

"You like it here, don't you?"

"I do. Really. There's something very calming about the place."

"That's what we aim for. Our customers...mostly they've made a decision. Come to an acceptance, or had a realization. It calms you, to be in that state of mind."

Jason Davies put his hands on Theo's.

"Can you tell me who recommended you?"

"Nobody. I just heard about it."

"Usually we only accept recommendations. How did you hear about us?"

Theo blinked. "I'm afraid I eavesdropped on a plane. I guess they thought no one could hear, because they were talking under a blanket, but my hearing is very good. I had to find the place myself, though."

He knew everyone was listening, because he had heard all the other interviews, both the successes and the failures. He hadn't identified why some failed.

"Tell me about yourself," Jason said. He had the questionnaire on the table before him. "It says here your greatest fear is bats."

"No! Not at all. The death of bats. That's my greatest fear."

Jason tapped his nose. "Is this an element of your disease?"

Theo felt his cheeks flush. He rubbed his nose. All his life, blood had drained from it when he was nervous, scared or tired. Children weren't smart enough to think of connecting it to bat's white nose fungus, but he thought of it himself and he didn't mind. He liked the similarity.

"No, this is just nerves. My fingertips go white sometimes, too. It's not life-threatening. Not like the bat disease. It gets carried from one cave to another by people who love bats and want to see them all. One of those ironies."

"People are a bit like that, aren't they?"

He asked Theo about bats, simple questions, leading him to feel comfortable, relaxed.

"All right. Look, come through."

Jason led the way through the gladiator door, through a short hallway to a bright-red door covered with stickers of unicorns, rainbows and puppies. *Family of four* b1952, b1953, b1975, b1980, d1984. Theo touched it.

"Father gathered them in the toy room and shot them all," said Jason. "Incredible tragedy. But don't things lose their awfulness over time? Become gossip, or matters of curiosity?"

Theo realized he was asking an actual question.

"It's still awful, isn't it? That the children died. And the wife." Theo thought he heard voices inside and the sound of a ball bouncing.

Jason smiled. "Yes. Of course it is. What doesn't kill you makes you stronger." Theo thought this made no sense at all.

Jason led Theo to a small, sunny alcove. A young woman sat there, sipping from a delicate tea cup. Her black hair was soft around her head.

"This is Cameron. She's going to ask you some questions, talk to you a bit about your questionnaire."

Theo sat down and smiled at Cameron. She smiled back.

"Would you like a cup of herbal tea?"

"No, thank you. I just finished one." Theo found it hard to contain his nerves, to maintain politeness.

"Okay then." She was very still and Theo was still with her. "What did you think of the questionnaire?"

He laughed. "It was pretty full on. I don't think I've ever thought about myself like that before."

Do you think of yourself as a good person? Is there anything that makes you feel guilty? How much do you give to charity each year? How many hours of voluntary work do you do each week? Do you feel guilty about the number of hours you do?

"I wasn't sure what the point was."

"The point is never meant to be clear in these things. We just want an understanding of you and your motivations. It's really an important part of the process. And, to be honest, we're not interested in helping psychopaths."

"I hope I'm not one of those."

She smiled. "You are not."

They talked for another hour. Theo hadn't felt so relaxed in a long time, and he hadn't ever talked about himself for so long. She seemed to understand about the bats, and didn't blame him for his state of loneliness. She spun her wedding ring periodically and he appreciated the signal; *this is all it is,* she was telling him. He liked things to be clear.

Jason joined them. "Feeling okay?"

Theo nodded. He didn't want to mention how he felt physically.

"Okay. So what we're talking about here is a second chance. You came to us, like all the others did, because you're desperate. You want to have another go at it. And you're tired of the pain, and the fear. Is that about right?"

"Yes." Theo's throat constricted and the word came out as a whisper.

"All right then. We need to sort out the paperwork." Jason opened the folder he carried and removed papers and a pen. "It will cost your life savings. I need to start with that. You need to begin this process with nothing to your name."

Theo had been prepared for a high price. "If I die I'll have nothing anyway."

"Exactly. That's all in the details. But then you will have to reconsider how you live your life. How you re-live it."

"What does everyone else do, given a second chance?" He wanted that as well.

"Everybody is different. Every single person."

Jason filled in the forms. Theo signed. He agreed never to kill, never to rape or maim. He agreed to live a good life, to make the most of his second chance. He signed the papers believing fully in this commitment.

"So...what is going to happen? Can I ask? What is the actual process?"

"We can talk about that tomorrow when you come back for your appointment."

"Come here? So is there a clinic here or something?"

"We can talk about that tomorrow." Jason said. "My suggestion is that you spend the day somewhere you care about. Somewhere important. Some will spend it with loved ones, but many prefer not to. There is nothing certain in this world and this is no exception."

Theo knew there were questions he could ask.

"It will take all you've got. We've discussed the money. But the life. You will be leaving your past behind. The people, the places. You won't want to visit your bat cave again."

"There are other bat caves."

"You'll feel nothing for them. That memory will be lessened, so much so that you will wonder where you read about it, if you think of it at all."

"I didn't know that."

"Make your visits. And decide. It's never too late to change your mind. But this may be your last chance."

Death's Door Café

Theo went to the bat cave, his first visit in 17 months. Only the memory of them remained but that memory was strong. Hours spent on a rough mat on the cave floor, his face covered, listening to them, feeling the flap of their wings. Close to half a million bats was the estimation, and through three generations of Theo's family there had been no harm, no damage. Then reports came in of the diseases they carried, and one scientist was bitten. Theo couldn't even remember now if the man had died; certainly there was a lot of fuss. Theo never believed it was the bats.

His father was determined. "Too many kids here to risk," he said, because there were cousins as well as siblings, all of them working on the farm, balancing it with school.

He was advised that fire was the best, the kindest way. That the smoke would put the bats to sleep and the fire would then burn the bodies so they weren't left with half a million corpses, just a pile of ash that could be swept away.

Theo's father made the children stay in the house, but it was an old place with gaps so the smell came through dead clear. They watched smoke billowing out, saw Theo's dad dashing out for air then back in again, and again, the whole thing taking most of the day. Theo's grandfather helped, and the brothers, all Theo's uncles, no women allowed to kill. Women inside keeping the kids quiet, baking up scones and cakes, stirring soup, all of them talking bright and cheerful as if a massacre was not taking place.

Theo never forgave them for that.

It wasn't as if the advice was right; the smoke did not kill them all, so many were burnt to death. And the fire did not burn them all to ash; the bodies piled at the entrance to the cave so that Theo and his cousins had to help dig the men out. Those bat bodies still warm, some charred, and the flutter of them, the sense they were still alive when they weren't. And the smell; he'd thought he was used to guano, that he actually liked it, but this was like poison.

It was years later a journalist came to confront his father with evidence the bats hadn't needed to die.

Theo's father cried as the journalist continued relentlessly to tell him...*you didn't have to. Those bats had lived in the cave for 150 years and you killed them.*

Theo cried, too. He said to his father, as he had said many times, "You should have saved the bats."

The farm was no longer in his family. His father was too sick to look after anything at all. His mother long gone. "Those bats. All that bat shit," his father said, coughing, furious.

The new owners didn't mind Theo visiting, as long has he didn't come knocking on the door for water. The bat cave was empty. Theo could see his own footprints in the dirt floor, and the broom marks from the last time he'd tidied up. Guano still decorated the walls and the rocks, and the smell of smoke, and the walls were dark from the fire. He lay on the ground and tried to imagine them back again, alive, generations of them coming and going and his family with no guilt on their heads.

It was there he decided. Imagine not caring anymore. Imagine not carrying this guilt, this sorrow. And this pain.

Theo couldn't eat or sleep that night. In the morning, he dressed carefully. A casual suit, a fresh, pale mauve cotton shirt, clean shoes, underwear he wasn't embarrassed by. Clothes he'd be happy to be buried in, if it came to that.

He felt as if the atmosphere at the Dusseldorf Café was charged, as if they were all watching him with envy.

The waiter brought him a carrot juice he didn't order. "On the house!", patting him on the back as if congratulating him.

Just the smell of it made Theo feel sick. He'd never been so nervous, so terrified, in all his life.

Jason came to his table after half an hour. "Come on through," he said. The other regulars all held their breath, it seemed to Theo. As if they could bring the magic to themselves by not breathing. He wiggled his fingers goodbye.

They walked through the gladiator door.

Death's Door Café

Jason said, "Did you manage to see anyone yesterday?"

"There's not really anyone I wanted to see. My family... we're not really in touch. Nothing in common."

Jason nodded, smiled, as if this was ordinary, something he heard all the time. "It's the people left behind who suffer when someone dies, so a loner leaves less grief than a father of three."

"But I'm still worthy. That's part of why I'm here," said Theo. "I want time to make a family of my own, one I choose and have a chance to mould."

"Most people don't like being moulded."

"I want a second chance, to make people care." Theo thought for a moment, then amended it to, "To find someone to care for. I don't want to die alone. This will give me the chance, it'll help me to find someone. It'll be different this time."

"How different?"

"I've made my money. I won't have to focus on that."

"You won't have much, though. Financially, it'll be like starting again."

"But I don't care now. I've done that. I want something else."

Jason touched his shoulder. "Good. That's very good. Now, the last thing we need to do is to get you to handwrite a letter. To cover us. It's a farewell letter of sorts."

"Who do I make it out too?"

"It needs to be to someone who knows you very well as you are now. You really have no one?"

Theo thought of his managers, his staff. "I've got people." He made it out to his vice-president.

He had little to say; he'd long since dealt with the business side of things, anticipating his own death.

"And then there's this." It was a promise of complete secrecy. "Do not tell others what happens. You may, if you are absolutely certain they are suitable, recommend someone, but do not bring them in yourself."

They walked.

They passed through a bullet-scarred door to a long hallway. "One of Ben Hall's gang died in front of this door. Shot to death." Jason poked a finger through one of the holes.

"There is a bat cave where that gang holed up," Theo said. "No one really knows where. Or they do but they want to protect the bats."

"So many connections," Jason said. "Now, what we have back here is a series of rooms. We're going to have a look at them, and you'll choose the one which suits you."

"How will I know?"

"You'll feel an empathy. Feel it physically, almost as if you could pick it up. One of these rooms will resonate with you. You'll feel a grieving, a sense of loss. One of these rooms will make your heart beat faster, or bring a lump to your throat. You don't need to know why; you need to listen to your body."

The door on Room One looked like it had come from a ship. Inside was a small children's room.

"A child died behind this door. It was so airtight and heavy, when the ship sunk he couldn't get out. He suffocated."

"Oh, God." Theo closed his eyes. He thought he sensed movement which made him dizzy. He reached out to balance himself on Jason.

"Let's look at the others before you make up your mind."

They walked. "What's...actually going to happen in the room?" Theo asked. "Once I've chosen it?"

"There will be some relaxation exercises. We always start with that."

Theo thought, *I'm an idiot. No one knows I'm here. Who knows what the fuck these people are doing. I'm insane. I should go.*

"Everyone feels nervous at this point, but I don't like to pre-discuss too much. It's better this way. Tell me about what you might do with your second chance. Your questionnaire wasn't big on helping others, Theo. Would you address that, perhaps?"

"I would," Theo said. "Because it makes sense." He wasn't sure that was true.

"You might be asked to do more good than you have done before. The universe may ask this, I mean."

Theo was silent. No one had expected him to do good before. "Of course," he said. "Whatever it takes." He had an absolute terror of death, after his experience with the bats,

Death's Door Café

and with his mother's passing. He wanted to avoid it for as long as possible; until he was deep in dementia and didn't notice his own dying, if possible.

The door on Room Two was narrow, with inlaid wood. It seemed Asian in influence.

"This is a popular one. Behind this door a Chinese prostitute was beaten to death over a hundred years ago." Theo leaned toward the door, wanting to touch the detail.

"This one?" Jason asked. He pushed the door open. The smell was overwhelming; incense, and perfume, as if both were present in living form.

Theo shook his head.

Room Three was a toilet with an opaque glass door.

"He died in the toilet. Fat and lazy. Heart attack at 42, lay on the floor, paralyzed, blocking the door. They couldn't get him out for four hours. Everything in the rooms is recreated precisely."

Theo shuddered. Stepped away. Put his hand over his face.

"Not that one, then. People do choose it, you'd be surprised. Smell and all.

The door to Room Four was a studded, shiny one.

"He slept through the hotel fire alarm and died of smoke inhalation. No one realized he wasn't safe."

Jason looked at Theo.

"This one could be for you."

He opened the door and they stepped inside. It was a typical, dull hotel room. The fan overhead spun slowly, slightly off kilter, and there was a sound to it like flapping bat wings.

Theo felt his throat constrict, his veins swell. He could hear them; the bats calling out, as they did when he was a child. Calling out to him, making him feel as if he belonged amongst them.

"It sounds like bats flying. Can you hear it?

"Everybody hears something different. We all see the same thing, though."

On the bed; it looked like a man, but there was no substance to him.

"We all see it," Jason said, comforting him.

The ghost on the bed shifted onto his side. His shirt tail hung out; it was crinkled.

"What I'm going to do now is to help you into a state of deep sleep. This will help us assess your physicality, now that we understand your mentality. It'll be comfortable, and you'll wake up with a sense of calm."

Theo felt a moment of panic. He looked for cameras, for some evidence that this was weird and wrong.

"Theo, really. It's okay. You've seen the others; you know it's okay. You really, absolutely know that. Let go of your fear and allow it to happen."

Theo closed his eyes. He thought he could hear the calling of the bats, but he often did. It was a memory. A guiding force. He felt himself slipping into sleep and wondered if this was all he was meant to do.

He shivered; it was cold. The ghost was gone, though there was a smell in the air of whisky, and aftershave, and soap. It was night outside, and that darkness with the flapping of the fan brought the bats to mind again. He curled up and wept with grief for those bats, lost generations, and for his father, who had killed them, and his grandfather, and for himself, because he had been a child.

He slept.

He dreamed his mother was burning the dinner and the smell woke him. There was smoke in the room, it was full of smoke and he could hear sirens and screams and he was hot, now. Flames licked under the door. He wrapped the sheet around his waist and ran to the window. It was bolted shut, double glazed. He found his shoe and hammered the window, coughed, coughed, his eyes streamed and his lungs burnt, he choked and coughed and collapsed, he could not draw breath and he could feel his eyes clouding, feel the heat leaving his body, then all was black.

He awoke feeling nothing. He wore his own clothing again and he felt cool, as if a breeze washed over him. He curled up, enjoying the comfort of the bed.

He curled up.

He had not been able to do that for some time; he felt flexible. He stretched out his arms, lifting them high.

"How do you feel?" Jason said. Theo had forgotten his existence, had not heard him enter the room, or, even, knew if he'd left.

"I don't know," said Theo. There was no guilt, he did know that. And the grief was gone, the sorrow for the death of the bats. There was room for something else.

It seemed the ache in his stomach was gone, and his veins didn't hurt.

"Give it a few days."

"I thought I died. There was a fire...did someone put it out? Is everyone all right? What about Cameron, is she okay?"

"There was a fire," Jason said. "We discovered that if we trick the body into believing it has died, it will recover from any fatal disease. We've had particular success with cancer. So we placed you behind a death's door, and we physically, in actuality, re-created the death. You DID die. You took some of the suffering of those who have passed before you, especially him."

"I feel as if the world must have changed," Theo said. "I feel so different, the world must have changed."

"You are a poetic man. But yes. This will suck the spiritual energy from all surrounds. You'll notice everyone around will be feeling lethargic for a day or two. We like to complete the process on Sunday evenings best. People pass off their reaction as Mondayitis."

Jason handed Theo a wallet with $500. "To get you started. Good luck. I've put my card in there. You're welcome to come back if and when you need to. We don't encourage debauchery of the body, but...well, this gives you the freedom to explore without the concerns others have. You will need to consider the financial element. For each visit we require at least double the last. Obviously, all you possess, but it needs to far exceed the amount you paid this time."

He led Theo to the back door.

"Could I say goodbye? I feel as if I know them all so well. And thank the waiters. They're so kind. And to Cameron."

"Best not," Jason said. "Not all of them will pass through the door. It's best for them not to know for sure until..."

The air outside smelt good; someone was cooking onions. He suddenly felt hungry. "A hamburger," he said to himself. "No, a steak."

He felt better the next day, and the next, then he saw his doctor.

"I'd call it a miracle if I believed in them," said the doctor. "But I don't. Good luck. Make the most of your second chance."

Theo did. He met and married a recovering drug addict who never needed another drink or another drug. He didn't invite any of his family to the wedding; as far as they were concerned he had disappeared.

He didn't miss them.

There were times, though, when a spinning fan made a light flicker, or when his ears picked up conversations he shouldn't hear, that he thought of the bat cave and its cold comfort and he did miss that, with an ache he could not ease.

THE GOLEM OF LEOPOLDSTADT
TARA ISABELLA BURTON

Into the clay she pressed her loneliness. She made a man in the image of her father, whom she did not love, and used a needle to poke letters into his back. She hollowed out his cheeks so that they were as hard and wolf-like as her father's; with her nails she made crosses in the eyes. Clara stretched the clay and pummeled it; she feasted on her tears and ignored Cornelius when he knocked.

"Papa's awake." He was dying.

She slipped the figure into her apron pocket and went downstairs.

They sat as they always sat: in silence. Papa, wheezing, up on the pillows. Cornelius in glory at their father's right hand. Mama twisting her fingers in her lap, trembling. Clara in darkness at the other end of the room. The shutters were closed; the electricity flickered. Cobwebs trailed up and down the bedposts. Clara could not breathe.

Papa reared up; Mama flinched. Papa kissed Cornelius on both cheeks and whispered a blessing Clara could not hear as she hollowed out her father's heart with her thumbs.

Cornelius was the anointed one; he was the hope of Leopoldstadt. He was the branch of David and he was the remnant. He was the child who had been born in darkness, and he was the boy who had survived. Women often stopped in the streets to gather him into their arms and weep, because he reminded him of the ones they had lost. In the brightness of his eyes he bore the promise of renewal. He was studying to be a rabbi. God had spared him. God had chosen him.

Papa had told them the story over and over again, the story of the childless officer's wife over whom the toddler Cornelius had once tripped in the Prater, who had poured out the fervent instincts of her motherly heart, and when the calamity had started had used her influence to spare the whole family from those railway cars. It was a miracle of God in a time without miracles, for God had singled Cornelius out as the rod and as its flower, to feed on curds and honey, and to survive.

God had not chosen Clara, who had been born three years after it was all over, colicky and pale, and raised in silent, spinsterish seclusion in her father's house. She was unfavoured; she polished the picture-frames. She turned away visitors at the door—Papa refused to face the ones who came to call. She cooked dinner; she helped Frau Moritz with the silver. She crept out at lunchtime, volumes of Papa's Talmud hidden in her satchel, and sat alone among the roses of the Volksgarten to read them, ecstatic with the thrill of transgression. She received Papa's curses with downcast eyes, and when he blessed Cornelius she turned away, swallowed, and reflected on the darkness outside God's wings.

God's hands had saved Cornelius, but Clara's hands worked in her lap, kneading as they had kneaded for nineteen years. Clay was the only thing she was good at. Twenty or thirty copies of her father lined her bedroom wall. Forty or sixty crossed and unloving eyes stared down at her when she went to sleep at night. She did not complain. She did not make a fuss. She only kneaded the clay, and leavened it with her hate.

"My son," Papa closed his eyes. "You have the voice of an angel. You have the mind of a scholar. You are beautiful and you have never suffered." His hands shook as he raised his fingers to the paintings. "You see what belongs to you. You see what you must do. You see what you will take from me when I am gone."

The paintings glared down at them. These were Papa's favourites, the ones Clara was not permitted to touch, the few Papa had not sold when he closed his gallery. The greatest collection in Vienna, Papa had said. They were Papa's legacy; they were Cornelius's inheritance.

"May you be righteous, my son." Papa coughed up spittle and blood. "May you be wise. You will redeem us all."

When she did not know better and her father had not told her better, Clara had wanted to be righteous, to be wise. She'd wanted to trace her fingers along the great scrolls, and to read the signs of holiness in the seasons, and to press beneath her palms the name of God. But God had chosen Cornelius, and Papa had chosen Cornelius. God had been stolen from her. God did not want her, and so she hated Him as she hated her father, and her brother, and this too she twisted into her clay.

Cornelius knelt before their father and received the blessing; Mama sobbed roughly into her handkerchief, and Clara worked her clay in silence. Her father did not call for her, and she did not answer him. She rose and went to her room, and when Cornelius knocked an hour later to tell her that her father was dead she did not reply.

"You're a fool." He quoted to her verses about fishhooks, about cows of Bashan about his God who was a vengeful God. He blazed with the righteousness of prophets and called her names of faithless women. His voice was high like a eunuch's and his cheeks were bright with his kingship and he did not even lower himself to cross her threshold. He named her adulteries and his words brought color to her cheeks. She listened to it all without blinking, and when he had finished she calmly put her figurine on the shelf to dry.

"That's it?" Cornelius leaned against the doorframe, and his hair gleamed golden in the lamplight.

"That's it." She did not look at him.

"*Three friends, said the Rabbis, has man. God, his father, and his mother.*" He smoothed the sleeves of his coat, as he always did when quoting the Talmud, and Clara imagined clawing out its many-colored thread.

"I have no friends." Her blasphemy thrilled her. Her father was dead, and with him God had vanished from the stars outside the window. The streets of Vienna were empty of shadows, of signs and words of holiness.

When he had gone Clara locked the door and put her

head in her hands. She did not cry—she *would* not cry. She would be stronger than Cornelius, stronger than God who had chosen him, stronger than the justice which she despised as injustice, stronger still than Papa who had cast her out, stronger than the dead. She would rage against God; she would fight His angel and win.

The idea appeared to her. She would seize hold of her birthright—she would smash open her father's desk and grab handfuls of schillings, grab the books which she was not allowed to read, overturn the paintings and fling wide the doors of the house onto Czerninplatz and invite the neighbors into their dark and festering halls. She would pack her suitcase full of clay men and sacred books, and then she would take the train to Budapest, and onwards to Jerusalem, and there she would stare into the face of God until she *made* Him listen to her, until He quelled her rage, until He brought her justice.

Mama was still wailing, and Cornelius was reciting the mourners' prayers, but she would not listen to them now. She forced her way past the cobwebs, through the dust, into her father's study where the mould crept at the wallpaper and the termites nipped at the wood.

Clara sat at her father's desk. Her palms trembled as she pressed them to the handles. She forced them still and then she pulled open the drawers, one by one, flinging them back, delving deep into them, overturning papers, snatching at documents, at coins and paper notes, at anything of value that she could use to buy a ticket, a night in a hotel room, a way out. She threw the drawers on the floor; she slid open the hidden compartments; she plunged her hand up to the wrist in her father's secrets.

She had trespassed; it was delicious. Papa could not stop her now—Cornelius could not stop her now! God Himself could not stop her!

She sliced her thumb open on a stack of papers; she sucked the blood from her fingers, and in that pause she caught sight of the contents.

It was an appraisal of Werner Kronenberg's *David*. She'd heard of it before, of course. It was one of the paintings that had hung in the Siebermayer ballroom before the war. Every

The Golem of Leopoldstadt

Jew or Gentile of note in Vienna had danced there in the last days of the Hapsburg Empire. But the house was abandoned now, and the Siebermayers were all dead, and the painting—like all the rest—had been taken.

She tore through the papers. Each one was like the last—a receipt, an appraisal, bearing the dates that made her flinch. *1939. 1943.* Her father's careful signature. Valuations, analysis, details about paintings that had been taken, information invaluable to those who held them. Information worth several thousand German *reichsmarks*—or a little boy's life.

"My father is a betrayer." She whispered it aloud; it gave her strength. "I was born because my father is a betrayer."

The miracle of the officer's wife—the miracle of Cornelius's bright blue eyes—the etiology of their salvation—all nothing more than stories—

"Cornelius is alive because my father is a betrayer."

This was Cornelius's birthright. This was Cornelius's inheritance. This was the shame that shuttered their windows; this was the stain that kept visitors from the door. Everything around them was ash, and bone, and *after*, and their father had picked at the carrion of Israel like a vulture. He had crouched at the door of his brothers and waited for them to be dragged out, one by one, and watched their houses as they burned. He had saved his only son.

She knew she should weep. But Clara could not weep. There was only joy.

"Because my father is a betrayer. Cornelius was not chosen by God.

"God has not chosen him."

God had not forgotten her. God had not cast her out. God had folded His wings around her; God had set His hand on her hand, and she was the first-born of Israel, and the hope of Leopoldstadt. She was the daughter of God who was forged in the very beginning, and would be there in the end, and she rejoiced in the whole world.

She was wild with joy; she breathed the breath of God. She flung open the shutters, drew in the moon; she aired the house of its shame.

Then came the rage.

She thought of her tears, and of the hatred she had nursed at her breast, of the darkness that was the darkness of her father, and the stain that was the birthright of her brother, of the times she'd felt God's wrath crawling up and down her skin and longed to tear it off in strips, with fishhooks, until she was clean again.

She returned to her room and took down another hunk of unformed clay. She kneaded another pair of arms, another pair of legs, another square, flat head with crosses for the eyes. She stretched and pressed the clay; she clawed at its limbs, and as she worked she murmured the secret name of God.

"Let there be truth." Her lips swelled with whispers. "Let there be truth."

She carved the letters into its back, the *aleph, mem, tav* which signified truth, and which God Himself had bound to life.

"Let there be justice. Let there be truth."

She closed her eyes and felt it stir beneath her fingers. She listened for the hum of life in her hands.

Clara knew what would happen next. She had read the words of the rabbis. She knew that God had formed man, and man had formed mud, and from that mud once in Prague there had risen a defender, who had shaken the evildoers like grain in a sieve, and that this defender could rise again, formed by the palms of those whom God had blessed.

She heard its first, wordless cry and she knew what she had done.

She rose quickly; she left suddenly. She swallowed down the beating of her heart and from across the Czerninplatz she saw the shadow that hulked through the house, and saw the first explosion, and the first few flames.

She understood. She understood why a voice, crying out in the wilderness, would cry out for the justice of the Lord. She understood the wail of Babylon, and the demand for scorched earth, for a reckoning. Her God was a vengeful God, and he punished unto generations.

Behind her, the hope of Leopoldstadt blazed and gave light to the first spike of morning. She walked onwards to the Danube, and from there to Jerusalem.

ROAD DEAD
F. BRETT COX

There was no cell service in our town. The nearest tower was in the next county. The closest place we could get a signal was the cemetery north of town. Danny needed to make a call and the rest of us didn't have anything better to do. Jake drove and Danny called shotgun. Rob and I were in the back. Before the turn to the cemetery there was a turn onto a dead end road and at the turn there was a sign that said Private Road Dead End. It had been there ever since I could remember. But there were smudges over the Private and the End like someone had tried to erase them and if you just looked quick it looked like the sign said Road Dead. Well hell Jake said and turned onto the road. What the fuck I got to make my call Danny said. Sorry man got to check this out Jake said. Goddammit I got to make this call make it quick Danny said. Good luck with that Rob said. I didn't say anything. I couldn't remember the last time I'd been on this road. Jake kept driving. It hadn't rained in forever and the car kicked up a lot of dust. The sky was overcast though and you couldn't see the sun. There were plenty of clouds. It just wouldn't rain. We got to the end of the road and there was a log cabin. That prefab shit Rob said. No this one looks old I said. And it did. The wood was so worn it was almost shiny and there were patches on it where it looked like someone had tried to chop the house down. Jake pulled over on the far side of the road from the house and cut the motor. He rolled his window down and we could hear music coming from the house. Classical music like the teacher played in humanities unit. It sounded familiar and before I knew it I said Bach. Danny turned around and looked at me. Lah de dah Professor he said. Rob snorted like it was funny. Then Danny said to Jake now what? Don't know Jake said. Make up your fucking mind I still got to make my call Danny said. Jake looked at Danny and said well fuck all right then. Jake got out of the car and started walking towards the house. Dumb shit always got to be chasing something Danny said. Then he started checking his phone. God damn this sorry remote ass place he said. Rob snorted again. Fucking Bach he said. Jake walked up at an angle to the front door and moved toward the side of the house. He put his elbows out to the side and got up on tiptoe and made a big deal out of creeping up to the house like he was one of the Three Stooges. When he got up to the side of the house he made another big deal of peering into what I guess was a window and then he kind of shook and went forward like he had tripped and then he wasn't there anymore. You couldn't tell if he had tripped and fallen in through the window or if he'd been pulled inside. Fuck Rob said. Danny was still fooling with his phone. What happened he said. Goddammit I said and got out of the car and walked across the road over to where Jake had been. There was a window all right but it was closed. I looked inside. They didn't have any lights on and it was hard to see much but there were a bunch of people. More than you would have thought would have been inside such a small place. Some were men and some were women and they all wore regular clothes. I didn't see Jake. One of the men was lying on some sort of table. He was strapped down to the table and it didn't look like he had any clothes on. He was shaking. Not like he was cold but like he was riding down a rough road. A couple of times he seemed about ready to jump off the table but the straps held him down. Some of the people were holding things but I couldn't tell what they were. You could hear the music like the window was open. There was another window on the other side of the room that looked like it was covered in plastic until you realized the whole wall was covered in plastic and the plastic had dark stains all over it. I looked again at the man on the

Road Dead

table and for a second I thought I knew him but then the one standing closest to him looked up. It was a woman. I don't know if she saw me or not but she stared like she was looking at something. I backed away from the window and into someone standing right behind me. I yelled and spun around. It was Danny. He and Rob had gotten out of the car and followed me over to the window. Fuck fuck fuck I said and ran for the car. Danny beat me there and got in and started it up. Rob and I piled in and we took off. We hauled down the road and turned and headed back up the main road towards the cemetery. What about Jake Rob said. I don't know I said. Danny didn't say a word but when we got up to the cemetery he pulled in and started driving up the path. The fuck you doing Rob said. Danny kept on as fast as he had been going on the main road. A loose rock flew up off the dirt and cracked the windshield. When we got to the very back past all the tombstones he stopped the car. The fuck you doing Rob said. Rob's right what about Jake we've got to go back I said. You looked through that fucking window fuck Jake it's his own goddamn fault Danny said. Then what are we doing here why don't we go I said. Danny looked at his phone and then looked and us. I've got a signal he said and got out of the car. It was Jake's fucking idea he said and walked away. Rob and I stayed in the car. I turned around and looked back at the main road. The tombstones ran down to the road in neat rows. One near the car had fallen over. Danny was standing by it talking into his phone low like he was trying to keep a secret but I could hear him. Hello? he said. Hello? I looked at Rob. Now what I said but now he was looking back at the main road so I turned back around. A car was pulling into the cemetery with another right behind it. About halfway up the path the first car stopped and then the second. The first car turned its lights on bright and the driver got out and then the rest of them. And Jake. Jake got out of the second car and started moving towards Danny but Danny didn't notice. He was still talking into his phone but now he was shouting. Hello? he kept saying. Hello? Hello?

THE QUIET ROOM
V. H. LESLIE

"Turn the music down," Terry said, standing on the threshold of his daughter's room. Some unspoken rule forbade him from going in, especially without permission. It was different for mums, he imagined; no part of the house was off limits to them, they could tidy and snoop in equal measure, unchallenged. But for dads, a teenage daughter's room was a minefield, a frightening place that only served as a reminder of how distant the days of childhood were. In truth, he preferred to stay outside.

His daughter, Ava, unaware of his presence, danced uninhibited to the music. The gap in the door allowed him to see more of her body than he would have liked, a body that had somehow grown overnight to replace the goofy child with pigtails and grazed knees. The clothes she wore seemed to belong to that younger Ava as well; too small and too tight, riding up to expose the body that had outgrown them, though Terry knew she'd bought them like that on purpose. Wearing as little as possible was the fashion these days and she was a dedicated follower, like all her friends. He should talk to her about that, about following the herd. But for now he just needed her to stop the music.

Terry rapped the door again. "Ava."

She was deaf to everything but the synthesized wail reverberating from her speakers. Terry raised his voice, "Ava, I won't say it again..."

"Dad!" Ava replied. Her voice was louder than Terry's,

amplified by embarrassment. "What are you doing up here?"

Terry was always amazed at how easily she could turn things around. Now he was in trouble for trespassing on her space. "Your music—"

"What?" Ava placed a hand behind her ear.

"It's too loud. Just turn it down."

She huffed as she walked to her stereo and turned it off.

"Happy now?" Her question was absurdly loud without the music to compete with.

"Yes," Terry said quietly. A poster of a very young looking man, tanned and shirtless, gazed back from above his daughter's bed. Terry pointed at it. "He'll catch a cold," he said, realizing as soon as he did how old he sounded.

Ava just raised her eyebrows, something she'd perfected to make Terry feel both chastised and insignificant. He wondered if she'd learnt it from Prue.

"You don't think maybe you have too many posters up?" Terry asked.

"It's *my* room, Dad."

It was *his* house, he wanted to say, therefore it was *his* room. But there was no sense in being pedantic. It was important for Ava to feel that she had a place. He supposed it was a good thing that Ava had become so territorial about her attic bedroom. The house had so many other good-sized bedrooms on the second floor, but she seemed to intent on having the smallest room, furthest from the nucleus of the house.

"It makes the room look a little crowded is all," he offered. He avoided what he really wanted to say, that he didn't like those half-naked men gazing down at his daughter. But there was no point rehashing an earlier argument; they'd already disagreed about poster-to-wall ratio and Terry had conceded. He couldn't start telling her what to do now.

Ava shrugged in a way that said she didn't care about his opinion. And why should she? He hadn't exerted any kind of influence on her life so far. Why should she listen to him now?

Terry realized he was hovering. "Dinner won't be long."

"Ok."

Terry looked around Ava's room one more time, trying

not to be disappointed at how much it conformed to a typical adolescent space. As well as the posters of manufactured pop groups on the walls, piles of clothes and shoes crowded the floor. They'd only moved in a few weeks ago and already the room had the worn look of a teenage den. It wasn't just the room but Ava's choice of music he found so annoying. He worried about her taste. Those formative years when he'd been out of her life were responsible for shaping her in all kinds of ways. He couldn't expect to change her overnight. But he wished she would listen to something else.

He made his way back down the stairs, conscious of the volume creeping higher again. It was clear now why she'd been so keen to claim the attic bedroom; it was so she could make as much noise as she wanted.

Terry walked through the old house, waiting for the pizza delivery boy to arrive with their usual order. It was a big house, bigger than it needed to be for just the two of them. There had been few properties on the market so close to Ava's school and of those it was the most affordable, though bigger and more expensive than he would have liked. Terry still wasn't accustomed to so much superfluous space. He walked through the house now, opening doors to rooms he wasn't sure how to use, how to fill, moving around the empty spaces before closing the doors once more. It was becoming a habit, a nightly tour. He tried not to think of it as some kind of vigil.

Though the house was old, the rooms lacked period features or individual characteristics. They were uniform, bare, gazing back at him with vacant expressions. All except the music room.

He hesitated on the threshold for a moment, drawn by what was on top of the piano. It was the first thing Ava had unpacked, the first thing she'd found a home for but Terry still wasn't used to seeing it. He just hadn't expected to bring Prue with them. The urn was much more plain than he would have expected for Prue. He would have imagined something more showy, more extravagant. But though simple in design, it still made him uneasy. He knew it was only ash and dust but it felt like he was facing an old adversary every time he saw it.

The sooner Ava decided where to scatter her mother's ashes the better. He'd tried to persuade Ava not to put it off, that doing it quickly would help her move on, but really it was because he hated Prue being in their home. The last time they had been under the same roof was thirteen years ago and, with the exception of Ava, he had no happy memories of that time.

Ava couldn't conceive of keeping the urn anywhere else. Prue liked the piano apparently and was especially keen on Liszt. The Prue Terry remembered didn't know the first thing about music, classical or otherwise. Prue's sister was the musical one.

Without looking at the urn, he walked towards the piano and pressed his finger to one of the shiny clean keys, cold beneath his touch. It let out a puff of dust. Terry pressed it again and imagined the effort inside as the mechanics attempted to conjure sound. A second silent exhalation was all he got.

Terry didn't know a thing about pianos but knew this one was busted. He would have thrown it out but for the fact the house was left so vacant, almost unusually so, that its presence seemed all the more engineered. It was almost a relief to find something from its past, even if it was broken. It was odd for a house of this age not to have more relics, Terry thought; old fireplaces, cornicing, fretwork banisters, any would have been typical of this period. The previous owners must have stripped it back to the bare essentials, purging it of its past with copious tins of magnolia. A blank slate.

Terry had moved a lot over the years and most of the homes he'd lived in had retained a few objects from the previous owners; mildewed white goods that were an inconvenience to take, unfashionable light fittings, the odd piece of furniture. And then there were the marks people didn't realize they left behind. Children's measurements on a doorframe, old photographs at the back of a drawer, a dent in the plasterboard from children play fighting too enthusiastically, or from grown-ups fighting for real. Terry liked to trace the narrative of the houses he lived in. The walls whispered their story through such scars.

But this house was silent.

Just like the piano. Terry pressed the key again, half expecting a clear shrill note to contradict him. But he only heard the click of the key as it moved and a whisper of air.

Terry sat on the stool. He wouldn't get rid of it. The piano was the only link to the building's past, a gift from the house. He spread his fingers over the keys, imagining himself a great pianist about to begin a concerto. He lifted his hands above the keyboard ready to bring them down in unison and glanced up at Prue's urn.

A shrill electric note echoed through the room.

Terry leapt back from the piano, stumbling over the fallen stool. He hadn't touched the keys and yet a sound filled the house, becoming a tune he began to comprehend— *The Flight of the Valkyries*, played on distant tinny notes. The new doorbell Ava had persuaded him to buy. Farcical, like the inside of a musical greeting card.

Terry rose quickly, closing the lid of the piano and hurrying to the front door.

Terry placed the pizzas and the dips on the table. He heard Ava bound down the stairs, surprised that she could hear the jingle of the doorbell over her music at the top of the house. She had a way of sensing food.

Ava piled her plate high, whereas Terry only took one slice at a time.

"You know we're going to have to eat real dinners sometime," Ava said with her mouthful.

"Why?"

"Because they're healthy. You're supposed to make sure I eat right."

"It feels right to me."

"Not for your cholesterol."

Terry, glancing at her plate, thought it a little hypocritical. "Well, what should I cook?"

"Pasta or fish. Vegetables and stuff."

Terry nodded, suitably admonished. He was reminded of one of the last conversations he'd had with Prue, her concern that he spoilt Ava too much.

"What do you normally eat?" she said between noisy mouthfuls, "you know, when you were on your own?"

Terry was quite content with sardines on toast, or pub grub from the local. But he always ordered a takeaway when he had Ava. He saw her so sporadically, sometimes only every couple of weeks that it always felt like a victory. Prue had not made it easy, so he equated seeing his daughter with a kind of celebration. It still felt like that, even though he was well aware they were engaged in a complex renegotiation of their roles. He wasn't used to being a full time father yet. For him, seeing his daughter everyday had not lost its novelty. Though clearly pizza had.

She was still waiting for an answer.

"Oh, this and that," he said.

"Well, why don't we go shopping tomorrow? Get some healthy food in?"

Terry smiled; when Ava wasn't being moody or answering back she was actually a pretty nice kid.

"I'd like that."

"I can make my chili surprise."

"What's the surprise?"

"You'll see." Ava smiled. "It was Mum's favourite."

Terry swallowed hard on Ava's use of the past tense but washed it down with his beer. He wouldn't have imagined Prue liking chili, too much spice for her bland palate. He was beginning to realize how little he knew about his ex-wife. They'd been little more than strangers at the end.

Terry smiled, taking the good mood to try to connect with Ava. "So how are you finding it? The house I mean?"

"It's ok. I like my room. But it's not very homely."

"No?"

"It feels empty. Even with all our stuff."

Terry thought about the piano room, the only room that felt occupied.

"Who lived here before?" Ava asked.

"No-one, apparently. Not for the last twenty years at least. Just been sitting empty."

"About time we came along then," Ava smiled, helping herself to another slice.

Terry smiled too. When she wasn't in that room of hers he felt like she was actually listening to him. He wondered whether it was time to deliver some fatherly advice, to address the way she dressed, to talk about her tidying her room a little more frequently.

Upstairs, Ava's music blared suddenly. Terry couldn't make out the words but the tune was melancholic, lovesick. Not the kind of music he would have expected.

"Sorry Dad," Ava said, getting up from the table and heading toward the stairs, "I must have forgotten to turn it off."

Terry listened to her footsteps as she ran up the stairs and the music stopped as suddenly as it had started.

Terry decided it was time to unpack the boxes. He'd been so focused on making a home for Ava that he'd literally left his work wrapped up, concealed beneath bubble wrap. Ava was keen for them to fill the house, to get as close to normality as possible. Besides, she would soon be up for school and he couldn't spend another day roaming around the old house, waiting for her to come home.

He took the blade of a pair of scissors to the first taped box, opening it to a host of chinaware. The tiny porcelain cups rattled as he delved inside. He worked in antiques—at least that was what his shop's frontage had said, but it was really bric-a-brac. "Antiques" sounded better; it implied that the object in question was in some way important. Customers wanted to know when items were made, who owned them, and they attributed worth generally to how well those questions were answered. Terry had learnt very early on that you could sell anything if you gave it a story. And what people sought most were unique stories. What Terry tried to do was to offer the mundane, the forgotten, the overlooked a good narrative. He'd largely succeeded. He'd made some exceptional profits on some lesser-known treasures, partly because of his expertise in restoration but mostly due to the calibre of his stories. Making something out of nothing was his trade.

Terry had decided to make this room, one of the many indistinguishable reception rooms, his workshop. He doubted that it had ever been used for that purpose before. The house felt grand, and though it didn't provide many clues, he imagined it had been designed with only luxury in mind. The reception rooms would have been filled with occasional furniture, countless armchairs to nestle into, little mahogany writing desks for penning love letters or replying to dinner invitations. As he unwrapped dainty teacups and their saucers, vases and ornaments, he thought that it was very likely that once the house would have been filled with such knick-knacks. Except that now, as he arranged them carefully on the table, they looked out of place. Absence and neglect had filled the house so entirely that everything else seemed like an affront.

"Dad?"

It shocked him into nearly dropping the teacup in his hand. He placed it down carefully. "Ava, you made me jump."

"Sorry. What are you doing?" Framed by the doorway, dressed in her school uniform but still rubbing the sleep from her eyes, she looked more like a child than ever.

"I thought I'd start work today. Come in, come in. Take a look around." He used his best shop voice.

Ava entered the room, picking up bits and pieces that took her fancy. She seemed to like the things that opened and closed, playing with the hinges or the catches, mostly timepieces or ornate pillboxes. She was opening the front of a carriage clock when something in one of the cardboard boxes caught her eye.

"What's that?"

Terry pulled it out and dusted it down. It was a black box, decorated with brightly coloured images of birds in flight. "It's a music box," he said. "Look…" and as he opened it, it began a to play the notes of a lullaby.

"It's beautiful." Ava reached for it. She ran her fingers over the surface.

"It's black lacquer," Terry said, competing with the mechanical tune, "undoubtedly nineteenth century, though the origin is harder to pinpoint. I'd say European, though it looks Japanese. There was a lot of mock oriental stuff then."

"It's beautiful," Ava repeated, holding it up in the light. "Look, there's a girl here," she said, delighted at her discovery, "and another this side but with wings." She turned the box around. "Is she an angel?"

Terry put on his glasses and examined it more closely. "I'd forgotten about this piece. No, she's no angel, I think it's Philomela. You see the bird this side?" He pointed, "The girl *is* the bird. She's transforming into it."

"Why?"

Terry shuffled in his chair. "Well, Philomela was very beautiful and her brother in-law wanted her very much. He engineered it so that she was alone in a cabin in the woods where he, er..." Terry searched for a euphemism. "Where he had his way with her. Then he cut out her tongue so she could never tell anyone what he'd done."

"Gruesome."

"Yes. But Philomela had a plan. She wove the story of his actions into a tapestry and sent it to her sister, who helped her escape. When the brother in-law pursued them, the gods took pity on them, transforming them into birds. Philomela was transformed into the nightingale, the bird with the sweetest voice. I suppose to compensate for a life of silence."

Ava smiled. Terry smiled too; he'd omitted the bit about Philomela's sister's revenge on her husband, how she had murdered their son and fed him to his unknowing father. Somehow infanticide seemed to tarnish the whole story.

Ava picked up the box. "Can I have it?"

Terry shrugged, "Well I'd say it would fetch at least £200."

"Really?"

"Shall we say... a clean bedroom and a hug?"

Ava pretended to think about it. "How about two hugs and I'll wash up instead."

Terry was so impressed with her bartering skills that he

was more than happy to forfeit the clean bedroom. "Deal."

They shook on it.

Ava turned before she got to the door. "One thing I don't get, why a tapestry? It seems like a lot of effort. Why not just write a letter?"

"A letter would have been expected. Only something more subtle would get past the guards. Sometimes we don't see the messages that are right in front of us."

Ava seemed satisfied with that answer and left Terry among his relics.

Terry spent the rest of the day in a frenzy of activity. He'd unpacked most of the boxes and sanded a few smaller pieces of furniture. The room smelt of varnish and woodworm treatment. Ava would be home from school soon and he was looking forward to showing her the progress he'd made.

He was repairing a Georgian chest when he first heard the tapping sound. He strained his ears, listening. A dull repetitive tap. Terry walked about the room, checking the various timepieces that were scattered about. It wasn't a ticking. It was hardly noticeable but it was there, a quiet but indisputable tap, tap, tap.

He walked out into the hallway. The tapping louder now that he'd left the noise of his workshop behind. It was a noise that would drive him mad if he didn't discover the source.

The doorbell broke him from his reverie and for once he was glad to hear it. Any sound was better than that incessant tapping. He jogged to the door, imagining he had wings like the valkyries, excited to see Ava after a long day. Except it wasn't Ava.

Terry froze. For a moment he thought Prue had come back. That she'd somehow wangled her way back into the world of the living to take Ava from him. Then the woman removed her sunglasses and he could see a younger face, kinder eyes.

Philippa.

"Some Gothic mansion you got here," Prue's sister said,

looking the place up and down. "I hope you've had a priest round to bless it."

Terry stood speechless. The resemblance had always been uncanny, though they were not twins. It was as if Prue was resurrected before him, but a younger version, closer to the woman he had married. He'd seen Philippa at the funeral of course, shocked then at how strong the resemblance had become over the years. They kept their distance. They always had.

"Come in," Terry said recovering. They leant in for an awkward kiss. "If you *dare*..." he added in an attempt to relieve the tension.

Philippa raised her eyebrows but followed him inside. "It's big."

"More rooms than I know what to do with. We have a music room, don't you know."

"A haunted library as well, I suppose, and a madwoman in the attic."

"We definitely have one of those," Terry said, relieved to see Ava coming up the path.

"Aunty Philippa!" Ava ran the rest of the distance.

"Mad as a hatter," Philippa agreed as Ava bounded into her.

"Why don't you give Aunty Philippa the grand tour?" Terry said once the hugging was done.

"Sure," Ava said, straightening her uniform. "If you care to follow me."

Terry and Philippa exchanged glances and fell in step behind her.

"Nice piano," Philippa said, stopping at the music room.

"It was here when we arrived," Terry explained. "The only thing the previous tenants left. But it's broken."

"May I?" Philippa asked, walking to it before Terry could object. She sat and pressed at the keys. Terry was reminded of the tapping noise he'd heard earlier, realizing that it had stopped in the interim.

"Silenced," Philippa said.

"Pardon?"

"I think it's been silenced. It's not broken. It's so people can practise without causing a racket. It can be reversed, I know a guy who could fix it."

"Really?" Ava exclaimed.

"I can teach you, if you like? I used to play," as she demonstrated with a silent flourish. "I'm a bit rusty but I'd be willing to share what I know. First things first," she said glancing at the urn, "let's get this piano to make some noise."

Terry found he could tolerate the quiet of the house in the daytime if it meant music in the evenings. Sitting in his workshop he listened to the snatches of melodies next door as Ava took her piano lesson. He could differentiate between them, Philippa's fluid cadenzas and Ava's hesitant and static playing. But Ava was improving. When Philippa left, Ava practiced on her own and he could make out the beginnings of tunes, the foundations of compositions he partially recognized.

It wasn't just the music that he looked forward to but the laughter. The house seemed alive with female voices. Sitting in his workshop he listened to his daughter's voice, laughing over the sound of the piano, and thought it was the most beautiful sound he had ever heard.

"Aunty Philippa said I need to practise more," Ava said at dinner.

"You play every day as it is," Terry replied, though he didn't mind Philippa's sudden involvement. In fact, he was surprised how naturally she slipped into their lives. It was important for Ava to have some familiarity, he reasoned. He helped himself to more of Ava's signature dish, the surprise being copious amounts of jalapenos. His mouth made an O shape as he tried to breath through the heat.

"But I want to get really good," Ava insisted. "I need to work on my tempo apparently and not rush the rests."

"Rests?'"

"The silent bits in between the playing. Aunty Philippa says silence is as important as the sound the notes make. She told me about this composer who wrote a composition of 4 minutes and 33 seconds of silence."

"I bet the audience wanted their money back."

"It was revolutionary."

"You can't compose silence," Terry said, pouring himself a glass of water. "It just exists. He didn't create anything that wasn't already there."

"But it wasn't there. Not until the composer closed the lid of the piano to mark the beginning of the movement. People listened more patiently than they would anywhere else because they were in a concert hall. Can you imagine how long four minutes of silence must have felt when you expected music?"

Terry thought of how quiet the house was in the daytime when he was alone in his workshop. But even then there were the sounds of sanding wood, the ticking of clocks.

"Except it wasn't silence," Ava continued. "People shifted in their seats, coughed. Some even walked out. That was the music he wanted the audience to listen to."

"Sounds a little lazy if you ask me," said Terry. "He wasn't the author of those sounds, he didn't plan that the man in the back row would cough, or that the lady at the front would tut."

"But he created the opportunity for those sounds, they never would have existed if he hadn't made the silence."

Terry looked at his daughter. He hadn't expected to have such a thought provoking conversation over dinner. Though still in her school uniform, she suddenly looked like a young woman and unmistakably like her mother.

That night Terry dreamt of the music room. It was full of people, dressed in black, sitting around the piano as if for a recital. Terry walked among them, noticing how still they all sat, their heads cast down. He saw instruments in their laps or at their feet. He tripped over a cello, the strings catching on his trousers, but it didn't make a sound. Nor did the cellist stoop to pick up the instrument. It was so quiet that even the sound of his footsteps seemed to have been silenced somehow. Terry stamped his foot, trying to make as much noise as he could, and when that failed he knocked over a set of cymbals, expecting the vibrations to shatter the

The Quiet Room

silence. But nothing dented the stillness of the room. He tried to address the gathering but his voice faltered, the people didn't even look at him. Terry grabbed the nearest man by his lapels and shook him roughly, but the man merely stared back vacantly. Terry tried to scream into the man's face, pouring all his confusion and rage into one almighty cry, but no sound came and his throat became hoarse with the effort.

In the background he heard the piano.

Dissonant notes at first, but gradually they merged to form the beginnings of a melody. He avoided looking at what was on top of the piano but glanced across at the keyboard. The lid was down. To signify the beginning of the movement, he remembered. But how could that be? The melody began to gain speed, the volume creeping higher and higher, the playing becoming more crazed, more erratic, building toward an inevitable and deafening crescendo—

Terry sat bolt upright in bed.

He breathed deeply, trying to steady himself, fancying he could hear the sound of his racing heartbeat. As it slowed he was conscious of another sound. He strained his ears and thought he heard the same dissonant notes from his dream.

It was the piano.

It echoed through the corridors of the old house, drifting up the stairs, filling the rooms and recesses with its melancholic air.

Ava.

Terry pulled aside the covers and began down the stairs. He pushed his dream to the back of his mind as he followed the melody to the music room, opening the door with a thud.

The music stopped.

"Ava?"

Ava sat at the piano in her nightclothes. Her fingers were stretched out on the polished veneer of the piano lid. Had she closed it suddenly when he entered the room?

Terry walked towards her in the silence. She opened her eyes slowly as if waking up. She looked around dazedly at her surroundings.

"It's ok," Terry soothed, placing his arm around her, gently bringing her to her feet. "You've had a bad dream. Let's get you back to bed."

As he closed the door, he looked one last time at the piano but saw only the urn.

Ava was quieter than normal the next day. She looked tired, as if she hadn't slept at all. There was no laughter during the piano lesson that evening either. Listening in his workshop, Terry could only hear Philippa's voice giving instructions between the playing. At the end of the lesson Terry walked Philippa to the door.

"Is everything ok with Ava?" she asked before she left. "She seemed a little subdued."

Terry shrugged. He wasn't ready to verbalize his concerns. "Teenagers," he offered.

Philippa looked at Terry for longer than was necessary before saying her goodbyes.

Walking back inside, Terry couldn't quieten his qualms. Ava had hardly uttered a word to him all day. Even at dinnertime, when she was usually so chatty. And she'd hardly touched her food. If something was on her mind he wanted her to be able to talk to him about it. He wondered if she could. She'd always had Prue befo...

Shhhhh!

He stopped in his tracks.

He was outside the music room. For a moment he thought he must have been speaking aloud, that Ava overhearing must have shushed him. But listening now, all he could hear was Ava's playing. He edged closer to the door. For a moment he was sure he heard two voices instead of one. Whispers, muffled by the sound of the piano. And in the background, a soft syllable. *Shhh. Shhh.*

Shhhhhhh!

Terry opened the door.

Ava sat at the piano. The lid was closed.

"Who were you talking to, Ava?"

Ava looked at her father bemused.

"Ava?"

Ava shook her head and made her way up the stairs to her bedroom.

The Quiet Room

The silent treatment continued for the rest of the week. Terry was reminded of Prue's sullen moods when they'd been together. She could go weeks without speaking to him if she wanted to. It was the worst kind of punishment. Terry hadn't expected Ava to inherit her mother's morose temperament; she'd always seemed so much more like him. Terry would have preferred Ava to shout at him, or skulk up to her bedroom and play her abysmal music as loud as her speakers would allow. But the house was as silent as his daughter.

The only exception was her piano lessons, when for a brief hour the house was filled with gentle refrains and familiar melodies. When Philippa left, Ava practised on her own, always the same song; the one he'd heard her play when sleepwalking. A sad, slow air that gradually built, stopping frustratingly short, just before the final crescendo. Terry wished she would play something else but she was as deaf to that request as she was to his pleas to open up.

The only time Ava said anything now, apart from the monosyllabic replies to his questions, was when she was alone at the piano. Listening at the door, Terry was sure he could hear whispers, hushed beneath the dark melody that had come to haunt him.

He resolved to speak to Philippa about it. Maybe she'd noticed something strange during their piano lessons. Seizing the next available opportunity, he took Philippa into his workroom and closed the door.

"Well, she follows instructions," Philippa assured him, "but she doesn't say any more than is absolutely necessary. Her playing though..."

"Yes, she's very good," Terry conceded. "Except that when she practises, she only plays the same tune over and over. It's driving me mad."

Philippa asked him if he could identify it. He hummed it instead, feeling a little self-conscious.

Philippa looked away. She shrugged after a few moments.

"Sorry, I don't recognize it. Listen, I'm sure whatever this is will blow over. Ava is adjusting." She placed her hand on his arm. "She's been through an awful lot."

Terry leant in closer, "That's not all. When you're gone I hear her talking in the piano room. Talking to…"

Philippa nodded. "I don't think you need to worry about that. She's obviously not ready to let go of Prue just yet. At least she's talking."

"I suppose." But Terry couldn't see past how morbid it was.

"Besides, why do you think people visit gravestones?" Philippa continued. "They offload. The dead have no choice but to listen."

When Ava went to school that day Terry went straight to the piano room. He needed to address the strange influence the urn was having on his daughter. Despite what Philippa said, there was something unnatural about the communication in the piano room.

He didn't give much credence to the supernatural, but he knew how stubborn Prue had been in life, and if anyone would flout the laws of death it would be her. He'd thought about replacing Prue's ashes with soil or something, wondering if getting rid of them would somehow restore normality. But it all seemed so underhand. He wanted to resolve this civilly, parent to parent. He'd practiced the words in his workroom but now, in the presence of Prue's urn, he was at a loss. He stared at the floor.

They'd managed to avoid each other pretty well over the years. When he picked up Ava he usually stayed in the car and honked the horn. But with death, a strange desire to see his ex-wife had overwhelmed him. He wanted to see what she'd become, to look down on the woman who had caused him so much misery. He remembered the last time he'd seen her in the Chapel of Rest; standing over her, he'd felt a strange sense of victory, one which hadn't involved the courts or social services. He'd won the right to his daughter just by waiting it out.

Prue had looked different, slightly bloated. He wasn't sure whether she'd put weight on over the years or if it was the effect of death. He'd read somewhere that a corpse had many of its fluids removed, to stop the natural bloating that sets in with rigor mortis and the body was pumped full of embalming fluid. He knew the dead were dressed up like this for the viewing public, a strange kind of charade; an attempt to stop the clock, to avoid the inevitable putrescence. Her face had been painted an unnatural shade, her skin alive with an artificial glow. He'd wanted to touch her cheek to see if it felt the same but he knew it would be cold and he didn't want to ruin the illusion.

He thought about how her body would have been doused in disinfectant and germicidal solutions. The body he had lain with, made love to in the back of his first car. The embalmer massaging the legs and arms the way he had once caressed them. The eyes posed shut with an eye cap. Worst of all was the mouth. The mouth he'd kissed. The mouth that whispered *I love you, I'm having a baby*, the mouth that had screamed at him a hundred times, or closed tightly in disappointment or anger when they'd exhausted words. All the things it had left unsaid, sown shut with ligature and a needle or stuck together with adhesive. He had known then, without any doubt, that Prue was gone. That the body before him was only an echo of her, the undertaker's artifice. In death the real face crumbles, the mouth rolls open, gawping in a way that Prue herself would have described as uncouth, expelling the soul with its final breath.

Back in his workroom, Terry finally began to relax. He wasn't sure if it was because he was surrounded by the tools of his trade, the reassuring ticking of the carriage clocks, or the silent narratives of the objects he'd resurrected, whatever it was, he felt consoled. He rummaged through his toolbox, forgetting what he was looking for but enjoying the sound of metal rattling. He wanted to make some noise. He felt like celebrating. He'd finally given Prue a piece of his mind after all these years.

He'd felt ridiculous at first, of course, speaking to the urn, saying the words aloud in the quiet room. It was absurd. But it was better than staying silent on the subject. It became easier when he imagined Prue in the Chapel of Rest. Then the words had poured out of him. They gushed uncensored from his lips, thirteen years' worth of latent discontent suddenly given voice. He'd shouted and sworn, threatened to scatter her ashes to the corners of the earth unless she left their daughter alone. The dead have no choice but to listen and he left the room feeling as if he'd finally vanquished his demons. That by speaking his mind he'd performed some kind of exorcism, that the house would finally be free of its strange deathly silence.

The sudden blare of music startled him.

Terry put his hands to his ears, shocked at how loud it was. It thundered down from the attic, louder than anything he had heard before. It made his heart race, filling him with an urgency to make it stop.

He raced up the stairs, towards its source. It was too loud for any melody, for words. It was an alarm, a war cry, an enormous echoing din.

Bursting into Ava's room Terry made straight for the stereo and turned it off. He sat panting on her bed, listening to his relaxing heartbeat, savouring the new silence.

When he finally looked up, he received his second shock of the morning: Ava's bedroom was completely transformed. Her clothes were neatly folded, the debris that had previously crowded the carpet put away. Her desk was clear of make-up and CDs, and in their stead were a pile of schoolbooks and a neatly arranged pad of A4 paper.

Terry stood and turned. The room was immaculate, spotless. Apart from the work on her desk, there was nothing else in the room. Even her picture frames had been removed, the walls bare.

For a moment Terry wondered what Ava's room had been like when she lived with Prue. He'd never asked her. He imagined that Prue would've run a pretty tight ship. He doubted she'd be allowed posters on the walls, to leave

The Quiet Room

clothes on the floor. Maybe these months living with him had been a rebellion against her mother. And if so, why had she reverted back?

Terry shook his head, bemused. He should've been glad that the images of bronzed hunks had been removed from his daughter's room, but it was all so sudden. And where had all of it gone?

Terry crouched, pulling aside the duvet to peer under Ava's bed, wondering if Prue had also snooped through their daughter's things. The space under the bed was pretty much empty as well, containing only the discarded rolled up posters and the music box.

Terry retrieved it and brushed it down, the black lacquer gleaming underneath the dust. He thought for a moment that maybe he shouldn't open it, that maybe it would contain something private, a diary or a keepsake. Maybe something that would explain her strange behaviour, he thought, justifying his desire to unclasp it.

Empty.

He waited for the mechanical notes to being playing. He wound the spring and opened the box again, expecting the action to spur the steel mechanism inside. But no sound came. Terry opened and closed it a few more times, each time anticipating the tinny mechanical melody. But it was silent. He'd take it to his workshop and see if he could fix it, wondering all while why Ava hadn't told him it was broken.

Terry ordered pizza that night on purpose, hoping that it would incite Ava to criticize him about his cholesterol again. But she ate her slice in silence, cutting it into small neat pieces instead of picking it up with her hands like she used to. He wasn't sure whether to come clean about going into her room—she'd always been pretty protective about her private space—but she'd soon discover her music box gone and besides, any reaction was better than none.

"I went into your room today," Terry said, breaking the silence. "You left your music on."

Ava continued eating.

"Your room looks pretty tidy. I'm glad you took my advice." But he wasn't glad at all. He preferred it when it was a tip, when she played her music really loud and ate her food with noisy mouthfuls.

Ava glared at him but still she didn't say anything.

"Anyway, I've taken the music box." Terry knew she'd know now that he'd been snooping under her bed, but he didn't care. "You should have told me it was broken. I'll try and get it fixed, if that's what you want?"

Ava put her cutlery down and looked at him again. Her eyes were softer this time, almost imploring. It frustrated him more than her anger.

"Ava, for goodness' sake, what's wrong?" he said. He heard his words reverberating in his head. He waited a few moments for her to reply and when she didn't, he stood. "Talk to me!" he yelled, knocking his plate off the table in his rage. It fell to the floor, shattering into pieces.

Ava raised her hands to her ears, closing her eyes.

"Ava, I didn't mean to scare you."

But she was up from the table in a flash, running up the stairs to the attic.

Terry watched her go, then he stooped to pick up the shards of crockery. He wondered at Ava's reaction to the noise. For though his rage had been voluble, and he watched the plate shatter, he couldn't remember it making a sound.

Terry gradually became accustomed to the silence. He went about his day as if his world had been muted. As if a strange cloud had descended over them, cushioning the usual sounds a household made. Ava withdrew into the silence, into the attic, only appearing for her piano lesson or for meals. He spent so little time with his daughter it was almost as if Prue had never died.

Terry sat in his workroom, listening, waiting for Ava's piano lesson to begin. Nothing happened for a while and then he heard Philippa's raised voice and footsteps on the stairs, heading to the attic. He headed to the music room, finding Philippa sat alone on the piano stool.

"What happened?"

"It's broken, I don't know how." She lifted the lid and pressed a key to demonstrate. "It's impossible, unless someone came in here and silenced it."

Terry sat down beside her, thinking about how his attempts to fix the music box had also failed.

"So Ava's still not talking," Philippa observed, "what's her problem anyway?"

Terry shrugged. He spread his fingers over the keys, pretending to be able to play. Without any sound it was easier to imagine the melody in his head, the melody Ava usually practiced. The imagined music distracted him from the alarm that was building up inside. Where was the sound going? Why did the house seem to prefer the quiet?

Philippa placed her hand on Terry's. He stopped moving his fingers in imaginary playing. He let it rest there under hers.

"You know," Philippa whispered, "before she took a vow of silence, Ava told me about why she wanted the attic room. She said that you hear things better at the top, that the acoustics are better the higher you are." She spoke the next words slowly. "The best seats in the house are in the gods."

Terry winced. They were Prue's words. Repeated often in mock enthusiasm when they couldn't afford the better seats, lower down. She believed them in the end, doggedly buying the seats the furthest from the stage.

"I lied the other day," Philippa said withdrawing her hand, "about the piece Ava plays all the time. I do recognize it. You do too. How could you have forgotten?"

Terry stared at the piano keys, hearing only silence.

And then he was sitting in the theatre, one sister on either side. He watched the orchestra pile in to murmurs from the auditorium. They were dressed in black formal wear, placing their instruments at their feet, or holding them in their laps. The conductor arrived and it became suddenly silent, the musicians and audience hushed. And then the tapping as the conductor counted them in.

They were in the gods of course. It had taken Prue ages to waddle up the stairs. But she couldn't be persuaded otherwise. Besides, they had no money then. She'd placed his hand against her stomach and he felt the baby inside swimming around to the music. At the interval, Philippa volunteered to help him get the ice cream. Prue was relieved to stay where she was.

They'd gone down together.

The theatre had a concave of private boxes. Relics from a time before, closed now for renovation. He was helping to restore them; it was how they'd known about the production in the first place. He was proud of his work. Prue never seemed to want to listen but Philippa was so engrossed holding the pile of ice cream tubs. It would only take him a moment to show her the balustraded parapet, the gilded plasterwork.

He closed the door. The wallpaper was decorated with nightingales.

They just made it back in time for the second half. The ice cream was soft. Prue never said a word.

That night Terry dreamt of the quiet room. He was expecting it, almost hoping for it. He felt as if he were on the wave of Ava's melody, rising and falling, building up to a final, inevitable climax. He didn't want to fight against it any longer. He felt himself carried along by it, up the stairs to his daughter's room, sweeping him across the threshold into the cold, quiet space. The posters were back on the walls. They looked even more obscene than before. He didn't want to see their oiled male torsos, their wanton expressions leering down at his daughter. He ripped one off of the wall, standing back in surprise at what was exposed behind.

A huge gaping hole. An enormous black pit, audibly sucking the air out of the room. He pulled down another and saw a similar void. He tried to peer into the darkness but couldn't see anything, couldn't concentrate on anything but the noise. He removed the other posters, revealing similar

The Quiet Room

vacuums, the sound deafening in the quiet room. Terry felt himself being dragged toward them, pulled toward the unknown.

Beyond the room, beyond the din, he could hear Ava's faint playing, the familiar melody barely a whisper. He latched onto its harmony and filled his mind with it, following its thread. He grabbed hold of the bedstead, then the desk, moving slowly through the room to the hallway, finally shutting the door behind him.

Silence.

He made his way down the stairs to the music room, this time prepared for the congregation inside. They were dressed in black as before, with their heads bent low as if in mourning. Terry didn't waste time trying to talk to them. He walked past them looking for the source of the silence. Ava was at the keyboard, her hands on the lid, her fingers dancing along the surface, playing her silent music. But this time Terry confronted what was on top. He could face Prue now that she was dead.

What he saw made him stagger. If he hadn't been condemned to silence, he would have screamed.

Lying on top of the piano was Prue's corpse. She looked almost as she did in the Chapel of Rest. Her eyes shut, her hands arranged demurely, but her legs wide open, revealing cheap stockings and a glimpse of her underwear. She looked like some slutty nightclub singer. Terry walked around the piano, an absurd bier, staring at the woman he had once loved.

He felt compelled to touch her cold skin, prepared to shatter the illusion. But just as he reached for her, she turned her head towards him and it wasn't Prue's face but Philippa's staring back, opening her lifeless eyes. And as he recoiled away from her she opened her mouth, ripping the embalmer's stitches from her lips and letting out the ear-piercing scream he couldn't make.

Terry woke with the scream in his mind. It was morning and glancing at his alarm clock he realized he had overslept. He wondered why Ava hadn't woken him, remembering then that Ava hadn't said a word to him for over a week. She had probably already left for school with nothing but the silence of the morning for company.

Terry put on his dressing gown and went up to her bedroom. He rapped a few times on the door and opened it, her absence confirming that she had already left. It was still a tidy, blank, shell, an empty cocoon that had facilitated her startling change. Terry wanted to take a sledgehammer to it, to break the unnatural silence with the sound of wood splintering, of plaster falling. He recalled shredding the posters in his dream, the delight it had given him ripping them from the wall, and he remembered the actual posters rolled up under Ava's bed.

He fell to his knees, thrusting his arm into the darkness to retrieve them. He sat on Ava's bed and unrolled the first of them, revealing the image of a bronzed torso, progressing to well-defined shoulders, then a muscular neck with a prominent adam's apple. He stopped at the head, realizing, as he saw the model's mouth that he was reaching the end of the movement, that everything was beginning to make sense.

The pinup's mouth was scribbled out with black marker pen, the messy scrawl forming a blackened hole. Could Ava have taken the posters down to give him a message, hoping their absence would tell him something, then scribbling on them in case he still didn't see. Sometimes we don't see the messages that are right in front of us, Terry thought, remembering the day he gave Ava the music box. Remembering the story he'd told her about Philomela. How do you ask for help when you are bound to silence? Why not write a message? Too obvious, he remembered telling her, it wouldn't get past the guards.

Terry shook his head. He could talk but he hadn't listened. Not really.

He got to his feet, straining his ears, listening now to the house below. You can hear everything better from the gods.

He heard a sound from the music room. He listened hard, but the silence itself seemed to be getting louder, sonorous, obscuring everything else. It was there underneath, barely a whisper.

Shhhhhh.

The Quiet Room

Terry raced down the stairs as he had in his dream, conscious that his footsteps on the floorboards emitted no sound. He pushed the door open as soundlessly and saw his daughter sitting at the piano. Her hands were on the piano lid, engaged in her silent practice.

Terry hurried to her side, turning her by the shoulders to face him. But her head flopped listlessly. Her eyes observed him vacantly.

"Ava? We have to leave. It's this house."

The silence buzzed around him like an angry swarm. *Shh. Shh. Shh. Shh. Shhhhhhh.*

Terry stood, tried to pull her from the piano, but she was a dead weight.

"Ava, come on, we have to go!" He knew he was speaking, he could hear his voice in his head, but the sound he made was swallowed up, absorbed by the quiet of the room.

The silence was enveloping everything, feeding on the sounds they made, stealing them, leaving nothing behind in its wake. A blank slate. Terry tried again to wrench Ava from the piano, from this parasitic house, but silence closed in around them. His mind emptied, blackness swirled instead, accompanied by the sound of air being sucked away. *Shh. Shh. Shh. Shh.*

Terry put his hands to his ears, trying to stop the pain in his head. He reeled against it, falling into the piano, knocking the urn from its perch.

It all happened so slowly in the quiet room that it had the same blurred quality as his dreams. The urn rolled to its side, silently tumbling toward the ground, knocking against the piano lid on its way down and releasing an enormous cloud of ash.

The particles swirled into the air, caught in a whirlwind, and for a brief moment Prue stood before them. She looked at Terry and opened her mouth into an exaggerated smile.

The house, he realized, created the silence for other sounds. Sounds suppressed or obscured, dormant or tacit. Sounds long dead, buried deep in the heart, called back again to speak out, amplified by the vacuous silence of the room.

Ava had tried to warn him, though she'd been bound to silence in her role as dutiful daughter. She'd always been caught between two parents and Terry felt a sudden overwhelming sense of sadness for his daughter.

Prue stopped smiling. Her mouth opened wider and wider, her face collapsing into a yawning, swirling hole. Terry stared into the hollow and saw only the darkness at the heart. A low rumbling like distant thunder emerged from the pit of it, then a cacophonous melancholy strung out into the room. He'd been the author of those sounds he'd realized, of her anguish and grief. But it wasn't too late—

"Prue," he tried to say, but the words couldn't compete with the piercing discord. He placed his hands to his ears. The notes became louder and louder, starting to come together, flowing into the familiar melody. Climbing higher and higher, as if to the gods.

The crescendo surged into the room from her mouth, spiralling around as if in flight. The music broke against him like a wave, and in awe he opened his mouth dumbfounded and swallowed it all down.

The dead have no choice but to listen, but Prue always answered back. He should have known she'd want to have the last word.

The sound of the urn shattering broke Ava from her trance. She glanced at the shattered remains on the floor then looked toward her father.

"Dad? Dad?"

Terry could feel the ash in his throat, silted around his larynx. A cloud of ash and dust rested in his gullet. He reached for his voice but felt only his absence. Yet in his mind all he could hear was music.

NIGHT PORTER
R. B. RUSSELL

Marianne had no choice but to take the position of night porter at the St. Denis Hotel; it was either that or have her job-seeker's allowance cut because she had already turned down too many other offers of work. She tried to tell herself that if she didn't think too much about the unsociable hours it really wasn't such a bad situation. Her shifts were from ten in the evening to seven in the morning, six days a week, and she reasoned that for several hours each day, especially those towards the end of her shift, she would be left alone to read; nobody would be looking over her shoulder.

Reading was what Marianne liked to do. Most of the jobs she had been offered would have reduced the time she could spend with her nose in a book (as her mother always said). Working as a night porter was a compromise she was willing to attempt, even if the manager, Mr. Lane, had been very uncertain about hiring a woman for the job. His fears appeared to be justified during her very first shift; at three in the morning a group of eight men, all drunk, tried to return to two rooms that had been booked for four people, and they became abusive when Marianne refused to let them all stay. She had been told by Mr. Lane, to use her initiative, but she had also been warned not to do anything to put herself, or other guests, in danger. Marianne told the drunks that she would telephone for permission to let them in, but, instead, she called the police. As the local station was just around the corner in Dern Street, the incident was cleared up surprisingly quickly. Quite where the men were taken away to didn't concern her; everything was in order once more.

On her second night Marianne booked an elderly couple into a double room just after midnight, only to have the woman appear an hour later to report that her husband had died. It was a heart attack, apparently, and entirely natural, but it still shook Marianne.

And on her third night working at the St. Denis, a guest set light to their bedding at two in the morning. More damage was caused by the Fire Brigade than by the fire itself, and evacuating the other guests caused chaos. Marianne stayed on after her shift to help to clean up, and for the following week there seemed to be no end to the work required to set everything straight again. She had to admit to herself that she had certain obsessive-compulsive tendencies; she hated disorganization and mess.

Marianne couldn't help wondering what might happen next, having called out the emergency services three times in her first three nights, but after those incidents everything seemed to go quiet. For the following few weeks the guests were all well-behaved and there were no dramas. A number of odd characters passed through the hotel, but after a while she failed to notice or even remember the more eccentric guests; they became simply names that she would enter into the register, faces she would never see again. The job was a compromise, but one that she could live with because every night she managed to find several uninterrupted hours to read. The only time she had to put her book down was when, once an hour, she was expected to walk up and down the corridors, on the three floors, just to make sure that everything was in order. She dutifully padded around the small hotel seeing nothing untoward, and hearing, at worst, the muted sounds of sexual activity, loud snoring, or the television playing quietly in the room of an insomniac. She would return to the book she had left at the front desk, and would continue to read, undisturbed, for another fifty-five minutes, until she would have to walk around the corridors once again.

And then, two months into her job, at about half past one

in the morning, while she was reading a Ruth Rendell novel, a large and expensive silver Mercedes pulled into the small car park in front of the hotel. A woman got out of the front of the vehicle and helped a young man from one of the back doors. She almost carried him across the car park and into the reception.

"A room for the night," said the woman, who was rather too well-presented in her sharply-pressed grey trouser suit, and too perfectly groomed for that time of the morning. Marianne had noticed that all of their usual guests would look rather uncared-for by the early hours.

"Just the one bed," the woman added. "My friend is rather tired and a little emotional. He won't be able to go home until the morning."

"Don't you think he ought to go to a hospital?" asked Marianne. There was nothing obviously wrong with him, but he appeared to be confused. He was not necessarily drunk, but it struck Marianne that he might be on drugs. He also looked a great deal younger than his companion, which seemed odd. His "supporter" had to be in her fifties, if not older.

"No, he's fine," said the woman. "Nothing that a decent night's sleep won't cure. How much is a room?"

"£60, with breakfast."

"I really do just want to go to bed," said the young man suddenly. "I feel a little wobbly on my feet."

"Look, here's a nice round £100 in cash," said the woman. "I'll happily pay the extra because there's a chance he might sleep in tomorrow and I don't want any fuss if he does. He'll miss breakfast, I'm sure, but he's bound to wake up and clear out before anyone needs to clean the room."

Marianne wanted to say no, sensing trouble, but didn't feel confident enough to turn them away.

"Is there a problem?" asked the woman.

"No, that will be fine," replied Marianne, deciding that the risk was worth taking. However, she insisted on seeing identification for the guest, and from the woman who was paying.

Marianne told Miss Fisher that she could take Mr. Charles up to 34. It was the room that Mr. Lane said should be used by guests who looked likely to make any kind of disturbance. It was the only bedroom in the hotel without any immediate neighbours, and was one of the few that had not been recently refurbished. The young man was helped up the stairs by his unlikely companion, and Marianne resolved that she would give them only a couple of minutes before going to check that nothing untoward was taking place. In her mind she uncomfortably played out scenarios involving Rohypnol and rape, but just as she was about to go up, Miss Fisher came back downstairs. Marianne was assured that Mr. Charles was fine, and the woman left.

Marianne returned to her Ruth Rendell novel, but found it hard to concentrate. She wondered whether she hadn't read too much modern detective fiction. Miss Fisher and her friend had worried Marianne, but she couldn't really explain why. She remembered that the extra £40 in the till needed to be either accounted for or taken as a tip, and in the end she decided to have it for herself. She had earned it in those two minutes when she had worried what might be happening in room 34.

The incident of the "tired and emotional" guest and her "friend" vaguely troubled Marianne all day. When she arrived at work the following evening, she asked the manager:

"Was everything alright after last night?"

"Fine. Any reason it shouldn't be?"

"A young man was brought in by a friend and he seemed the worse for wear... I nearly said 'no', but in the end I put him in room 34."

"I've not heard of any problems."

And so began an ordinary, uneventful evening. Marianne was steadily busy until one o'clock but there had been nothing demanding to attend to; in between guests coming and going she had tidied up the reception area and the office. Once it was quiet she returned to her Ruth Rendell paperback and the rest of her shift slipped by without her really noticing it.

Night Porter

Marianne had the following night off work. She kept to her usual routine, going to bed at seven in the morning, and getting up again at two in the afternoon. Over the past few months she had become increasingly frustrated by living with her mother, and had considered moving out. She was finally earning some money and could probably pay rent for a room somewhere, or even a small flat. However, now that her hours didn't coincide so frequently with her mother's, she was more content with the present arrangement.

She read during the afternoon, and went out just before her mother returned from work. Marianne had an hour to browse in a local bookshop before it closed, and finding a Henning Mankell paperback she hadn't read before, she decided to treat herself to dinner in a local pub. A regular wage was still a novelty, and it felt wrong to pay for a meal when her mother would have been happy to cook for her. However, it felt good to be out, and she started to read her book as she waited for her food, and then as she ate.

Marianne was interrupted just as she was finishing her meal; some old school friends had arrived to celebrate a birthday, and she stayed drinking with them until after closing time. Before she had taken her job as night porter she would have declined the invitation to go on to a club, but she was still wide awake, and they spent the rest of the evening in The Milky Way on Mill Street. Marianne would have liked to have found somebody to take home, and once again regretted not having a place of her own. However, relationships were going to be even harder to find now that she kept the hours she did.

At work the next night it was very quiet, with very few guests booked into the hotel, and all of them back quietly in their rooms by eleven, which was how Marianne liked it. She tidied up the reception area and wiped down the tables and the insides of the windows. It had turned cold and there were occasional snow-flurries outside, which seemed to keep people off the streets. When everything was tidy, Marianne sat at the counter and continued reading her Henning Mankell paperback.

She had walked the corridors twice that evening, and was back at the reception desk with her book when she happened to look up, and stare out of the glazed front door. She was wondering whether the settled snow really amounted to even a centimetre, when the Mercedes drove into the car park. She recognized it as the expensive silver model that had brought Mr. Charles as an overnight guest only the week before. Once again, the older woman got out of the driving seat and helped somebody else out of the car. As had happened the previous week, she had to support this second person as they made their way to the front door.

"Miss Fisher," said Marianne in her most neutral, professional voice.

"Good evening. You were on the desk last week, weren't you?"

"Yes, when you paid for a room for Mr. Charles."

"That's right, and I can't believe that I'm in a similar situation tonight... My friend's name is Fitzpatrick. He's had a very, very long day. I made the same mistake as with Mr. Charles of taking him out to a restaurant rather than bringing him straight here... He really will be no trouble."

"I would rather not book him in, not in this state."

"But you let my other friend stay."

"I did, but I shouldn't have done."

"Was he any trouble?"

"No."

"Well, then. Mr. Fitzpatrick is just the same; tired and a little drunk."

Marianne could not make up her mind what to do. During her job interview Mr. Lane had put various awkward scenarios before Marianne and he had obviously been pleased by her common-sense replies. This wasn't as clear-cut a situation as any she had been asked about, though, and she hesitated.

Miss Fisher had to prompt her again for a decision.

"Room 34 is available," Marianne agreed reluctantly.

Night Porter

"That will be £60. I will need to see identification, as before."

"Of course."

Miss Fisher smiled, but Marianne did not feel able to trust the woman. She recognized her own prejudice against this self-confident older woman, with her heavy make-up and expensive clothes. And she hated herself for agreeing to do as the woman asked. While Miss Fisher took Mr. Fitzpatrick up to his room, Marianne went to put the cash in the till and found that she had, again, been paid £100 in notes. This time she put the difference into the charity box.

As before, Miss Fisher was back down again in less than a couple of minutes. Once the Mercedes had driven away Marianne went upstairs and stood outside the door of number 34, listening, but she could not hear a sound. The young man was probably asleep, or trying to get to sleep, but this time Marianne knocked. She had decided that she would have to be honest and say that she was concerned; worried because he had looked so ill. It might get her into trouble, disturbing a guest, but her conscience insisted that she had to take the risk.

There was no answer. Marianne knocked once more. It was still strangely quiet, so she went down to the office and made a new electronic card key. After knocking again at the door of room 34 and still receiving no reply, she unlocked it and walked inside.

Marianne was immediately hit by an icy cold. Her first thought was that Fisher had left the window open to help the young man sober up, but in the streetlight that flooded into the room Marianne could see the window was closed. The room was empty. Nor was Fitzpatrick in the *en suite* bathroom.

Marianne checked the window, wondering if the young man had climbed out of it, but it was firmly locked from the inside. Anyway, there was quite a drop to the street below, and down on the pavement there were no footprints in the snow.

Fitzpatrick couldn't have passed Marianne on the stairs, and the lift hadn't been used. The disconcerted night porter went back down and looked at the security tapes in the office. They showed that the young man had not come back through the lobby at any time; he had simply disappeared.

She couldn't decide what to do. She considered calling the police, but where was the evidence of foul play? The guest was free to leave whenever and however he chose to, and the fact that she had not seen him go could always have been her mistake.

While she tried to decide what to do, Marianne made sure that her note of the name and address of Miss Stephanie Fisher was recorded legibly, and as an afterthought she made a separate note for herself. She told herself that she was being unreasonably over-careful, but in the office she played back the digital recording from the security camera in the car park and took down the registration number of the silver Mercedes. Just to be sure, she copied the file containing the footage from the front desk camera into a new folder on the computer; she did not want it to be erased after a couple of days.

Marianne found it impossible to get back to her Henning Mankell book. It suddenly grated on her that the novel was set in Sweden during a heat-wave, while in Britain it was snowing. She was also annoyed to discover that she had previously been reading the Mankell books "out of sequence". But the cause of her discontentment wasn't really the book.

"I don't know," said Mr. Lane simply. "I asked the cleaner and she doesn't remember having had to do anything in room 34 for weeks. To be honest, I'm not going to worry. Your Miss Fisher has paid the bills and nobody's done anything wrong. Although we can't think of an explanation for a disappearing guest, that doesn't mean there isn't one."

"If she comes in again, wanting a room for another young man, I'll refuse to book them in. And I'll call the police."

"If you really think there's something illegal going on, by all means tell them to try another hotel."

And that is exactly what Marianne suggested when Miss Fisher arrived the following week. Once more it was a young man she brought with her. They had all been the same kind of pretty-boy that annoyed her; she preferred her men a little more, well, masculine. They had all been under the influence of drink or drugs, and Marianne had read enough crime novels to be able to imagine all manner of reasons for Fisher dumping them at the hotel. They could well have been robbed or abused. Prostitution was possible. The only part of the whole story that Marianne did not understand was how the previous guest had managed to disappear from his room, and why.

"Which hotel do you suggest?" Miss Fisher asked, pleasantly enough.

It was three in the morning and, although it wasn't snowing this time, it was bitterly cold outside. The man was even younger than the previous two, perhaps even younger than Marianne herself. She was uncomfortable when she realized that she actually felt something maternal or protective towards him, and Marianne asked herself if turning him away was the best thing for his safety. If she booked him in, then at least she would make sure that this time she kept a close eye on him. She would put him into a different room from where the only other way out would be though a window into an inner courtyard.

"Room 18," she said. "I'll have to come up with you."

"There really is no need," said Fisher. "I can take Mr. Evans up to his room."

"I need to reset the lock on the door," Marianne lied. "It will only take a second."

All three of them went up to the room with Marianne leading the way. She opened the door with her master keycard and explained, as nonchalantly as she could, that it would now be reset. She then made sure that Fisher's key worked and she handed it over to her. The woman took the young man inside and Marianne used her master key to go into the room opposite, which she knew to be empty.

She watched through the squint in the door, and when the Fisher left Marianne waited for her to walk down the corridor before she came out. She listened to the woman going down the stairs, and although she couldn't hear the woman crossing the hall past the unmanned reception desk, she felt the slight change in pressure as the front door opened and closed.

Marianne risked getting into a great deal of trouble, but, nevertheless, she opened the door to room 18 with her master key and walked in.

"Please excuse me," she said, immediately noticing how cold it was in the darkened room. "I do apologize, but I..."

Her first reaction had been to look towards the window again, to see if it was open, which it wasn't. But her attention was immediately taken by the young man standing just inside the brightly-lit bathroom. He was wearing only a tee-shirt and his hands were tied to the door handle with what looked like a dirty strip of some white material. He was obviously distressed; he was gagged and the look in his eyes was at first wild, but then suddenly hopeful, pleading. Then he looked from Marianne to somebody else who was inside the bathroom with him.

Suddenly that person pushed past the terrified young man. The first thing that struck Marianne was that the man who appeared was really very, very old. He had a long face and his wrinkles were deep, like the cracks in dried earth. He was also completely bald. He was dressed in a brown suit that, even back-lit from the bathroom and almost entirely in silhouette, appeared dirty and stained. In one hand he carried a hotel towel, and in the other he had a huge hypodermic syringe that looked like it was made of corroded brass.

"You shouldn't be here," he said with a low, quiet but insistent voice.

"I'm the night porter," said Marianne, without thinking.

"I know, Night Porter," the man said. "Can we agree that you have seen nothing here? Would you like to leave and never think about this again? It would be for the best."

Marianne reasoned that she could be out of the room and downstairs, phoning for the police, long before the old man caught up with her. But the young man was staring at her, trying to scream at her to stay and help him.

"No," said Marianne, shaking, still considering running. "*You* can leave."

"I will, when I've finished."

And the man was across the room with an unbelievable

Night Porter

speed and agility. Instinctively Marianne flung the door
open to run out and it crashed into him.

That should have given Marianne enough time, but
as she reached the stairs she could already hear the man
coming down the corridor towards her. Marianne vaulted
over the banisters between the two sections of the dog-leg
stair and managed to get her footing right as she landed. She
took another leap into the reception area and ran across to
the desk. She immediately picked up the telephone and hit
nine three times before looking up.

The man was already standing by her as they both heard
the distant, tiny voice asking which emergency service was
required.

"Police," said Marianne, upset by how shaky and thin
her voice sounded. How had the man appeared so quickly
beside her? What did he intend to do with the syringe he was
holding?

But the old man just smiled at Marianne, and walked
away, backwards. Although he appeared quite calm, and
the movement was effortless, the man seemed to move too
quick; he was at the stairs and climbing them backwards, too
soon, before he should have done...

"The St. Denis Hotel," Marianne added into the
mouthpiece of the phone. "A guest is in danger, room 18..."

She put the receiver down on the counter and unwillingly
returned to the foot of the stairs. She looked up, but the old
man was gone; he would already be in the corridor. Marianne
followed reluctantly, and when she saw that the first floor
corridor was empty, she made herself walk along to the door
of room 18.

She hesitated before going back inside, but room 18
was now empty; both the old man and the young man had
gone. It took a great deal of courage for Marianne to look
around the door into the bathroom, and she wasn't sure if
she really felt any relief in finding nobody there. The only
signs that there had ever been anybody in room 18 were the
horrible piece of material still attached to the door handle,
the towel on the floor, and the state of the sink. There were
dark marks on the white porcelain, as though somebody had
been washing something very black and oily in it.

The police took seriously the call from Marianne. The security tapes clearly showed Miss Fisher and the young Mr. Evans, leaving the silver Mercedes and entering the hotel lobby. Fisher was traced through the number plate and questioned, but Marianne was told that she could have nothing to do with the disappearance of Evans. Traffic cameras clearly showed her driving away as soon as she had left the hotel. Evans had apparently been acting as Miss Fisher's "escort" that night, quite legitimately.

The old man with the bald head didn't appear on the security tapes at all. There was only a partial shot of Marianne herself at the telephone calling the police; unfortunately, the cameras were angled too far towards the front door to show the whole reception desk.

Marianne was given a couple of weeks off work, paid, by Mr. Lane. It was very good of him, thought Marianne, who felt bad taking the money when she didn't intend going back. How could she return after what had happened? The idea of being alone in the hotel at night was unimaginable. Well, not quite alone; there would be guests, of course, locked away in their rooms. But who else might be behind the closed bedroom doors? The old, bald man?

Marianne continued to keep the hours that she had done when working at the St. Denis. She didn't admit to her mother that anything had happened at the hotel; instead she would go to The Milky Way until five in the morning, and then walk around the streets, sobering up in the cold dawn until she could go home after seven. She would still go to bed at the same time, although she would now be getting up at more like four in the afternoon.

Not that she could sleep; Miss Fisher and the old man insisted on invading her thoughts as he lay awake in bed, threatening to enter her dreams if she dared to lose consciousness.

Night Porter

Marianne had never been a regular anywhere before, but The Milky Way made it easy for her. She knew one of the barmen who worked there during the week, and at the weekends her old school friends would turn up. It was dark and full of alcoves where she could hide away and nurse a drink for hours if she had to. However, she soon got to know several other regulars, including a middle-aged man called Anthony, who she was becoming quite attached to. Anthony was an insomniac, and, distressingly, probably an alcoholic. Marianne worried that she might end up the same as him, but she enjoyed his company, and he seemed to tolerate hers. Marianne knew that she could not keep up the lifestyle indefinitely, not least because the St. Denis Hotel stopped her pay after two weeks, and the little money she had saved was already dwindling. She was convinced that her mother would find out what had happened, as Mr. Lane telephoned every week to ask after Marianne, leaving messages on the answer-phone. (Luckily, Marianne had always managed to intercept and erase them.) The hotel manager was trying to make it easy for her, Marianne knew that. She also knew that at some point she would have to re-apply to the benefits agency, and Lane could easily tell them that she had just walked out of the job. Then there wouldn't be any money coming in for at least a month.

It was three weeks later, perhaps four (Marianne had lost some sense of time), when she saw Miss Fisher walk into The Milky Way. It was a weeknight, and not at all crowded. Having bought drinks at the bar, Fisher sat at a table at the back. With her was yet another young man.

Marianne had been talking to Anthony. At some point in their friendship she had told him about the hotel and Fisher. She now pointed the woman out to him.

"Ask her," he said, and because Marianne had finished her fourth glass of wine, and felt safe in such a public place, she did so.

"The police have already interviewed me," Fisher insisted, uncomfortable at having Marianne confronting her across the table.

"I know, and they could *prove* nothing," said Marianne.

"Because there's nothing to prove! You gave them a description of the man they need to talk to."

"It's too much of a coincidence," Marianne dismissed the reply. "You're in league with the bald old man."

"I really don't know him. Look, I'm here for a quiet drink with my friend…"

"Another one of your escorts?" She turned to the young man, who looked confused at the sudden appearance of Marianne and her accusations.

"I hope she's paying you well?" Marianne asked. "I don't know what services she'll ask of you, but if she tries taking you back to a hotel afterwards, don't let her. There'll be an old man with rusty hypodermic waiting for you."

"Please, Miss… Night Porter," said Fisher. "Please leave us alone. Otherwise I'll have to call the management."

"And tell them what? I'm a regular here, don't you know?"

"I like to have company of an evening. I'll take a companion to a restaurant, or a bar, or sometimes a club like this. When my young friend is tired I drop him off at a hotel with a couple of hundred pounds in his pocket to thank him."

"And that's when they meet your bald friend…"

The young man had been looking increasingly uncomfortable, and Marianne watched in amusement as Fisher opened up her purse, handed him some notes, and told him that he could go.

"I hope you're feeling happy with yourself," said Fisher, as the young man walked away.

"If I've saved his life, yes!"

"And how, exactly, have you done that?"

"By saving him from you, and the old man who disposes of your 'escorts' for you."

"And how does he dispose of them?"

"I don't know," said Marianne. "Perhaps he injects them with something to dissolve them… so all that's left is an oily, fatty mess in the sink!"

Fisher laughed, to which Marianne took exception. She hadn't realized how drunk she was, or how tired. She realized that she had voiced a private fantasy that really was too fanciful. She decided to leave Fisher and the scene of her minor triumph, resolving to walk away without looking back. She made her way back to Anthony and apologized to him, saying that she was going home. She was depressed that he simply said goodnight and let her go. She looked back at him on her way out, and he was heading for the bar.

As she was leaving, Marianne went in to the ladies'. She sat on the toilet and replayed the scene with Fisher in her head, confused, unable to decide if she had made any sense. As Marianne walked out of the cubicle she heard the main door open and Miss Fisher walked in.

"I have nothing to hide, Night Porter," said the woman.

"You drug your young victims," said Marianne, wondering why she was continuing to be confrontational when all she wanted to do was leave.

"No, I don't drug them. I buy them a decent meal and they usually end up drinking too much."

"It's called prostitution."

"No, they only act as company. Nothing sexual happens."

"No?" asked Marianne. She was relieved to have been able to get past the woman, and was now close to the door, able to leave.

"Night Porter, how I envy you," said Fisher. "And the young men I pay to keep me company. I admire your youth, your vitality, your innocence..."

"Bullshit."

"You could help me meet young men. There would be something in it for you..."

Fisher had come forward, almost without the younger woman noticing, but Marianne pushed her away. Suddenly there was a flurry of arms and legs as Fisher slipped backwards on the wet floor, and, when she fell, there was a horrible sound as her head hit the dirty cracked tiles. The woman didn't move, and immediately an almost black liquid started to flow from out under her head. In the dim, ineffectual light it took a few moments before Marianne realized what it was. But she didn't have time to find out how badly Fisher might be hurt because she was frozen by a blast of cold air. A cubicle door had opened. She had thought they were alone, and she was confused to see that it was the cubicle she had, herself, just come out of.

Suddenly there was the old, bald man with the deep wrinkles. He looked at Marianne, then at Miss Fisher, and he smiled.

"I'll finish her off for you," he said. "In a few moments there will be nothing."

"I don't want to know," said Marianne, backing away.

"Good, good. Then we can agree that you have seen nothing here. Leave and never think about this again."

"But why help me?" asked Marianne, although her voice was so quiet she hardly knew whether she had articulated her thoughts.

"Why?" asked the old man. "I was always there to tidy up for you before. And I'll be there when you need me again."

THE STATUE
MYRIAM FREY

A s usual, Benjamin had found himself the longest and most cumbersome piece of wood—most of a young beech tree in this case—and dragged it behind himself for ages, ploughing the damp, black forest soil as he went. Julie was investigating a brown heap of crumbling leaves just this side of compost. She was fascinated with micro-organisms and her plan was to observe some live decay under her microscope later that day. She had been given it for her sixth birthday and she had since examined every body fluid and foodstuff known to her, putting Benjamin off milk because of the red and purple blotches all over it. Spring was late this year; it was early April, but there were still small patches of snow at the base of some of the larger trees. The soil was faintly gurgling and hissing and the branches of the trees were strangely tense with the impending eruption of millions of buds.

Sarah led the way and turned around to tell the children to step it up a bit. The sunshine earlier in the day had fooled her into putting on her soft-shell jacket. Now she was freezing and she needed the loo. Patrick had chosen a different route, presumably to jump into their path as if out of nowhere when they least expected it. The lack of foliage would make this a tricky one, Sarah knew, but her husband's resourcefulness with pranks was legendary. Benjamin finally let go of his tree, having grown tired of pulling it along. Their path took a turn to the right and then they saw Patrick, standing on a tree stump, arms to his side like a soldier. Sarah had witnessed this many times, but it always gave her the creeps to see him like this, unblinking and as if carved in stone.

The children giggled. "Dad's a statue!" Benjamin screamed and quickened his step because he knew what was coming. His dad would jump off the tree stump with a huge roar and grab whoever stood nearest to him and give them a messy cuddle. Sarah and the kids walked cautiously past Patrick, who didn't move. They shot nervous glances over their shoulders, expecting him to be all over them any second now, but he wasn't. After a few metres, Sarah turned around to face Patrick and warned him that they were going to start dinner without him if he wasn't coming. "Maybe he wants to see how long he can stand like this," Julie suggested. "Mrs. Moll made us do that in PE and it was really hard." Sarah agreed. It was just the kind of thing he would do.

When they got home, the children kicked off their muddy boots and went straight for the couch. Sarah picked up the phone to call Patrick. She let it ring until she heard it go off in their bedroom. She rolled her eyes, wondering once again why her husband had bothered to buy a mobile in the first place. He always seemed to mix up his settings so he couldn't hear it, or he forgot to take it altogether.

Sarah cut open a roll of ready-to-bake pastry dough and spread it on a large baking tray. She pricked it with a fork, sprinkled ground hazelnuts and started to grate apples over it.

"Mum? Where's Dad?"

The children had just put in a *Madagascar* DVD and were waiting for the anti-piracy disclaimer to fade.

"He'll have bumped into someone. You know Dad."

"Yeah," Benjamin chuckled, "we know Dad!"

Once dinner was in the oven, Sarah started to worry. She went upstairs and called Michelle, their emergency babysitter from next door. She appeared on the doorstep ten minutes later in tracksuit bottoms. Her hair was wet. They walked into the living room together.

"Julie? Ben? Look who's here!"

"Michelle!" Julie jumped off the couch and threw her arms around the girl's neck. Sarah knew she was her daughter's favourite babysitter in the world, but dodgy friends and a rumoured weakness for weed confined her to the substitute bench.

"Where are you going, Mum? You didn't say you were going out."

Benjamin didn't like sudden changes in schedule.

"Sorry, Ben. I didn't know earlier. Dad's met some friends on his way home and they've invited us over for a drink and a bit of a chat."

"But, why can't *we* come?" He was upset now.

"Because it's Sunday night, dummy," Julie said and stared at her brother with mock exasperation, clearly for the benefit of Michelle, who was supposed to think of her as very grown up.

Sarah put on her down jacket, a woolly hat and a pair of sheepskin gloves. It was still light outside, but as she got closer to the forest, dusk started to fall like something creeping out from between the trees. She walked up the forest path they had used on their way home, hoping to find something, anything, that led her to Patrick. By now, she was convinced that something was wrong. And then she saw him. He was still standing there, in the same position, hands by his sides, chin tilted up.

"For fuck's sake, Patrick, what the fuck do you think you're doing?" Sarah called when she thought she was within earshot. He didn't flinch. Walking closer, it occurred to her that, for some reason, he might not be able to see or hear her. When she was level with him, he still didn't move or acknowledge her presence in any way. She touched his hands, which were cold. She pressed her own hands to his chest and felt his heartbeat. Clearly, he was in some kind of altered state; perhaps he had hypnotized himself without knowing it. Sarah tried to shove Patrick off the tree stump, hoping it would wake him up, but he wouldn't budge. She started to push against his hip with both hands. Nothing. She tried to prise away his shoes from the wood and make him topple over. She could easily lift Patrick's shoes, but only because they were no longer attached to their soles. The soles and much of Patrick's feet had somehow sunk into the tree stump. Sarah tested the moist, half-rotten wood with her fingers before she climbed up to face him. She tried to rub some warmth into Patrick's arms, then took off her down jacket and placed it over his shoulders. She put her hat on his head but couldn't manage to slip the gloves onto his hands, because his pale fingers were impossible to separate from each other. She willed herself to take deep, regular breaths and hugged him until it was completely dark in the forest. Sarah kissed Patrick and jumped back on the path. "I'll be back, don't you worry. I'll get you out of here."

Sarah sneaked into the garage and started to pile everything she needed into a wheelbarrow. She put on Patrick's ski jacket and hunter hat, which she was glad now they'd already put in storage in the cellar. She quietly let herself out again. The way to the edge of the forest was short, yet she couldn't be sure any of the neighbours weren't watching from behind their curtains, and so she decided to take a detour over the muddy field adjacent to the back gardens. She sank in to her ankles with every step she took and the wheelbarrow was near-impossible to push. She ended up dragging it behind her, with the effect that she lost her cargo several times and had to pull it out of the muck.

By the time she had returned to Patrick, she was covered in mud and badly out of breath. She sat down and hugged his legs for a moment. Then she set to work on the tree stump. She wasn't too sure where to cut. She couldn't tell how deep Patrick's feet had sunk into the wood and she didn't want to risk hurting him. She decided on a hand span from the top and hacked the crosscut saw into the back of the stump. She'd once had to cut a piece off a large trunk on a company outing and she'd done remarkably well, but this one wasn't lying on a sawhorse and it was wet and much tougher than she'd expected.

It took her the best part of an hour to cut through to the

middle. She'd lost the all-important rhythm several times and it took an incredible effort to pull the saw out again when that happened. Also, she soon discovered that she would have to cut out wedge by wedge because of Patrick's weight pushing down, which made it impossible for her to slide the blade back into a single cut. When she had sawn out a deep enough section of the stump, she started to cut down from above, in front of her husband's toes. She placed the wheelbarrow behind the tree stump, embraced Patrick and tilted him back like a toy soldier. His muscles relaxed and he collapsed into the wheelbarrow. He looked very much like someone who'd passed out in an armchair. Sarah could remove the half disc of black wood from around his feet with comparative ease. They were not injured as far as she could tell but she cursed herself for not having brought replacement shoes or at least a pair of warm socks. She secured Patrick to the wheelbarrow with lashing straps, covered him with a picnic rug and started to push him down the forest path. There was no way she was going to be able to move him over the field and so her best hope was that it was dark enough now for people to have stopped staring out of their windows.

In the garage, Sarah made the emergency call. Afterwards, she loosened the straps, gently tipped the wheelbarrow to one side, and let Patrick slide onto the picnic rug she'd spread out on the floor. She covered him with a thermal blanket from the car's first aid kit. Then she stowed the tools, all the while rehearsing a plausible version of what had happened. Patrick had passed out in front of the garage after he'd returned from the forest. She and the children had no means of knowing he'd arrived at the house. He must have lain there, in front of the garage, for several hours. He couldn't be woken up and was evidently suffering from hypothermia. Surely the paramedics would know where to take it from there.

It was nothing. At least that was what they said. Patrick woke up in the ICU the next morning and couldn't remember a thing. Not the statue thing, not the tree stump, not even the walk. They ran all sorts of tests on him: cardiac assessment, blood panel, the works. They gave him a sick note for the rest of the week, just to be on the safe side, and he returned to his former life feeling relaxed and fully recovered.

Sarah was the only one who noticed a change in Patrick after the incident. He had become calmer, more even-tempered. He never raised his voice anymore and there was hardly anything that seemed to really upset him. For some reason Patrick had developed a great fondness for footbaths, which he would take in a fairly deep angular window cleaner bucket every night while watching the evening news. It was only after a couple of months that Sarah realized that by the time the weather forecast was on, the bucket would always be empty.

SHADDERTOWN
CONRAD WILLIAMS

D oes he like to hear her talk about Manchester in the days when she was young, and fit enough to do what young girls did? He seems to. Sometimes, when she talks, she drifts away a little. It's as if she's transported herself back to the Pendulum or the Twisted Wheel or all-dayers at the Merry-go-Round. Back then her lungs were pinker, more elastic. She could suck deep the air that carried the oxygen to send her careering around those sprung dance floors like something electrified. "They called me 'Place'," she tells him, "because I was all over it." Her name, though, her real name, is Peggy. Billy calls her Peg.

Now she finds it hard to get out of her chair. Walking from one room to another brings on a panic that threatens to fill her up completely. Her mouth is constantly open. Her shoulders are hunched from years of fighting for breath. There are some good days, but mostly bad.

Peggy doesn't see Billy as often as she'd like. She won't drive because lorries induce panic attacks when they overtake her (50, inside lane). She won't go on the trains or the buses because she doesn't want to suffer an incident; she doesn't want to die going blue in the face while a bunch of strangers stare down at her. But she loves Billy as if she had given birth to him. His mother, Jill, isn't around much (a young woman, still got it, and wants to enjoy it while she can... party, work do, weekend away... you don't mind, do you? You wouldn't begrudge me, would you? I mean... let's be frank, we don't know how many more opportunities Billy will have to… well, I don't need to spell it out, do I?) and leans on Peggy a lot to provide childcare. She doesn't need to say the things she does, but she says them anyway, as if that will persuade her to spend more time with her grandson. She doesn't seem to hear when Peggy tells her she'd be happy to spend all day with him, every day with him. It's no hardship.

Except, it is. Peggy's husband, George, died three years ago. She's had to have a bed made in her living room now, so perilous are the stairs for her. She shuttles between the tiny kitchen and the living room, to all intents and purposes a ground floor flat while the upstairs gathers dust. Terry, her son-in-law, installed a tiny cubicle shower in the far corner of the kitchen, under the stairs, spending most of his time swearing and sweating and eyeing her violently as if to say *I wouldn't have to be here if only you'd do what your name suggests.* She has to sit down in order to use the shower. Not because she runs out of puff but because she'll bang her head on the rose if she doesn't. When Billy comes to stay, as he has done today (girls' afternoon in Liverpool, shopping and cocktails and then a nightclub… I'll try not to be late to pick him up tomorrow) he has the bed; she goes to sleep in her armchair, the armchair George claimed for his own. She can still smell the oil from his scalp on the headrest.

Each time Billy comes to stay she's momentarily broadsided by the look of him. He seems different. Bigger, more energetic. Sometimes she gets this funny feeling that it's not the same boy. Sometimes he's surly or rude. Sometimes he's a little reserved. Sometimes he marches straight into the kitchen and helps himself to what's in the biscuit barrel. He can never sit still, even when they watch morning cartoons together after breakfast. She gets tired and breathy just watching him fidget. He's like his dad in that respect. Or maybe his dad just doesn't like being here. Terry's always first out of the door when it's decided they'll leave, car keys jangling from his finger. Claustrophobia, he says. He doesn't like being crammed into a tiny living room with so many people. It doesn't stop him getting in a small plane on his annual jaunt to Magaluf with his golf pals, though, does it?

"What do you want to do, Billy? I've got a jigsaw puzzle

somewhere. Or there's these colouring books you left last time."

"I've been inside so long, Peg. I want to go out."

"Don't your mum and dad take you out?"

A shake of the head. He's always got the pilchard lip on him. He used to laugh a lot when he was a baby.

"What did you do yesterday?"

"Mum and Dad stayed in bed because they had overhangs."

"Who got your breakfast?"

"Me. I can get my own breakfast."

"But Billy, you're only six. How do you reach the bowls? Do you never have a cooked breakfast?"

"I had lollipops."

She feels anger move through her but it's strangely languorous, like the torpor that comes when she puts a sleeping pill under her tongue. She no longer gets a proper rage on her as she used to. It's far too taxing.

How does Jill allow herself to be like this? Peggy never treated her like this when Jill was Billy's age. She wasn't brought up to be so... unmotherly. They had fresh fruit and vegetables always. Peggy never opened a tin that contained anything that came out of the ground. Jill was out rain or shine. She had scabs on her knees up until she was a tween. A right tomboy, she was.

He wants to go out.

"Okay," Peggy says. "Okay."

"Where are we going, Peg?" Billy asks, once they've struggled on board the bus. A man stands up to allow her to sit and she's momentarily put out by that; he must be ten years her senior, but she sits anyway, and Billy stands in front of her, his left nostril encrusted with pale green gunk, every button on his coat missing.

"We're going to the Land of Far Beyond," she says. "Or is it Upside-downville? Or is it Shaddertown? I forget."

"Oh, Peg," he admonishes, but he's smiling. Being here on the bus, with its peculiar smell of diesel and damp and worsted coats reminds her of trips out with Jill, over twenty years ago. Condensation on the windows. Every bump and gear change felt through the bones of your arse. They went ice-skating in Altrincham. Afterwards they'd drink hot chocolate and compare bruises. Peggy's lung capacity hovers around the twenty per cent mark now. She might be able to get one ice skate on but that would be enough to finish her off for the afternoon.

When it comes, it feels as though there are fingers, too thin and hard to be real, gripping her shoulders and bending her backwards. It's how she imagines it must have been for Christ on the cross. Hyperexpansion of the chest muscles and lungs. An inability to expand. The shallowing of air. Should have stayed in and watched *Balamory*. Should have had an easy day. Teach him how to play Old Maid. Get him to read to her. *Owl Babies. We're Going on a Bear Hunt.* Sometimes she dreams of being chased, something clawing at her from the darkness, something trying to grab hold of her and get the job done properly. She tries to sand down the edges of her fear with hopes that it might be George reaching out for her, but how could it be, when the hands are tipped with such ghastly, denuded fingers?

The bus stops outside the library and they get off. What breath she can muster churns from her mouth in a frantic grey torrent, as if it is aghast at what it has experienced inside her lungs. Each breath she takes feels shallower than the one before.

"Right, come on," she says, and she likes the way Billy's ears prick up. She's got her voice on. The voice that must not be disobeyed. She'll try to be full of vim and verve for him. For her Billy. She won't show him her grey, failing side though it seems to be winning these days. *Death, coming up on the rails.*

Where did that come from? She suffocates the thought before it can bloom in her mind.

She smoked for fifty years, every single day. Never less than twenty cigarettes between rising and retiring. She started when she was twelve years old. When she couldn't cadge money for fags or pinch them out of Mum's handbag, she'd roll brown paper into tight tubes and smoke that. She liked the way Marlene Dietrich looked when she smoked. Peg copied the hairstyle, and did her make-up the same. The cupid bow lips. Smoky eye shadow. George used to call her

"Well, it doesn't matter. We're not oversubscribed. How old is your son?"

"I don't have a son. I have a daughter. She's twenty-six going on five."

"It's just that some of this tour will be me talking about things and it might go over his head. Nazis and that."

"It'll go over mine as well, then. I wouldn't worry."

Soon there's a group of half a dozen standing in the damp, wearing variously disappointed faces.

"I'm Clive," says the guide, consulting his clipboard. "I'll be showing you around the forgotten chambers of Mancunium today. I hope you brought stout shoes and a torch."

Peggy stares at her flats. At least Billy is wearing his boots.

"Have you got a torch on you?" she asks. "Don't boys carry things like that around with them all the time?"

"I've got a light on my bike," Billy says.

"Never mind, look. Everyone else has got one. We'll stick close."

The guide talks for a while about the hotel, how it would have been Hitler's north-west nexus of operations had the Nazis successfully invaded Britain. German bomber pilots were expressly forbidden to release their payloads anywhere near the hotel for fear of damaging it. The guide's voice is the endless gritting cycle of a cement mixer. Billy fidgets. The cold is clinging to the ends of Peggy's fingers like a needy child. What has all this talk of architecture and Nazi plans, and Rolls meeting Royce, and the Beatles being thrown out because they didn't adhere to the dress code... what has all this got to do with the tour? Underground Manchester. As Jill might say, *this is not doin wot it sez on the tin dot co dot uk LOL!!!*

Eventually it's time to move off. It's a little way to the entrance to the tunnels, explains the guard, reminding them that they have signed waivers that abrogates the tour company from all responsibility should someone be mown down by any vehicle, including a bicycle. Somebody says something about litigious culture. Someone else says something about the nanny state. Billy, in a too-loud voice, tells Peggy that this morning he did a poo that looked like Uncle Derek's moustache.

Soon Peggy has become the back marker. Maybe they should just peel off to a cafe for hot chocolate. She'll get Billy a comic. He'll be happy with that. He's only six after all. What was she thinking, bringing him here? But the talk of tunnels and torches has excited him. *Do you think we'll see any rats? Do you think we'll find the goblin king?*

Peggy looks at the thin face of the guide and bites her tongue on *Look no further.* She has to concentrate on her breathing, so she smiles and winks instead. She can feel the tubes in her lungs winking too. Once, when she was young, she could drink in litres of air. She'd do it to tease George, who liked it when her chest expanded. *Look at you,* he'd say. *All fulla love.*

Dark spots crowd the edge of her vision, as if they've already started along one of the tunnels.

They've stopped again. They're on James Street standing in front of an unassuming brick building with large wooden gates and a tower. The guide tells them, through his mouthfuls of cement, how this building was the entrance to the main tunnel of Manchester Guardian, an underground telephone exchange built in 1954 when the Cold War gripped the world. The tunnel would have been able to withstand the blast of a twenty kiloton atomic bomb, preserving communications links even if the city had been razed. There was enough food to keep people going for six weeks. The toilets had restful scenery painted on the walls. The guard laughs. "Of course," he says, "by the time the tunnel was ready, the Soviets had developed much larger bombs that would have obliterated the place. Waste of money if you ask me."

The guide eyes Peggy's shoulders, bowing like the spine of a pitched tent in high winds. She's waiting to be taken to one side, the dropped voice, the reiteration of point twelve on the terms and conditions, people with health problems such as high blood pressure and heart defects should be aware that there are a number of stairs to be negotiated during the course of this tour. When it comes she maintains eye contact and tells him she's fine. "We're nearly there," the guide says.

"I'll look after you, Peg," Billy says. In the past Billy has

Shaddertown

made monsters from clay to scare her bad cough. She has a drawer filled with them. They are drying out now, crumbling golems, but she refuses to throw any of them away.

"Then I've nothing to fear," she says.

The entrance to the tunnels is through an office at the rear of a busy department store. They descend well-lit steps covered with linoleum, bypassing two office workers texting feverishly. To each other, Peggy imagines. At the bottom is a heavy, padlocked door. The guide pulls out a single bronze key from his pocket. Brandishing it like Neville Chamberlain with his piece of paper, he unlocks the door. The sound of the tumblers turning sends echoes into the space beyond. Peggy thinks: *leave now. Take Billy to the football museum instead. Take Billy to the helter-skelter in Spinningfields. Take Billy away.*

But people are jostling for position, and she feels herself being herded through the doorway by those behind her, and she reaches for Billy's hand and he squeezes it and everything will be fine.

The temperature drops the moment they pass through into the gloom. The guide is ahead of them and he's saying something about how they were going to install a simple lift but it's logistics, you know, but she can't properly hear and it doesn't really matter because she's here for fun with Billy and it will all go over his head and her head. Soon there's no light and people start flicking on their torches. Some of them are poor, cheap affairs, casting not enough light to illumine the low ceiling above them. Peggy gets closer to a couple huddled together who are carrying a large, powerful rubber-cased torch that seems bright enough to find its way between the cracks in the brickwork and surprise people up on the surface.

It's dank down here; the cold has a raw, weirdly elderly touch to it. It's ill-tempered. Impatient. It's like being prodded, an old aunt wearing too much make-up pinching your arm before declaring there's not enough meat on you to last till lunchtime. Billy's hand is warm inside hers. Her left foot disappears into a puddle and she almost loses her shoe. The cold judders along her leg like in the cartoon she watched with Billy where Bugs Bunny, or Daffy Duck, or whatever cartoon animal it was hits a petrified tree with an axe. If the cold reaches her heart she's sure she'll stop moving and shatter into a million pieces. The thought makes her want to laugh more than anything else though. Silly old carrot, she thinks. Just think of the bath and the rum-laced hot chocolate you'll enjoy later.

She used to laugh a lot. God, George could pull a giggle from her, and often when she was determined to be angry with him about something. But he was one of those people it was impossible to remain annoyed with. Now if she so much as chuckles or titters or snorts it can bring on a fit of coughing that convinces her she might die. She no longer watches the funny shows she likes on TV. She tries to avoid spending time with the girls who know how to tickle her: Penny or Jenny or Flo.

The guide is at the front. His voice comes to her in strange swells and beats, like the rhythm of the sea on the shore. He's saying something about the Manchester and Salford Junction canal. He's saying something about a shelter from the German bombings. There are steps coated with slime, and pieces of rubble lying around where the brickwork has started to fail. Great arched ceilings stippled with stalactites. Some day they will cease to take people down here because of the risk. The doors will be sealed off and whatever is left down here will be trapped for good. *Watch yourself here!* Part of a wall has collapsed into one of the arterial corridors, partially blocking it.

Shards of graffiti are picked out by the lunatic splashes of light. She can't make out the names, or the deeds, or the insults. Scraps of old warnings from the war remain. The guide reads out a few: *No insobriety. No rowdiness. No unseemly conduct.* In a corner of this particular... what do you call it? Chamber? Cellar? Crypt? (no, let's not do that... let's not give ourself a reason to be fearful) there's a dummy slumped over its knees, dressed in a red-checked flannel shirt and black jeans. Its head looks to be made from polystyrene. People giggle and point. It looks punched in, crumbling. It reminds her of George, how she found him that morning after breakfast when he'd gone upstairs to get dressed. It was as if death had upset him so much that he had the time to sit down against the foot of the bed and cry into his chest about

Shaddertown

it. But think of George thirty years younger at the Twisted Wheel, dressed to the nines in blazer and brogues while she was always at sixes and sevens over what to wear. His hair scraped back with the ubiquitous back-pocket comb. The Oxford trousers and sports vests. The smell of sweat and Brut. The amphetamines; the jaw grinding. Juicy Fruit and Doublemint. He moved so hard and fast on the dance floor she was scared sometimes that he might break. The heat and the smoke in that place grew so thick that it condensed on the ceiling and returned as a light yellow rain.

They move deeper into the Manchester underground and her mind sinks with it. She remembers how slim she was back then, and how taut the muscles in her calves from all the dancing. George could almost enclose the span of her waist with one outstretched hand. Where did they get their energy from? The calories they must have burned off! And afterwards, in George's little Hillman Imp, they'd drive up to Saddleworth with the windows open and they'd be smoking and singing rare-soul classics and they'd make love in the moors for a while, or in the car if it was too cold, and back to George's parents' house in Longsight as the sun came up, just in time for bacon and eggs with George's old man before he went off to the bleach factory.

All those days of twists and shimmies. The miles covered more or less on the spot. All that energy spent. The endless cigarettes. And throughout it this was down here: coldness and damp and coursing water. *The Land of Far Beyond. Upside-Downville.*

The guide's voice slaps against the damp brick and falls at his feet. He's saying something about how dark it really is down here. He invites everyone, for thirty seconds, to switch off their torches and to put their hands in front of their faces. *You won't be able to see a thing.* In the split second between this palsied light and the utter black that follows, Billy tugs his fingers free of Peggy's hand.

"No, Billy," she snaps, but then the delighted yelps of alarm get in the way of her warning and all she can think, as she swings around, trying to catch hold of Billy's arm, is: *This is what it is like for George every single day.*

She shuffles forward a little, blindly groping (just as we

used to, George, out on those wild, black moors, remember?) but she succeeds only in bumping against a figure that recoils at her touch. The feel of her (must have been a her, too thin an arm to be male) is waxy under her fingers, but maybe that's because she's so cold, and anyway, people these days wear strange waterproof fabrics and...

"Billy!"

She hasn't shouted like that for a long time, maybe not since Jill was a teenager. Billy doesn't answer. People are still laughing about the dark. It's a darkness she has never known. It seems so deep as to be beyond understanding. Even in her own bed, when her eyes are shut, the colour is not nearly so extreme. The guide says: *this is what it must be like to be profoundly blind.* He says: *it is literally blacker than the grave.* In the absence of light, his voice seems different, as if it is wetter. She doesn't understand how the light can alter the acoustics of a place. Maybe it can't—of course it can't—so then it must be her own rising panic that is adding juice to his words.

"Turn the lights back on!" she caws, but the effort of shrieking Billy's name has deflated her. *Kippers in a smokehouse,* Jill used to sing, cryptically, to the tune of "Mirror in the Bathroom" and it's only in recent years Peggy's realized she must be referring to the lungs in her chest. She thinks of the tar marbling them, like bitumen she used to tease from the road on hot summer days. She decided she wouldn't follow George into the earth. When she goes she'll face the flames. She imagines the crematorium workers who would have to shovel her out, their faces when they see those two smouldering lumps, tacky with crude fuel, burning on long after the rest of her is dust.

It's been much longer than thirty seconds; minutes, it feels like, before the torches spring back to life in a contagious relay. They seem much brighter than before, even the cheapest model causing her to avert her gaze. She hunts for his tiny shadow, the little cowlicks of bed hair. She claws her way towards the guide, but already he is off through the archway—*Mind your head! Mind your head!*—and everyone pushes forward to see what's coming next. No queuing down here in the dark. No manners in the Mancunian shafts.

Shaddertown

The light is shrinking from the chamber
we don't abide that shine in shaddertown
and she spins, spiked with adrenaline, ready to lash out
at the owner of the grinning little voice that hissed at her. But
there are only the etiolated shadows of the departing, jerking
and frisking against the walls.

"Wait," she calls out, but she barely hears herself. Billy
must be in the middle of that scrum of people. She has to
believe that. If he were here, in this darkening room, he would
call out for her. He's always calling her. *Keep up Peg! Peg, can
I have a biscuit? Peg, where are my toy cars?* He'd call out to her,
if he were able. Did he fall? She peers into the gloom but she
can't see any figures, other than that damn stupid dummy.
Maybe he's hiding, playing a daft game. She hasn't the puff to
admit defeat. *I give up. I give up. Ally Ally in come free.*

She staggers from the chamber and one of her shoes skips
off her foot as easily as if it had been snatched away. She
crouches and pats the earth around her, but she feels only
soil and brick dust. Forget it. Billy needs me. I need Billy. She
leaves the chamber and she's slowing down because the light
has dwindled to such an extent that only a dim graininess
remains. The hubbub of excited voices has gone and now
she can hear the rumble and squeal of her chest, her breath
coming in shallow plosives. She's straining so hard to hear
beyond that for Billy that her ears might bleed. She can
imagine Jill with her arms folded across her chest. She can
imagine triumph in her face, more so than any grief, and her
heart is pierced with double the guilt.

Perhaps they've found Billy and he's all in a tizz, blubbing,
they can't get any sense out of him so they take him up to
safety. She has to find out. Maybe someone will realize she's
not come up after them and they'll come to help. She'll make
damn sure that cement-mouthed chocolate teapot of a guide
loses his job, that's a given.

Peggy makes her way through the archway and along the
corridor, tensing herself for obstacles she might trip over. Her
one shoe carves sharp *skrit-skrit* noises into the walls. Peg-leg.
Ha, George would have loved that.

She's almost at the end of this corridor—she can smell
the canal, and feel cool air coming from what must be some

sort of junction up ahead... that surely means she's close to the steps where they descended, doesn't it? — when she hears another grating in the rubble behind her. She turns, hoping it might be Billy, but instead she sees a pall of smoke funnel through the archway she's just vacated. It's lit palely within, a soft, mellow light, the colour of burnt amber. It shifts constantly, contracting and expanding as if powered by some internal engine, though it might just be the ebb and flow of air through all of these tunnels. Some trick of light and shade. A weird internal example of marsh gas. Billy, maybe, acting the goat. He had a torch all along and now he's playing tricks on Nana.

She draws in breath and the pall swings towards her. She speaks and as his name trickles out of her, the pall contracts. What is this? Is this consciousness shrinking? Is she about to faint? She mustn't, for Billy's sake. The moan might have come from her, it, or the tunnels but it doesn't matter. She rounds the corner and there are the stone steps, muddy and wet and subtly gleaming, like barely-set mortar.

Fear is at her heels, but also the awful feeling that she might be making a mistake and leaving Billy behind in the dark. She turns and sees the pall rounding the corner as if it was on a thread attached to her shambling feet. And she thinks: *every toxic inhalation.*

She's right to go up. She can report Billy missing if he's not with the rest of the touring party. Within ten minutes there will be a search party down here.

o you wish... you think you can climb these steps in ten minutes o my o you!

But it's her only choice. Billy will be found, but only if she gets out of here. She plants her shod foot on the first riser (thirty steps, just shallow ones, not as steep as those at home, but three times as many... come on old girl, you can do it... you used to glide up the steps at the Oasis as if they weren't there, and then dance all evening to Blue Dice or The Gordons or The Needles) and begins the long haul to daylight.

She counts each step and she does not look back. *Four, five, six...* she sucks at air that has turned intractable. It sits, niggardly and hot in her chest, as if her lungs were strangers to their job. She tries to imagine George up ahead, reaching out to her from the dance floor, the light catching in the oil in his hair and the rings on his fingers, the polished buckle on his high-waisted trousers. He looks lean and wolfish and sizzling with nervous energy. Young again. Christ, what she'd give.

Come on Peg, come on my Lili, let's give it some rice.

Eight, nine, ten... But there's something rising behind her too. Something within that bronze fug of smoke, she thinks, that is not so pleased to see her progress. She imagines a Billy trapped down here for decades, a Billy that is fish-grey, his eyes pale from the lack of sunlight, his skin mucoid and failing, touched by iridescent green flashes. She imagines that happy, chubby boy emaciated from hunger, lost in the maze, trying to find his nana. Clawing at the air for her.

My love for you renews my might
I'm warm again, my pack is light

By the time she gets to thirty steps, to forty, to fifty (*out now? I should be out by now?*) her legs are moving more quickly, and—miracle!—her chest seems less congested. She feels her ribs expand beyond any point they've achieved in fifteen years and the light is thickening around her, so bright, so playful she feels she might be able to reach out and touch it, cradle it in her hands like molten gold. Now, though, she smells the stale stink of old smoke in her wake, as if it's trying to catch up after all these years away. Her lungs ache in recognition. She might be able to summon enough breath, should that snatching grey claw ever manage to land on her shoulder, to power a scream.

THE VAULT OF THE SKY, THE FACE OF THE DEEP

ROBERT LEVY

They left me here during the evacuation. Old shrunken and childless widow with broken hips and no one to check on her, knees that lock beneath soiled nightgown and sheets, I listened as it all played out on my now-dead transistor radio. "Only three days," my wageless nursemaid Natalia said, "I'll be back in three days," and she never returned. No food for a week, well-drawn water long emptied from the bottles at my bedside in this patchwork cottage with the windows covered in newsprint since the light hurts my eyes, the same way it hurts to look at you. So blindingly blue. Now they're gone, from Pripyat to Chernobyl, all of them gone, eighteen miles in every direction around the plant. Such a waste. And I'm reaching the end.

Fitting fate to die alone, but then you came. Part of me hoped you would. And now you're here. Just as you were then, so very long ago.

Come closer. No, closer still, for you and I must speak on what I pray will be my last night on this godless earth. I might have had a few more days or weeks if someone else had come for me, but no matter. One day is just as good as another.

Tell me your name. I've always wanted to know.

No?

So then you came to listen. In that case I'll talk, and tell you what you want to hear. If only you'll do me one favour.

Yes?

Then I'll tell it.

I was born at the turn of the century as Irina Aleksandrovna Semonenko, named after the Grand Duke's daughter. Our only royalty, though, was my father, who was indeed a king but only of the local tavern, where he would rule over his court of drunken loyalists. Member of the Black Hundred through and through, and I remember his second pair of workboots lined up against the wall in the hallway, wondering when the first would walk home from the fields, his swollen feet inside. He was not a bad man, as far as fathers go: as a breed they are largely absent. The worst kind are the ones who are always hovering about, and he was a mercifully empty space in my childhood.

My mother, however, took great joy in her children, the four that lasted through infancy. We would dance around her dress hems, making mischief which might earn a hard slap on the head; that didn't mean the same thing then as it does now.

There was no school in those days, certainly not when this place was called Lokachkiv, so family was everything; my oldest brother Ivan was the one who taught me how to read. There was no going to Kiev then, no modern means of transport or pleasure to occupy our time, and when there wasn't work there was boredom, which hung heavy over all of us. Especially the men, who would drink and drink more until their thoughts turned to either hatred or lust.

Now that I think on it, that's why we're talking now.

When was it? Was I six years old? Or was I seven? It's hard for me to put it in place, all that time before the revolution we were supposed to forget. My strongest memory from that time is of you; that's how I knew you'd return to me, once the accident happened at the plant. I said before I had hoped it, but actually I knew. I knew.

You ruined my wedding night, did you know that? The night I became a Petrova. You came to me in a dream and gave me a horrible scare. Sergei had to stay up with me until morning. I was so afraid, over nothing. I tried to talk with my friend Elizaveta about you years later but she just laughed, as she did the night it happened. I never mentioned you again.

Where was I? Pardon me. I keep thinking I hear someone calling me. My mother perhaps, crying "Irinotchka" with anger from the kitchen, for I've done something wrong. But she's dead now.

Then again, so are you.

This has become a village of ghosts, and in a way, it's your fault, your people's fault, I mean. They're the ones who invented this way of turning energy into destruction. And now you've gotten your revenge on us, made us flee our homes as we once made you flee, and I suppose I can't really blame you for that. For there was a time when some of the men of this province wouldn't think much more about slitting one of your children's throats than they would peeling an apple; it was almost their national duty. So try not to judge us too harshly, if you can. Especially Ivan, God rest his soul, may he live on in heaven's embrace. He of the three of them was the drunkest, and if I hadn't gotten him from the tavern that night, then they might never have done what they did. But maybe that's just the wishful thoughts of a dying old woman.

And you. Come even closer, sit on the edge of the bed. Right here. Take my hand. I know you came to hear about yourself, not me. All young men are that way. You're more handsome than I remember, especially for what you are. And so young. So very young. How old are you, sixteen years? Seventeen?

I can feel pins and needles on my face, pricking at me. Is that you?

Your skin is the color of the sky that first night after the accident, has the same radiant bluish glow that there was in the clouds over the plant, one month gone now. Natalia propped me up in bed before running off with everyone else to the hills and rooftops to watch. So bright.

Is the accident what brought you back? I heard a program on the radio once, regarding some foreigners, from the Orient, I believe, who could think something so strongly that they could will it to life, so that it walked free in the world. Is that what you are? Or perhaps you were here all along, watching me, and the radiation just illuminated you, made you visible to the eye. I don't know about such things, the old superstitions weaned from us by the state, only what I hear on the now-dead transistor, or what I might hear from Natalia, who is a gossipmonger; she talks a lot, and never listens. You're a good listener.

So you want to hear a story you already know? But why? Are you my confessor?

If you insist, then, I'll tell it. It will be my last tale.

That night Alexander and Yuri found you, our mother had sent me to bring them home; your cries hurried me along the rain-slicked streets and that's when I found the three of you at the corner, my brothers bent over you, taking turns kicking you in your sides. Your skullcap had fallen off, and Yuri ground it into the mud with his heel. I ran inside the tavern and screamed, "Ivan, Ivan, they're beating a Jew in the gutter," and the whole town seemed to spill outside to watch as your blood started soaking into the dirt. It was Ivan who stumbled forward and shouted for them to stop, and a grumble of disappointment passed through the crowd.

You got up, or at least on one knee, and Ivan reached out his hand. You looked so peaceful then, not afraid, peering with wonder between the curls on the sides of your head as if looking up into the face of God himself. When you went to take his hand he grabbed you by your wrist instead and dragged you through the crowd, which roared its approval and trailed after him. I ran alongside you, watching as you tried to keep your head from hitting the stones; maybe it would have been better for you if you had managed to concuss yourself, I don't know.

The alley behind the tavern reeked of urine and sick, and there was a wooden barrel there against the wall, high as Ivan's waist and nearly full with rainwater and vomit. He pulled you forward as he held your hands behind your back, tipped your head into the barrel as Alexander and Yuri lifted you from your feet. The crowd cheered.

Our father stepped out of the back door of the tavern then, and when he saw what was happening his face lit up with pride, radiant. He began to clap his hands above his

head and started the crowd in a Black Hundred rhyme. Oh,
let me see if I can remember it...
"Remember the crown, for the good of Russia,
Strike out at the heart of thieves,
Take up the sword, and make it prosper
May it bloody our enemies."
Something of the sort.

I watched you begin to drown, your body convulsing
like a fish on the floor of a boat, and then your legs twisted so
hard that my brothers, laughing, dropped you into the barrel
before lifting you again so that only your head was beneath
the water's surface. I turned to the crowd then, everyone so
much taller than me I could barely see their faces, though I
do remember seeing young Elizaveta Baranskaia—Natalia's
mother, she died just last year, God rest her soul, may she
live on in heaven's embrace—with a great smile on her lips.
How much fun they were all having. I laughed along with
the rest of them, clapping my hands and stamping my feet
into the mud. But part of me felt for you, it really did, for
I didn't know how to swim and I have always feared the
water so.

Maybe that's because of you.

I started to turn away but there was a strong hand on
my shoulder and I was made to face forward, your legs just
twitching now, barely struggling at all. "Irinochka, what are
you doing?" my mother said at my side, holding me. "You
must watch." And I did.

After a few minutes my brothers lifted you out of the
barrel, and your dead face had gone blue. But not the blue
of you now, the steady blue glow of a toxic cloud, but rather
a face mottled with white and red blotches. The crowd
continued to carry on, and my mother abruptly scooped
me into her arms as she made her way through the crowd.
"Okay, time for bed now, sweet one. All good little girls
should be in bed."

All good little girls should be in bed. And now I can't get
out of mine.

And now I'm done. Eighty more years gone, and I'm
done. Over there on the wall is a portrait of my husband

Sergei, God rest his soul, may he live on in heaven's embrace. Everyone loved him so. When I met him I was nearly your age, and he reminded me so much of my father. So loved.

How does it feel, then, to be hated? To be despised, hounded from your homes and hunted down in the streets like dogs until you're driven out or dead? Of course, your people have their own land now; the world should have thought of that sooner. Such a waste.

Oh, it's time, it's time, I must leave my bed for the very last time. Won't you help me, so I can see the midnight sky once more? I've told you the story, so that you might be free of it, if that is why you came. But now it's time. And you promised.

That's it. Slip your hands beneath me. Oh, pins and needles, pricking everywhere. It's your skin, you unholy thing, it's on fire with power like sunlight, penetrating me. That's it. Lift me up. Not too roughly, I'm all bones and loosened flesh. Only a monster like you would hold me now.

Carry me to the front door. That's it. Careful. I'll help keep your skullcap upon your head, if you'll let me. Now, over the threshold, like a bridegroom from the cinema. Look, there's my cat Misha. So skinny, what have you been eating, my dear, nothing but weeds? Oh, my garden, my once-beautiful garden, who will tend you now?

One moment. There. Look around, do you see them? There. Right there. And there. What are those things, glowing blue in the darkness at the edges of the field, watching us as we pass through the garden gates? Are they your people? They frighten me. So many of them. So many of them so young. Look at her, that child there, her face is familiar to me. Perhaps she and I passed one another on the street one summer's day, when I too was a girl. So bright, blinding radiance, it hurts to look. I'll close my eyes, and never open them again.

Is that the sound of my mother, calling me from the kitchen? It's too late for that.

Now, do as you promised, monster Jew. I can't do it myself, for that would be a sin. Help this old woman down to the well and throw her in, so that I too may see the true face of God.

APPLE PIE AND SULPHUR
CHRISTOPHER HARMAN

The Greyhound bus wheezed to a stop, its doors hissed open and the driver said, "Only seats for two more."

"Not to worry," Malcolm said, usually the spokesman in these situations. "Karl doesn't mind standing." He grinned at Karl. "Yeah, thanks mate," Gareth said, in his uninflected voice, swinging his rucksack off his scrawny shoulders and preparing to board.

"Sorry lads," the driver said, not looking all that sorry. "There's no standing in the aisle allowed. Not safe on these roads. Go over the limit of thirty-nine and my job's on the line."

Karl was too tired to smirk at the rhyme and the jobsworth who was pretending not to have noticed it himself. Passengers watched from presumably every seat but two.

"Could one of us *sit* in the aisle?" Malcolm said. He smiled, teeth clenched.

"Nope," said the driver, looking ahead, mentally filing his fingernails.

Each waited for one of the others to volunteer to tramp alone the three miles to the village on the hard, winding, up-and-down blacktop. A lot to expect after five hours of the horseshoe of hills, then the knee-capping descent down Wetherlam—all under the late summer sun.

The driver revved the engine to indicate his reserves of patience weren't unlimited, then, as the three conferred, the doors whispered that a decision had been made for them and the bus moved off.

Apple Pie and Sulphur

"When's the next?" Karl asked, aching, hot. A disappointing end to the last of their roughly tri-annual hikes, the final get-together before Malcolm and Gareth relocated to the east and south coasts. He'd enjoyed today, though he'd never liked the walking as much as the views from the tops, the spread of hills like the backs of faceless beasts with muzzles buried in lakes, rivers and forests. Before the sun had burned it away, mist strands were like sheep's wool snagged on coarse pelts of woodland, stuck to glue-like yellow blobs of gorse.

"An hour—and that one might be full too. The Tilberthwaite Country Fair is on today." Leaf shadows dappled Malcolm's bald crown and owlish face as he examined the Ordnance Survey map. Karl and Gareth watched the bus disappear, along with what had been the prospect of a beer or two in Connerstone, then the Stagecoach service's uninterrupted hundred mile run to Manchester.

Karl said, "I can hear it, the fair." A faint voice over a Tannoy system, commentating, cajoling.

"Don't think so, Karl," Malcolm said, making one ear bigger with his cupped hand. "It's two or three miles away."

Sheep shearing, wrestling, dog races, stalls selling everything from jam to woolens held little appeal for Karl, nor stifling shuffling crowds.

No longer audible, the festive noise must have been blown elsewhere.

Gareth pushed his glasses up the bridge of his sweat-shiny nose and lifted his slim-line camera to frame a stile in the stone wall. An arrow sign pointed to Guards Wood. Malcolm said it was the start of a longer route to the village which would be kinder to their feet, and offer more shade. He looked at them for agreement and they nodded, having no better suggestion. While Gareth immortalized the partially rotted stile, Malcolm edged his barrel-like torso through the gap. Karl and Gareth followed.

A path went by a thin band of ash and birch. Karl guessed it was Guards Wood which glowered, a green-flecked massive wall of lumpy tar three or four tilted, misshapen fields away. The dark cloud directly above could have been the woods' blackness reflected against the blue sky.

"That might get us before the finishing line," Malcolm said, relish at the challenge in his energetic stride along the ash path. His map was stretched between his hands; it was more necessary here than it had been up in the hills, where there had been one clearly indicated route. Sheep watched them approach, their faces stupidly noble, before prancing away under bouncing burdens of ragged wool.

A gate overgrown with weeds was the first indication of a dilapidated property; it was enclosed by a chaotic hedge with upright slates, the size of encyclopedias, running along its base. Gareth snapped at them with his camera. A crooked tree grew through a partially collapsed roof. There was a crumbling barn and a grassed-over yard. A farm once, so long out of use it no longer stank.

"They've all got stars engraved on them," Karl said, peering down at the slates.

"Pentagrams," Gareth said, blasé, as if you saw them all the time.

"What, to keep demons out?" Karl said. "These broken ones where they got in? Actually, the sheep do look sort of devilish."

"Now chaps," Malcolm said, "we'd better get a hurry on. The only evil here is that dratted black cloud."

Karl thought Guards Wood could run it a close second; it looked dense, airless.

They paused at a tree with gnarled twisting branches hung with shriveled bulbs, unlikely to mature into eatable apples. There were several opened bottles hanging from strings. "Shooting practice?" Karl wondered aloud. His heart pumped as it never had on the steepest slopes.

"None are broken," Gareth said. "Looks like the old method to catch wandering demons."

"Dear-y me, Gareth," Malcolm said; he'd no time for such nonsense.

Darkened by foliage, a thick branch high up looped in a graceful extended S laid on its side. It didn't seem to belong. Karl sucked in a breath as it shifted position. No, *he* had. Warm air hissed through leaves.

They walked on. In the ten minutes since the road, Karl hadn't spied one other walker. He reflected that dedicated hikers kept to the hills. This was landscape you glanced at as you drove by it. It looked abandoned, sheep its custodians, masticating grass and watching with disdain as the three of them passed.

Five more minutes elapsed and the wood was a towering wave about to break. Malcolm stopped, eyed his map as he might a willful child in one of his classes, and complained at the scale being too small. A horsefly landed on it, mistaking it for the world. He batted the fly away and wiped at his gleaming forehead with his handkerchief. Being honoured with a name must mean the wood was of a size and character to deserve one. Karl couldn't think of anything in its favour other than the shade it would offer.

"Ready?" Malcolm said, as if the brief stoppage had been primarily to give his companions a rest.

The path rose to a sagging stone wall. Malcolm went first, striding over the broken remains of a kissing gate.

No diminution of the heat. Karl felt they'd entered innumerable stuffy rooms, defined not by walls but by the pillars of the trees, furnishings a matter of masses of brambles and other unidentifiable greenery. Maybe they should have avoided the wood, the way the birds had. Sunlight falling into distant glades and rides darkened the heavy cover elsewhere. The mix of trees suggested it was an old wood. That was the extent of Karl's arboreal knowledge and it was confirmed not long after. Gareth stalked forward, camera poised, towards a collapsed wooden frame the size of a TV screen. Under cracked glass, words, some not eaten by insects or dampened to illegibility.

"... birch, oak and ash, natural to ... kingdom. Ecosystem thrives ... maintenance of a continuous canopy ..."

Karl thought the choking underbrush wouldn't be as continuous if, as he suspected, woodland overseers weren't as scarce as the birds. He'd no sense of how far they'd penetrated the wood—and there were no longer sightings of sunlit glades. Close, heavy air pressed. Pattering on leaves began slowly like hesitant applause.

"I think the trees have told the black cloud we're here," Malcolm said, shrugging off his rucksack and pulling out his waterproof. Gareth and Karl did the same.

They walked like beggars, heads bowed as the air filled with rain and the swishing of their waterproofs. They stepped carefully over roots intersecting the path like prominent veins on a wet hide.

Karl couldn't be bothered remonstrating with Gareth, who was close enough behind to be kicking lightly at his heels. The hissing of millions of leaves sieving the rain focused into unintelligible whispered words directly behind his ear. Gareth hadn't been previously given to japes and Karl was about to suggest he shouldn't start now. Then he noticed his friend walking stolidly several yards ahead.

Karl flung himself around. Puddles had formed on the empty path. The rain hissed and crackled like fire. His own flapping wet trouser legs had kicked at his ankles.

"Sun's back," Malcolm called out.

Some distance ahead a glade overflowed with buttery light. Karl's limbs un-stiffened. Abruptly, the rain stopped but for sporadic fingertip taps on his hood.

Moments later they stepped into a wide break lined with gorse. There was a litter of rocks and stones from a glacier that could have passed just yesterday. An empty wedge to the right in the trees revealed a pin-prick flash of a distant windscreen, a section of the lake like a bent nail, a flank of the mountain whose summit they'd reached in time for sandwiches and the midday news on Karl's headphones.

They walked down the ride until it was clear the right-hand path Malcolm said to look out for had been grown over, or broke away from a different glade entirely. But here was another path heading off to the left just short of where the ride ended in dense foliage.

"Can't see it on the map but it's got to lead to somewhere," Malcolm said.

"Paths *always* lead somewhere," Karl complained, stopping, rebellion inside him. "Let's go back and look for the path on the map."

"The map's not reliable here," Malcolm said. Karl felt the same about the wood. The trees looked too dense to even let a path through but Malcolm and Gareth were heading into them.

Karl followed and after a moment turf was light and

springy underfoot and there were cushions of moss. "Had this place in mind all along," Malcolm said, his grin signaling how untrue that was.

Like a faulty TV picture, the whitewash flickering between the dark tree trunks. At their feet, a winding series of stepping stones, flush with the grass. They ended at a short length of fence into which was set a low gate with a sign across it, *Journeys End Refreshments*. "Should be an apostrophe before or after the 's' in 'journeys', but I'm prepared to forgive on this occasion," Malcolm said.

"I've some water left if you want some," Karl said. "Let's just get back. I want beer, not tea." Hidden here, the house's saving grace was not being made of gingerbread.

"Keep hold of your water, Karl," Malcolm said, lifting the latch with a sharp snap.

Karl went through last, the latch raining a rusty powder onto his fingers.

The whitewashed cottage was at the end of a long narrow lawn. Around the door was a trellis of faded red roses. There were windows at each side and two upstairs—all with closed shutters apart from the one to the right of the door. Murk behind the large single pane of glass.

They dropped their rucksacks by a lone round table halfway down the garden by the wall. "I'll parley with the natives," Malcolm said, anticipation in his face at what a delight this was certain to be.

"Sure there are any?" Gareth said to Malcolm's back. The closed shutters and dark window gave Karl hope but then a face appeared in a gap in the doorway, and he noticed a shape, vaguely visible in the window.

A hefty someone. More likely a female, to judge from the profusion of banana-sized and sharp-pointed crescents of yellowish hair around the solid base of the dark block of the head. Working at a sink or worktop?

A few words were exchanged and Malcolm called back, "Apple pies and tea do for you?" Gareth said "yeah" and Karl raised his thumb, rather than his voice and affront the stillness of the trees. Malcolm had gone to the un-shuttered window where he stooped to a book on the ledge. He wrote into it then was strolling back to the table.

He asked Gareth how many photos he'd taken. Gareth checked, said "thirteen".

"Lucky for some. A good day, don't you think, Karl?"

"Not bad," Karl said. The trees had twisted it out of shape, the house stopped it dead.

Malcolm said, "I envy you, still having hills on your doorstep when we're gone."

A hundred miles was no "doorstep"—and walking alone held no appeal, even if he'd known how to read maps. That's why he'd joined the Hill Billies. Malcolm and Gareth had joined separately at the same time. A disparate trio of physiques and personalities bound together from the first day in a loose camaraderie. The Hill Billies group had folded four walks later. Karl had a vague notion the three of them had infected it in some mysterious fashion, thus ensuring its demise.

He couldn't feel the breeze carrying the sounds of the country fair down corridors between the hills and over the dense carpet of woodland. Many voices, with one amplified and surging over the rest.

Karl said, "Hear that—?"

"Stand by your beds, gentlemen," Malcolm interrupted, smoothing the altar-white tablecloth.

Tall and very slim, the young woman carried a loaded tray and approached with quick small steps of her tiny feet. The close-fitting maroon garment she wore down to her calves had a sheen in which darker shades billowed like smoke.

She placed the tray on the table; the pies had strikingly golden crusts and pillows of clotted cream. Karl tried to catch her eye, just to see if he could. She had large wide-apart eyes. Supposed to be an attractive feature, weren't they? He'd beg to differ. Malcolm said, fulsomely, "Thank you. You've saved our lives." Her lengthy thin-lipped smile encouraged him to go on.

"How's business? You're quite hidden away." He could ask questions like that.

"Coming to an end," she said, her voice sibilant, how the trees would talk if there were a breath of air. "We're going home. We aren't from around here."

Apple Pie and Sulphur

"No?" Malcolm said. Still smiling, and as if she hadn't heard his invitation to expand, she turned and went back to the cottage.

"See her teeth? Like a baby's milk teeth," Karl said, pushing at his apple pie with his spoon.

"Except for the incisors—they were a grownup's." Gareth was observant without ever being obviously so.

"Arms too small," Karl said. "Perfectly proportioned, just ... too small."

"Oh, we are pernickety today." Malcolm lifted a hideous china teapot. "Shall I be Mother?" he said, as always proceeding to be.

They drank and ate.

"Eggy. Too much egg," Gareth said. Karl agreed—the strong flavour of egg yolk in the pastry battled with apple. "You fussy eaters," Malcolm chided, smiling under his cream moustache.

He and Gareth finished theirs first. Malcolm lifted his cup. "To new beginnings." His declaration rebounded off the trees like not-quite-articulated responses. Karl and Gareth echoed it in restrained murmurs then all three silently contemplated Gareth's imminent departure to a life as a notably youthful mature student in and around Falmouth Art College, Malcolm's recent appointment to a deputy headship at a Grimsby primary school. Karl was closer to a sacking than promotion at North West Energy's call centre after losing his cool again and hanging up on an irate customer last week. A tally of two strikes; a third and he'd be out.

"It's a word I use sparingly, but 'heavenly' just about sums up this place." Malcolm leaned forward; a self-satisfied little gust of laughter. "These establishments—" Low-voiced—this was for their ears only. "They're uniquely English. There's usually an attractive young girl at front of house. Mother is formidable, matronly, has a farmer's wife build, keeps to the kitchen." They glanced to the window in which the shadowy bulk was motionless, as if watching them back. Malcolm went on, "Dad's even more in the background. He does the books, the DIY. Always mysteriously busy. Probably early-retired from some significantly more demanding professional occupation." Malcolm sat back. He was fond of making affectionately astute observations and was pleased with this one.

"Not surprised they're packing up," Gareth said. "Can't be much passing trade." Other people's financial situations always interested him where nothing much else about them did. Despite a handful of exhibitions and positive reviews, photography wasn't proving lucrative. He scraped a living from part-time jobs. He got out his camera, a small neat basic model he prided himself on finding wholly satisfactory for finding the strange in the ordinary.

Malcolm patted the solid mass of his stomach. "That was lovely. Simple and comforting." With a slight frown, he smacked his lips around a lingering aftertaste. Karl pushed aside his plate, a third of the pie uneaten. Neither of the others offered to finish it off. Malcolm got up. "I'll go and pay."

He walked across the grass. Standing before the cottage, he pressed both hands to his stomach, frowned, then pushed at the door and stepped inside.

A listlessness came over Karl with the lynchpin of Malcolm gone. "Come *on*," he said, impatient after three minutes or so.

"He could get a Trappist monk gabbing." A skill Gareth didn't have and probably didn't envy. He got up and walked to the cottage door. He adjusted a function on his camera and photographed the slab of the doorstep, then stooped to the book on the window ledge. He wrote into it then tipped his head as if he'd heard a sound from the doorway. He went to it and stepped inside.

Karl listened. No voices, no birdsong, no brush of tree foliage. The treetops waved to such a slight degree it could just as well have been the blood pumping through his eye sockets. He felt observed, and not from the trees, though he had a peculiar sense of them "facing" the garden and cottage. Not from the window either; dense gloom within.

He stood before the window a moment later. Nobody inside. A bare plaster back wall; no sink or cupboards as far as he could tell.

It was an open foolscap-sized book on the window-ledge.

Apple Pie and Sulphur

On facing pages row upon row of signatures with attached comments all written in a brownish red ink. A visitors' book. Gareth Shuttleby's was the last name, written in a tiny pinched hand, with, typically, nothing else added. On the preceding line, "Malcolm Goodey" in a controlled flourish that would have looked more fitting on a legal document. A fulsome comment next to it: "Excellent: a Heavenly enclave." One empty line left to fill at the bottom of the right-hand page. Karl took up the pen: it was cold between finger and thumb, a smooth texture like polished bone. The silence was acute; the trees, like an audience bound in shadow, made for a sense of intense expectation—he couldn't think what else might.

Writing his name would feel like giving too much of himself. He felt a new-found appreciation of his anonymity answering calls at North West Energy. There, he was nameless—he liked things that way. No, he'd keep "Karl Crier" to himself. He couldn't help thinking Malcolm and Gareth should have been equally reticent. He very much wanted to leave but first he had to find out what they were finding so compelling in the house. Malcolm might be deep in conversation but surely not Gareth.

He pushed at the door and stepped inside

—and down.

Shock, at the unexpected drop of a foot or so. An odour of leaf mould and mildew. Dirt underfoot and the remains of rotted floorboards, beneath the layer of dead leaves. There was a landing—and no way up to it with the wooden stairs below, collapsed and rotten, strangled by some parasitic weed. "Hello? Anyone?" he said, his voice tight. Why hadn't either of them cried out when they stepped into this place? Karl just wanted to cry. Nobody had lived here in years, yet the girl had brought out food—he could taste it now and felt queasy.

Rough stone walls exuded coldness and damp. His boots pushing through leaves, he peered into the gloom at the back of the house. A florid tongue of leafy branches thrust down through a window to feed on weeds, rubbish and glass shards.

Discoloured chunks of white ceramic, mingled in

rotted leaves on the floor, were the only indication that the room at the front may once have been a kitchen. Lighter than elsewhere, the space was harder to endure. Stepping backwards his foot squelched something soft. He looked down and his stomach rolled at the half-embedded worm wriggling in the decayed apple.

Stepping back outside, he saw that the visitors' book was no longer on the window ledge. Were the staff and Malcolm and Gareth enjoying a joke at his expense as they hid not far off in the trees? In the gloom of the house he could have missed some other doorway—but nothing would persuade him to venture back inside.

"Yeah, very funny," Karl called out, nodding as if it were. "You can come out now." He thought someone was about to when he glimpsed movement.

Sunlight outside deepened the gloom in the kitchen, occupied again. The more he stared, the less he wanted the two shapes with the girl to be more clearly delineated. Alone out here, he refused to believe the human-sized pepperpot had a crescent of horns around a black muzzle with nostrils you could fit fists in. It and the girl were in the shelter and deep shade of a fleshy black canopy, like a warped mattress. In the pillar-box thick stalk that supported it were several dark pits like empty eye sockets.

The girl held a book before her. Karl could only think it was the visitor's book. His limbs felt calcified. How long before perusal of the book was transferred to him? Twisting, he felt rooted in the lawn before a supreme effort freed him. He ran, grabbed his rucksack and then the gate's latch snickered drily and puffed rust onto his hand as he pushed.

A random fleeing until the woods expelled him. More unknown paths dipped in and out of further misted islands of woodland, rose and fell on meadows and pastures ruckled like mouldy green bed linen. An arrowhead of geese honked laughter in and out of low cloud. Sheep fled from him on stick legs, matted fleeces leaping.

He was able to triangulate from the positions of the mountains a tortuous way to the village. A chill, a faint fuzzy patina of grey on tree and hill, as if summer had shifted into autumn in under an hour.

Apple Pie and Sulphur

Connerstone offered little relief. Damp grey stone, grubby whitewash, faded stucco. Rumbling cars glided in slow lines. Voices bloomed and diminished on the crowded paths outside a mini-gallery, the gingerbread shop, *Souvenirs and Gifts*, cafes and pubs. He sensed lassitude—people filling the time before departure. Grey light washed colours from their clothing.

At a convulsion in his stomach, Karl tasted apples and foul eggs. The girl had been real but those companions must have been distorted reflections from the garden and the trees. Going inside to demand an explanation he would have found that out for certain—and the whereabouts of his friends. His phone would clear up the latter mystery.

Malcolm's recorded voice introduced and instructed like a deliberate delaying tactic before Karl could say, his voice clipped, "It's me. I'm in the village. Are *you*? Ring me back." From Gareth's number a ringtone like a robotic cough.

There was just over an hour before the Stagecoach service was due to leave the terminal. He'd kill time until then. He wandered, as much in the roadside gutters as on the paths.

He was returning along the main street when there was the unhealthy rattle of an engine and a bus began to draw past him. Karl looked up at the passengers. They were still, listless, like prisoners, each pair in their tiny shared cell. Despite the state of the bus—a drab grey, dented, rust patched—their clothing suggested they were tourists or day-trippers rather than users of a regular local service.

Gareth, in the middle of the back row, was neither. Karl stumbled, recovered, looked again. *Gareth?* Lacking any livery, the bus clearly wasn't part of the Stagecoach fleet they were booked onto in less than an hour's time. So what was Gareth doing onboard?

Karl kept pace, leaping, waving, shouting. Gareth stared forward, oblivious, his expression even more closed-off than usual. People on the path went about their business with bovine intent, Karl's antics of no interest. The bus picked up speed. Some obstruction up ahead had been cleared, but then, short of that, it took a squeaking left-turn into a side road.

Entering a moment later, Karl could see no sign of it

though he heard the diminishing rattle of an engine from within the trees bordering the village.

Karl went and sat in the Yewdale Arms. A grey cast to the light in the window. Wood panelling was dull, as if sandpaper had been applied to it. He barely touched his Guinness. It couldn't have been Gareth on the bus. That would make no sense. Behind glass and the reflected street, just someone *like* him.

Later, when he arrived at the bus terminal, the Stagecoach vehicle was ready to go and nearly full. None of the passengers were Malcolm and Gareth. He could have taken his seat but the puzzle would have gnawed at him all the way home. Waiting outside the coach, he rehearsed to himself the diatribe he'd aim at the pair should they appear in the next moment. At a loss when they failed to, and as the coach slowly pulled away, he tried their mobile phone numbers again. No replies. He left the terminal and wandered again, bewildered.

There was a corner building with books on three floors. He browsed in the local section. In slim stapled volumes no references to Guards Wood; the origin of its name was lost in the hills, or knowledge of it buried in Connerstone Church graveyard. Guarding against what?

On the uppermost floor he looked over the roofs of the village to the upland approach to the fells. A dense fur of woodland draped over an incline must be a near edge of Guards Wood. Were Malcolm and Gareth still up there?

A dull silver mass edged into his eye corner and Karl gasped. The bus had shuddered to a halt on the opposite side of the road below. He was certain this was the same dilapidated vehicle as earlier.

With the passenger door at the front on the far side, it was hard to tell if anyone alighted or got on. No bus-sign or shelter, no line of traffic to hold it up. That it had stopped directly opposite him expressly to display Malcolm in the rearmost window seat was nonsense, though coincidence seemed even less likely. Karl's heart vaguely complained as he ran down three flights of compressed stairs and out onto the path.

He stared across the road, and was struck that nobody

stared back at his agitated presence—least of all Malcolm. Karl looked down at his own body in an involuntary check that he was fully present. For a moment he was unsure if it was Malcolm in the back seat, such was the unfamiliar set of his face. He and all his fellow passengers could have been victims of some terrible and inescapable fate. Pictured in a bracingly honest coach holiday brochure they couldn't have been any more motionless.

Karl now knew for certain this was the same bus he'd seen on the main street. And that was definitely Gareth on the far side of Malcolm, still in the middle seat and facing down the central aisle. It was better that they were here. He could forget about Guards Wood now.

He ran, preparing to knock on Malcolm's window—and the bus moved off. He yelled and waved frantically with both hands, saw the staring unyielding square page of the driver's face in the side mirror. He sprinted after the bus until it took a turn into a tiny estate of grey-pink rendered rented houses. Its trundling speed in the confining streets was sufficient for it to elude Karl. It had exited at some point, for Karl knew he'd covered every yard.

He sat on a bench by a deserted tiny playground with his head in his hands. If this was a practical joke, to all appearances it was affording Malcolm and Gareth no pleasure. He returned to the bookshop. The manager didn't look up from his examination of a till receipt and when he finally acknowledged Karl's presence he'd evidently forgotten him hurtling by earlier like a book thief. He hadn't heard of *Journeys End Refreshments* though he knew Guards Wood.

"Everyone does. If you've any sense you go round it."

"Me and my friends went through," Karl said, an ache in his chest like grief.

"Still there are they?"

"No. I've seen them on a bus. It was outside just now. Didn't you see it? Grey. Looks a wreck."

"Yes. Better the bus than the woods," he said, oozing complacency. "You should have joined them."

"*They* should be joining *me*. It wasn't the bus they were supposed to be on. I've seen it twice now. Couldn't get their attention. We had seats booked on the Stagecoach run to Manchester."

It no longer felt like any consolation, the three of them safely out of Guards Wood. Karl slipped out into the street. Voices and traffic sounded like they were from radios turned down low. If he was slumped in a chair outside Journeys End, replete with apple pie, when was he going to stop haunting this washed-out Connerstone and wake up?

Later, he walked between darker shadings of slate and stone. Hints of evening in touches of chill air from side roads. Cloud like the thick-ribbed drab sand of a seabed. In an alleyway between shops he got out his phone. The same gratingly breezy recording of Malcolm's voice. Gareth's repetitive coughing ringtone was like something dying.

He booked into the Beaumont Hotel. That evening, in the bar he sat at a table and drank mineral water. Coming down from alcohol would exacerbate the ache of abandonment that rippled wider than the sundering from his friends.

A large shaggy dog, an unidentifiable cross-breed, wandered, accepting crisps and peanuts before retiring behind the counter. A sudden odour of cider or raw apple broke into Karl's fascination with the flames in the wood burner. A waft of rotten eggs had him standing. Deep snorts and porcine squeals under the counter. A sinuous movement of a shiny reddish brown embedded itself into a group of voluble young women. Whispering laughter was like a vapour around their harder chuckles. It dispersed as he stood before the group; none of them was the girl from Journeys End. It took a moment for them to notice him staring. He returned to his seat and gave it up soon after. Nobody else appeared to notice the sulphurous smell which the dry heat of the wood-burner intensified until it was more than he could stand.

The streets were as empty as the paths and glades of Guards Wood, and as silent—until he heard the rattle of the engine. It drew him through the village and had faded to nothing by the time he was in sight of the car park, a crossword puzzle layout demarcated by wilting flowers in stone troughs, low walls and head-high shrubs.

The bus was in a corner. Approaching warily he saw that

the grey wasn't paint, but the absence of it. He was reminded of favourite toy cars, taken from the toy box so often they began to lose their lead paint and reveal the matte metal beneath. Deep scratches in the bodywork. Rust wounds. Lifting his gaze he saw threads of bright orange where cracks in the glass caught the sodium light.

A double shock seeing the seated figures in the dark interior, hearing the engine cough suddenly like a diseased thing. He staggered back as, moaning through its length, the bus moved off. Karl followed until it was heading through the exit and withdrawing like a bloodless tongue into the stone jaws of the village.

Visible through the rear window, four heads on the back row, five if that right-hand corner seat had been filled. Later maybe, the passengers' dispersal to hotels and bed-and-breakfasts—though their continued presence was making them seem as integral to the functioning of the bus as the sick engine.

The crowd awoke him. A vast crowd, an ocean of voices dragooned by an overwhelming voice soaring and swooping above them. It couldn't be the country fair again, not at this late hour, and in any case the sounds weren't entering via the leaded panes of the window.

He got out of bed, opened his door a few inches. Nothing audible from downstairs, other than a sound that soon he identified as a lazy flap of turned pages.

In the soft illumination of night-lights he went down the stairs. The multitudes, gone now, could have emanated from a TV or radio.

The visitors' book was on a walnut occasional table. Cold air laid a page finally to rest and stiffened Karl's limbs.

On facing pages, names. The latest entry had Gareth's precise tiny signature. The preceding name was Malcolm's.

Were they in this hotel? A coincidence—or they had discovered he was staying here. They must have booked in late—any earlier he would have seen them in the bar, unless they'd chosen to hide in their rooms. Speculating on how their reunion with him might proceed, he drew a blank, couldn't in fact envisage any kind of reunion. Again no comment by Gareth's neat inscription. Malcolm had written "Heavenly enclave" rather than come up with something new for the Beaumont. Similarly, there was a single space waiting to be filled at the bottom of the right-hand page. The ink was the same reddish brown as in the book at Journeys End. There was even an identical make of pen, fawn, shiny, like a long slender bone of a bird.

Karl flipped over the book; the front cover had a reddish brown encrustation like the scab over a healing wound. He pressed his splayed fingers into it, wanted to press it out of existence. He stepped away from it. "Heavenly enclave" flattered Journeys End, the visitors' book for which was before him now. In the morning, oh yes, in the morning, he'd slam the book down onto the reception desk and demand an explanation and—

A footfall at the end of the passageway to the staff quarters, a shadow poised in the doorway. Karl said, "What's this doing here?"

Placing a finger on the last two names in the visitors' book, the paper felt smoother. He looked down—it was cleaner, newer—and he didn't recognize the names. There was a column for dates in the left-hand margin. There was a blue biro chained to a blotting pad.

The manager said nothing; he wasn't even present.

After breakfast, a crackling like fire after Karl had keyed in his friends' mobile phone numbers. Later that morning his phone battery was dead, and his charger was in his flat in Manchester. He could be there himself by evening if he caught today's Stagecoach run.

At midday he left the hotel and drank in a coffee shop and watched pedestrians and vehicles. He browsed unthinkingly in souvenir shops and outdoor clothing emporia. He was in dread and hope of seeing the grey bus. If, bizarrely, Malcolm and Gareth were still onboard he'd find some way to get on. He'd confront them, shake them out of whatever stupor held them. He wouldn't be taking that empty back seat, he'd be ensuring two more would be vacant.

Mid-afternoon he sat on the churchyard wall. Unshaven and in the clothes he had climbed mountains and slept in, he was as noteworthy as a lamppost to the apathetic crowds on the path.

A sustained snort from the open back doors of a butcher's van shocked him. A hiss of airbrakes had him covering both ears and retreating into the church. His gaze skittered over the visitors' book in the porch and he entered the nave where he sat on the back pew.

In a side chapel as dark as the bole in a tree, a bank of candles in transparent votive holders cast a lurid red light, rendering the priest's face demonic.

Cries from the street, masses of them. An amplified voice barged and blundered. Karl shook his head; a country fair can't have instantly manifested itself in the graveyard. He didn't believe in it even when the priest said, "Now that's a glorious din." His eyes retained a faint redness when he turned to face Karl. "Hell is other people, it's been said. That's true enough." A toothless smile, if it was a smile. "You can't escape it."

Filling the long slits of the side pockets in his soutane, his hands must have been enormous. He was bringing the darkness of the chapel out with him. Karl didn't want to hear whatever else the man intended to say and left.

Outside he listened. Only village sounds, muted as if heard through thick canvas. The fair must have been a recorded event, blasted out of the open window of a vehicle going by.

The graffiti-decorated porta-cabin was indicative of how the police viewed the general run of tourists' issues in the village. What would they make of this one? Inside there was a tiny TV screen over the desk: Karl couldn't tell from the tiny busy figures if he was seeing the streets outside or the exterior of some obscure daytime drama. It held the apple-chinned officer's attention until Karl repeated himself in a raised voice, and even then he looked to the window first as if Karl had called from outside.

Karl omitted details that would demolish his chance of a

fair hearing. The officer dragged his pen across the incident book opened out on the counter. He began asking questions; where was Karl from, did he have a job, did he live alone? "I don't think I can help you here. Looks like your … *friends* are alive and well. Not sure you're in good shape though. You look like death warmed-up. Take my advice and take yourself back home—wherever that is." A place the officer appeared to have little faith in.

The village was like floating debris on a sluggish stream. Shutters came down on the front window of the greengrocer's. Battered suitcases were being loaded into the open wound in the side of a coach.

In the Yewdale Arms Karl sat at a table close to the bar, drank scotch and placed his ticket on the table before him. Seat thirty-nine. Would the company accept it for today's service? At home, at work, he would let the mystery resolve itself.

The priest entered and Karl felt a curdling sensation in his stomach, a taste of apple and bad eggs. Sitting opposite him, the priest crossed his black-trousered legs, entwining them down to his coal-black shoes. He nodded at the coach ticket. "Thirty-nine—you're the last. They aren't going anywhere without you. You must accept the inevitable."

"They?" Karl's back prickled with cold, his front baked as if the priest exuded heat.

"'They' are a delightful family—but homesick." Dreamy reminiscence on the priest's face. "They've been stuck here for ages and can't return until they've met their quota of names—thirty-nine to be exact. Thirty-nine is a number replete with diabolical significance." He snickered. "Sadly for them, thirty-eight isn't."

"Names?" Karl pocketed the ticket. If the coach left at 4:50pm, same as yesterday, he'd be away from this lunacy.

"Yes, obviously you haven't signed the book. They aren't happy about that. That's the payment they required for that sumptuous repast."

Karl wanted to swing with his fist at the delta of throbbing red veins in the priest's temple. In the soutane's side pockets, an outline of abnormally long fingers. The man's stomach rumbled like magma. A taste of apples and foul eggs crumpled Karl's face.

"Go to Hell," Karl said. His frown felt half way down his face.

The priest's sigh seemed to issue not just from his crooked mouth. "I wish." On one side his gleaming forehead drooped like wax to his cheek as airbrakes screamed. Karl got up, quivering.

In the tall window, just under the curtain rail and in the plain glass over the lower half of frosting, a band of faces blurred, stilled.

Malcolm's and Gareth's gazes passed through Karl as unheeding of him as subatomic particles.

Bubbling pitch behind him. He turned to see the opening to the Gents door narrowing under the bent arm of the self-closing device. A hot, layered and meaty stink made him gag. He rushed out, swallowed air in the street, felt nauseous. No bus in sight but it didn't matter, as he knew Gareth and Malcolm were no longer aboard.

There was a bottleneck of tourists at the entrance to a side road. Motionless forms beyond a ferment of people entering and exiting some establishment a little way down with a "Closing Down Sale" sandwich board notice outside. He crossed over, keeping his gaze steady. Two people; Gareth and Malcolm, he firmly believed until the sinuous slenderness of one couldn't possibly be Gareth nor the obesity of the other Malcolm.

Though the pair had gone by the time he'd made his way through the crowd, Karl sensed they'd found a better spot from which to observe him.

On the corner, the butcher's shop; in its window a pig's head with tiny eyes stared glassily at him from a bed of lettuce leaves and apple halves. Then his attention was drawn to a narrow maroon pennant, rippling off its pole and tumbling down the other side of the petrol garage's shallow pitched roof.

At the terminal shortly before 4:50 the driver told him the coach was full and that his ticket was for yesterday. The coach slid away. An official said there were no more services to anywhere before tomorrow. Karl returned to the Beaumont and booked another night. He tried not to be upset by anything other than what this was costing him financially.

He could hear guests packing, prior to departure in the morning. With frequent pig-like squeals of door hinges, the hotel was a sty.

He watched TV for four hours before hisses and grunts underlying the actors' voices had him switching off. He made no other preparations for sleep other than to close his eyes and wait for the last door to squeal savagely on its hinges.

Later, out of the darkness, came the turn of a page. He stared at a slight swaying of the curtains for minutes before leaving his bed and parting them down the middle.

At the dead centre of the deep window ledge was the Journeys End visitors' book. He closed his eyes, willed it not to be there, and looked again.

Thirty-eight names, and a space opposite number thirty-nine. There was the pen, a slender piece of bone carved to a point. He'd tear the book to pieces-throw them into the stream. His fingers were curved like talons when he heard the voice.

"Greetings this fine night."

The words shook through him. A male voice, not loud but like a mountain speaking. Karl looked into the deep-set window in which the grotesques were reflected.

Deep snorts and squeals from the porcine thing loosened the flesh on his bones. Next to it, a twisted flourish, a cartilaginous shiny length in shades of reddish bronze emitted harsh whispers, like escaping gas. They were both in the protective shadow cast by a great fleshy dark cap that extended some way past the walls and ceiling it rendered insubstantial. Holes in the massive thick trunk watched him intently. He thought one of them had spoken.

This was the window of Journeys End again, except that he and they occupied the same side of the glass. Tight as a family. Inseparable.

"We fed you well." Like gravity speaking.

"Yes. De-delicious." His voice was the last toothpaste squeezed from a tube.

"You must sign our visitor's book." In the monumentally deep and reasonable tone a planetary pressure to comply.

Apple Pie and Sulphur

"I prefer not to put my name to things," Karl managed to say.

"Your name is important to us."

Karl let out a bitter, tremulous spurt of laughter. In the glass, the scatter of holes that observed him would have been light-years deep if light had been conceivably involved. Seen directly, not reflected, he thought he'd be gone into them, never to emerge. They didn't want that—what they wanted was what was happening, his fingers grasping the pen.

Hissing in his head. Snorts and grunts rooting hungrily in his guts.

"You want to be with your friends, don't you?" The voice—from the floor of the universe. "Come with us."

"Where?" he said, though the question seemed spoken through him.

"*Home.*" A triumvirate of yearning inhuman voices sent the curtains billowing. He felt a void the depth of his skin away.

"Whose home? I'm happy here, thank you."

With the lie, resistance began to drain through his right hand and into the bone pen which was moving into position over the empty space on the page.

As the nib drove home, he obstructed it with his free left hand.

White hot pain awoke him to daylight. Grey-blue light around the edges of the closed curtains. Voices; doors opening and closing. Vehicles were moaning on the main street.

A small painless black wound in the back of his hand. There was no pen on the window ledge to have caused it. No book either.

In the dining room he couldn't eat breakfast. Afterwards, at the reception desk, the manager finally noticed him and Karl asked for his bill.

The manager had chicken skin. His upper lip was bowed in a smile but not the lower.

"I'll pay by cheque."

"If you tear out the slip, I'll stamp it for you."

The manager stamped the hotel name and passed the slip back to Karl.

The pen had scratched Karl's unruly signature when he noticed its bony hue. He dropped it and it clattered hollowly onto the desk. The scratching had scored through the cheque to the scabrous book beneath which the manager deftly pulled away. Speechless, Karl pointed with his wavering pierced hand in a tempest in which the manager's ears flapped and his long fingers rippled like thin pennants.

The hotel leaned four ways in turn. Doors banged open and shut, open and shut. Easy chair cushions plumped and flattened like lungs. The floorboards rippled like conflicting currents in water. Stair risers rose and fell like wreckage on rough waters. Pictures floated as far out from the walls as cords attaching them to hooks would allow. Horseshoes clip-clopped randomly over rough plaster walls. Insane celebration, everywhere.

The halves of the front door opened and shut like heart valves. On an out-swing he darted through onto the path and looked up at the swinging Hotel Beaumont sign. The building was alive and he was too close. He backed, and it came from his left before he'd time to think about evading it. A violent impact; a thought struggled in his head, died.

The earth shook beneath him; a dry heat. Through the bars of his eyelashes a column of figures approached, some slipping out of sight to either side, some would be in touching distance soon. He shrank back and down.

"Call off the search," a familiar voice said.

He opened his eyes. Malcolm and Gareth hauled their rucksacks up into the overhead rack. Malcolm looked at his ticket, then at the tiny brass stud on the back of the seat next to Karl's. "You don't mind me taking thirty-eight, do you Gareth?" Malcolm said, plumping himself down. *And I'm in thirty-nine as stipulated on my ticket here in my hand. All seats taken. We're ready to go.* Karl's mouth twitched towards a smile.

"So, Karl, where the heck did you get to?"

A new note to the engine and the crocodile skin of grey

tarmac became grey silk as the coach glided out of the station and turned onto the main street. Connerstone sharply delineated after the fuzzy imposter in which everything had been like a watercolour left out in the sun.

"Speak to me, Karl," Malcolm said, joining thumbs and tips of middle fingers to make a big circle.

"Journeys End," Karl said.

Malcolm looked at him as if trying to work out several conundrums at once. "They certainly do." Gareth and Malcolm looked at each other, then Gareth aimed his camera at Karl. The lens brought to mind the vague pit of a dark tree bole.

"Not now, Gareth," Malcolm said. "Are you all right, Karl?"

Karl thought about that. "Not sure."

"Okay." Staring at the headrest before him, Malcolm formulated a response. "There was a deluge in Guards Wood. Next thing we look around and you'd gone. We spent ages calling out, wandering. Thought you must have headed to the village. When we got here we walked up and down the main street, had a drink in the Yewdale then came here and here you were, out like a light in the corner. So, a happy ending."

Try telling your face that, Karl thought. He watched Malcolm and Gareth as intently as they watched him. No hint of a struggle to contain mirth or gaiety. It's all me, Karl thought, and wasn't he glad about that? Walking at the rear he could have slipped on a wet root, hit his head and knocked himself out. Meanwhile Malcolm and Gareth could have walked on, oblivious. What if some instinct for self-preservation embedded in a state deeper than sleep had subsequently guided him to the village and the coach in time for the return trip to Manchester?

No sinister fracturing of reality. He was here, now, thinking rational thoughts, in the company of his friends and heading home. This was the best outcome after the trio of monstrosities, the priest, the hotel manager; they'd stirred to life in his unconscious, representations of his dread of the future, his only friends gone to distant places, his unsatisfactory job in that wet miserable city. Now he could let his friends go, bring a better attitude to his job, appreciate wet glum Manchester.

The miked stone-dry voice of the driver came over the speakers. "Good evening ladies and gents. Hope you're seated comfortably. We are finally leaving. Home again jiggety-jig."

Karl longed to get there. Gareth clicked his camera at the pattern of the rubberized flooring of the aisle.

Outside the village, the coach followed Connerstone Water to the north where the road began to wind as it rose. The declining sun painted hillsides, flashed through scatters of trees. Areas of woodland cover thickened, darkened as the sun became an indeterminate crimson low in the west. At a high elevation there was no more climbing. Ranks of mountains on all sides under an empurpled sky dusted with pink cloud and salt stars. Subsequent to a series of dips, the hills were taller; suspended between peaks the sky had insidiously become dark as graphite.

The coach increased its speed where caution might have been advisable. Karl thought the driver was keen to get home. *Me too,* he thought.

No chatter. Looking along the gap between headrests and windows Karl saw heads leaning.

"You should get some shut-eye," Malcolm advised Karl. "And get your doctor to check you out first thing in the morning."

Not long after, Malcolm was following his first piece of advice and snoring softly, puzzlement verging on anxiety in his furrowed brow. Most eyes were shut if the jerking heads, visible between the headrests, were any indication as the coach swung and dipped around the interlocking buttresses of mountainside. No moon, no stars, no lights of farms or isolated hamlets. Karl supposed the darkness was stretching the distance to the motorway.

Malcolm's body leaned against him, pressing him into the window. He noted many minute scratches. The glass was of uneven thickness, as if it had approached a liquid state in extreme temperatures and oozed, subsequently hardening again. At the bottom of the frame, where the exterior bodywork bulged out slightly, he noted a matte grey. As his

Apple Pie and Sulphur

heart turned over, he told himself the whole coach wouldn't be that non-colour. He pushed Malcolm back so he was snoozing upright. Gareth's head was tucked down into his narrow chest.

This must be another route bypassing by miles the approaches to Windermere, the next town. The road would level soon, the mountains step back and valleys spread wide. To be endured until then, the shrouded distances, at once vast and claustrophobic. Without stars or moon, an elusive ambient light must be lending these eminences the greater part of their massiveness, comprising as many precipitous walls as slopes.

A pull forward, the bus on a descent. A diffuse redness was intermittently visible below. It couldn't be the sunset at such a low point in the soaring encompassing terrain.

Karl envied the others sleeping. Closing his eyes, the dark spreading through him was like sleep and he didn't resist.

When he awoke, a faint red tincture glinted off some surfaces, glowed on others. Elsewhere, intense gloom monumentalized natural features to produce awesome battlements and redoubts, soaring pillars and spiked bridges. Daylight would make the mountains sane again, and hours prior to that the coach would be entering Manchester.

Malcolm's expression suggested his dream had become tragic and terrifying. Karl wondered if he should wake him. The road had leveled off. Either it was an extraordinary sunset behind and below the miles-wide dark edge ahead, or artificial lights of a size fit to illuminate a gargantuan sunken stadium.

The bus came to a stop. The engine cut out but the window glass continued to vibrate. Karl realized a gigantic voice outside was responsible. Tiny cries flocked around it. It awoke Malcolm, Gareth and the rest of the passengers. Was it the same voice he'd heard scraps of since coming down from the hills to Guards Wood? There had been the country fair at Tilberthwaite and there were, he presumed, others. Late as it was, this fair had yet to conclude. He'd get Malcolm to identify the vast hollow in the mountains on his map when they got home.

The driver spoke over the microphone in a voice that brushed like a yard broom. "When you've made your way off the vehicle, you'll be taken to the place in three groups."

Such stupendous numbers, their cries like the pipings of an asthmatic chest a continent wide. But the voice of the Master of Ceremonies dominated them all. It exclaimed unintelligibly between screeches of uncontrollable laughter. The speakers amplifying the voice Karl pictured as being as tall as buildings, and in untold numbers.

The passengers were getting out of their seats.

"You know I've never actually been to a country fair before. Wonder how long we'll have?" Malcolm's eyes bulged, the desperate calamitous dream continuing in them.

"Should be time to take a picture or two," Gareth said. Not good ones if Gareth couldn't control the wild shake of his hands holding the camera.

The doors weren't open yet. Gareth, Malcolm and Karl standing at the end of the aisle, numbers thirty-seven, thirty-eight and thirty-nine, would be the last to leave. Karl looked past his appalled reflection into the darkness. The mountains were like gigantic workings under a rock-solid sky. From precipices, immense silhouetted birds launched themselves and flapped lazily as if on hot up-draughts and appeared to be biding their time.

Conflicting rhythms; the limping beating bass note in Karl's chest, the running sensation in his head, someone on inner highways coming to convey news that would congeal his blood.

From the canopy of the fungal growth, growing from the thick stalk up against an adjacent cliff, she emerged, a rippling sheaf of molten maroon. Outside the closed door she looked along the windows, her tongue flickering out of her long-lipped smile. Karl heard her hiss, unless that had been the doors opening. "Make haste," the driver ordered in his blow-torch voice.

Intense heat entered, and there was a powerful odour of sulphur—and apples to remind them all of home.

SUMMERSIDE
ALISON MOORE

The Irvings had acquired "Summerside" unseen in an auction, paying a paltry sum for this run-down Victorian property. They found the house unbearable over the winter, but even when the spring came round, it was no better. If anything, it was growing colder. They tried changing the curtains and painting the walls. Mr. Irving favoured something bright, a happy shade of yellow. His wife wanted white or magnolia; the closer to white the better, she said. They settled in the middle, with a pale yellow, "wheat". But when they looked at it on the walls, they wondered if it was bright enough.

They had an extension built, and in due course they locked the door between it and the old house, living only in the extension and just trying to ignore the other part. As winter approached again, though, they vacated the premises altogether, moving in with Mrs. Irving's parents on the far side of the village.

They decided to let the extension. They had, after all, to recoup the money it had cost them to build it.

Mr. Irving, showing Anna Harris around the outside of the property, tried to explain about the old, locked-up part of the house. "No central heating," he said.

"It's standing empty?" said Anna.

No, said Mr. Irving, it wasn't empty. All the furniture was still in there. It had been left just as it was. Anna thought of the war, of air raid sirens that meant people had to go quickly to a shelter without stopping for anything, and fire drills at school when you had to get out without even collecting your bag.

She put her face close to the kitchen window, cupped her hands around her eyes and peered through. Mr. Irving told her about wanting yellow and his wife wanting white and settling for "wheat" and then looking at it on the walls and wondering if it was bright enough, if it was bright enough to make the room happy.

"Happy?" said Anna. "You thought the room was unhappy?"

"You know what I mean. The house as a whole," said Mr. Irving, gesturing towards its dismal façade—Anna thought he had said, "The house is a hole," and she nodded, looking at the tatty window frames, the broken stone step—"is rather impressive, but it has been neglected. Let me show you the new extension."

He took her to another door that let them into the extension, into the living area. Mr. Irving indicated the sofa that folded out into a bed, and the television. He showed her the kitchen, which was really a utility room with a sink, a microwave oven, a portable hob like the one Mitchell took camping, and a kettle. There was no bathroom but there was an outside toilet that was, said Mr. Irving, just fine.

"But isn't there a proper bathroom in the old part of the house?" said Anna. "Isn't there a proper kitchen?"

"There *is*," said Mr. Irving, "but that's all locked up now."

"Can they really not be used? Are you saying it's condemned?"

"It's not condemned," said Mr. Irving, "but you wouldn't want to use them. I'll show you the outside toilet."

Anna moved in. The lack of space was not a problem because she was not bringing very much with her. A coat cupboard doubled as a wardrobe. The windowsills were her bookshelves. Each morning, she folded away her bed, and ate her breakfast at the little coffee table in the living area. She washed in the utility room. It was like being young again, she thought, just starting out in the world with what little you have.

"I'm on my own now," she told herself, taking a deep breath. "I'm making a new start." She had left behind a life that was not good for her—an unhealthy relationship, an unpleasant job, a polluted town. *You'll never leave Mitchell*, her sister had said. But look at her now; she had done it, she had left him.

Or if you do, you'll go back.

It would soon be a new year and Anna was making plans. She would try again to read *Ulysses*. She would visit art galleries; she would take a beginner's course in Art History so that she could understand the paintings she saw.

Had she been buying rather than renting, she might have taken a lodger, for the company. "But you wouldn't want to live with a stranger, would you?" said her sister, on the phone from Spain. Anna would have liked to live with her sister, but her sister had emigrated, starting a new life with a man Anna did not like. He reminded her of their father. "Have you seen Mitchell?" asked her sister. "I bet you go back to him in the end."

Lying awake in the fold-out bed, Anna listened to the radio. At one o'clock in the morning, the lady on the radio said, "Sleep tight," and Anna switched off her lamp and went to sleep.

Standing at the sink the next morning, washing herself with a flannel, Anna thought: *What I want is a bath.* She wanted to slip into hot water, to feel her muscles unknot, to wash away the world. She went to the door that stood between her and the old house. She put her eye to the keyhole and looked through, seeing the pale yellow of a kitchen wall. She could hear something. Still crouching, she listened to the rhythmic knocking sound. With her mouth close to the door, she said, "Hello?" and as she spoke she saw a small boy run past her window. Standing up, drawing aside the net curtain, she looked out at the garden. She thought of it as a garden even though it was slabbed. She saw this boy, who was perhaps six years old, circling the house, hitting the walls of the old part with a stick. She moved towards the door but she couldn't go out because she was still naked, holding a flannel in her hand. She picked up the phone and dialled Mr. Irving's number. She was going to ask him about the boy but when he answered she said to him, "I want a bath."

"I'm afraid," said Mr. Irving, "I can't let you use the bathroom; I can't let you into the old house."

Anna finished washing with her flannel at the sink.

She was in the utility room again at lunchtime when she saw that the boy had come back. She had been spreading oatcakes with low-fat cheese (she was trying not to eat bread, not to eat wheat, because it left her bloated, left her feeling bad inside). The boy was standing on the broken doorstep, hitting the old front door with his stick. Anna went outside and said to the boy, as she approached him, "What are you doing?"

"Waking the ghosts up," he said, turning to look at her. "What are *you* doing?"

Anna wondered what he meant, and then she saw that he was looking at how she was walking; he was watching how she stepped carefully over each crack in the paving slabs.

"Oh," said Anna, smiling. "Don't you know about the monsters that live under the cracks? If you step on the cracks, they come out and get you."

Now they were both standing outside the old part of the house, next to the door, which Anna reached out and touched. She put her hand on the handle and turned it, although she could not have said why; she knew that the door was locked and had been locked for months. The door did not open. Anna bent down, opened up the letterbox and looked through. She had a sense of old air getting out, touching her face like warm breath; there was a smell like vegetable soup.

When she stood up again, the boy had run off.

Summerside

Every wash with her flannel at the sink in the utility room increased Anna's craving for a bath. When she stood at the locked internal door, it was as if she could feel the bathroom's humidity pressing against the wood, as if she could smell bath salts leaking through the keyhole and the cracks. She kept thinking about how it would feel to climb into a full, hot tub. She did not have the key to the door, though, and in the end she had to force it, causing some damage to the frame.

Carrying a towel, shampoo and soap, she stepped through into the old kitchen. She looked around, seeing a fine stove, a family-sized table. *Summerside*, she thought; a lovely name for a family home. She stood and listened to the quiet house. (*Summercide*, she thought, like matricide and patricide and suicide.) She moved further into the room. She saw the wheat-coloured walls and felt nauseous, bad inside. That pale shade of yellow was not enough. The stale air filled her nostrils, her mouth, her throat and lungs.

She walked towards the stairs.

If anyone knocked on the door of the extension in the weeks that followed, they went away again without an answer, until rent day came around again and Mr. Irving arrived looking for Anna. Letting himself into the living area, he found the internal door broken open. Not wanting to step into the old house on his own, he fetched his brothers.

He is going to let the extension again—he can't afford not to—but he will impress upon his new tenant that the old house is out of bounds. He has not mentioned his previous tenant's breaking and entering, her being found dead in the bath. He has mended the door frame.

As he hands Katie McKinsey the key, receiving in return a cheque—her deposit and a month's rent in advance—he notices that the boy, that damned boy, is hanging around again. He was a nuisance when Mr. Irving and his wife lived here. They had to keep chasing him off the property.

Mr. Irving would shoo him away but Katie McKinsey seems delighted by him. Mr. Irving knows that she is alone and has no children.

Katie keeps asking about using the kitchen. "I like to cook," she says, standing outside the old house now, turning towards the kitchen window. "I like to bake cakes."

"You can make cakes in the microwave in the utility room," says Mr. Irving.

Katie is at the window, peering into the kitchen with her hands cupped around her eyes. "I bet you like cakes," she says, turning to look at the boy, who is stamping about on the paving slabs. "What are you doing?" asks Katie. The boy looks at her but does not stop. What he is doing is stamping on the cracks. "You don't want to wake up the bears!" says Katie.

"There aren't any bears," says the boy. "And I don't think it's monsters either, but there's something down there."

"Is that right?" says Katie, standing outside her new home with the key in her hand, and she laughs, but no one else does, and after a while she stops.

THE SPACE BETWEEN
RALPH ROBERT MOORE AND RAY CLULEY

"What's that?"

They were in the kitchen of a multi-family home, two or three apartments on each floor. Trying to decide if this was where they wanted to move.

Don turned around.

The apartment was right under the building's roof. There was a short wall under the slanted roofline on that side of the kitchen, following the pitch of the ceiling. Set in the wall was a door only two feet tall.

He raised an eyebrow. "That's where we'll have to move next."

Carolyn clicked over in her high heels to study the door more closely. "It is sort of charming. Kind of like a dwarf door. Or it's creepy. But seriously, why would anyone do that?"

"I saw them before, when I was in college." And at the beginning of his career, when this was the only type of place he could afford. "The space closest to the roofline isn't usable as living space, since the ceiling is so low. So they box it in for storage space." He reached down in his dark business suit, pulled the door open.

Through the floors he could hear the other, unseen tenants sharing this same house. So unlike being in their home, where the only sounds not coming from one of them came from the ice-maker, or the air conditioning. Rising up from below his black shoes came muffled voices that sounded like a girl arguing with her boyfriend. The only phrase he could make out was, Great tits!

Carolyn's quizzical face. "You're not eavesdropping, are you?"

His embarrassment. "No." He clicked the door closed.

The apartment was small. Kitchen in front, bedroom in back. That was about it. Carolyn poked her head inside the bathroom off the kitchen. Toilet, sink with long rust stains under the taps, old-fashioned tub with a plastic shower curtain celebrating goldfish.

"What are you thinking?"

She hugged herself. "I'm thinking the clothes we're wearing are too good for this place." Gave him a wounded look, apologizing.

They took the apartment.

They had to sell nearly all their furniture. Didn't get anywhere near as much as they expected. While he was in the front foyer boxing up what little they could fit into their new home, he realized he hadn't seen her in about an hour. Walked up their central staircase, found her sitting on the master bedroom carpet, under a window. "You okay?"

Red face looking up from the carpet. Wordless shrug. Brave smile. "Yeah. I'm fine." Got herself up. Gestured helplessly at the window, the wide green lawn below, the blue pond in the distance, its weeping willows. "I know, really silly. But oh my God, I used to love that view. I'd look out that window every morning while I had my coffee."

Once they had everything moved into their new place, carrying it up the three flights of stairs themselves to save money in moving expenses, Don sat on a cardboard box marked Kitchen Utensils and said, "Before we unpack anything, let's assemble the bed. Because we don't know how long we're going to last tonight. We can always do the rest over the next couple of days." Still perched, he reached over, clicked the dwarf door under the ceiling open. Heard nothing. Shut it.

Carolyn, in a better mood now, accepting what had happened (she was like that), raised a slim forefinger. "Even better idea. Why don't you put the bed together, because we

The Space Between

both know I'd just be standing around watching, and while you do that I'll go out and buy us some food for our first night in our new home."

They ate at the kitchen table, by candlelight. Ribeye steaks, fettuccine tossed with olive oil and garlic, tossed salad greens with slices of Gorgonzola.

Don's strong jaw moved as he ate a hot, red chunk of the steak. Eyebrows going up. "These are from Angelo's, aren't they?"

Face rising bravely, fork still in her salad. "I figured, What the fuck? We'll get back to where we were. We're just between places right now."

They didn't have a cable connection, so when they got into bed they listened to the radio.

Carolyn slid her bare legs out of her side of the sheets at one point. "Be right back."

He listened to another oldies song by himself.

Heard her clear her throat behind him.

She was standing in the bedroom doorway, in her nightgown. In this dim light she looked younger. He wondered if he did, lying in their bed. "I figured we should christen our new home," she said.

He sat up on his pillow as she sauntered into the bedroom, hands behind her back. Bemused look on his face. "I'm not sure what I should say."

Both hands coming out from behind her back. A small black bowl in each.

"Oh."

"Remember when we moved into our first apartment? What you surprised me with that first night?"

Don looked down into the bowl she handed him, saw the scoop of red and green swirls. "Peppermint ice cream?"

Don volunteered to take a few days off from his job-hunting to get the apartment in order while Carolyn went back to work. He figured he'd unpack all the boxes, set their contents out on the kitchen floor, then decide where to put everything.

The General in charge of an army in retreat.

Looked around the shabby kitchen. Is this what the rest of his life was going to look like?

About halfway through sorting all the worldly possessions they still had, he realized there just wouldn't be enough space for everything in these two rooms. He glanced at the walls. Put up shelves? He saw the door leading under the eaves. It was ajar.

Don went to the door with the intention of closing it. But as he neared he heard faint voices. Or one voice. He opened the door wide. Squatted beside it.

Yes. One voice. Faint. "Can you get up? Can you hear me? Sweetheart?"

He barely thought about what he did next, crawling into the storage space. A little shuffle forwards on hands and knees, head and upper body only a short way in. Tilted his head down as if to drink from the dust. Listening. He heard the sound of footsteps receding and he shuffled after them, the crawlspace earning its name. He was glad to be wearing jeans and his old college sweater; dust swirled around him. Cobwebs broke against his face. He pulled them from his skin with a grimace and the pause had him inhaling dust enough to cough. When he'd finished he could hear nothing else from below. Cocked his head one way then the other, straining to hear.

"What the hell am I doing?"

Wiped his face again and began a slow retreat, emerging from the hatch into the kitchen feet first. Legs. Backside. Kneeling, he wiped his palms on his thighs—"Quite enough of that"—wondered if talking to himself was what he had to look forward to now. He nudged the door closed again— snick—and turned back to the kitchenware spread around him. At least they had plenty of storage space for whatever they couldn't fit into the drawers and cupboards—the passage he'd just explored seemed to follow the wall all the way around, beyond the kitchen, and behind the other rooms. Other apartments. He wondered if they were all the same size. Wondered if his neighbours were on their way up in the world or sliding their way down. Whether they were on the ladder or the slippery slope, watching everything they lost as it whizzed past. He told himself it was only temporary, as no doubt everybody else did. But he couldn't even lie properly any more. Not to himself, anyway.

Don grabbed handfuls of cutlery and dumped them into the appropriate compartments, feeling condemned with each metallic rattle. A man fastening his own chains.

"I met one of our neighbours," Carolyn said, arriving home. She kicked off her high heels in the hall with twin sighs.

"Me too."

She went to Don with a quick kiss, passing him to drop her bag on the kitchen table. "Hey, great job."

Don was pleased by her effort to admire his effort but the truth was clear enough on her face. Their kitchen was that of a Wendy house. Pans that once hung above a central work surface were now stacked one inside the other beside the oven. Where before they'd had their espresso machine with bean grinder, their pasta press, their cake stands, now they had a kettle with containers marked Tea, Coffee, Sugar. Tea in bags. Instant coffee. Little changes that made more of a difference than they should. He had stored a half bag of beans in the freezer even knowing they'd never grind them.

Carolyn took it all in with a tight smile that he somehow loved and hated at the same time. It only faltered when she saw how carefully he was watching her. "It's all right," she said.

Don couldn't agree but didn't want to contradict her either. "Tell me about our neighbour," he said.

"Well." She went to the fridge. There was still half a bottle of white. She poured herself a small glass, raised the bottle to Don. When he shook his head she topped up her glass with a little more. "Nice lady. About my age. From somewhere east, judging by her accent. Welcomed us to the building and asked *a lot* of questions." She sipped her wine.

"What did you tell her?"

Carolyn wrinkled her nose at the wine glass but took another sip anyway. "You're Dimitri," she said, "A Greek sea captain who wants to set off in his ship for parts unknown. I'm Dolly and I design 'artificial companions'—" she made speech marks in the air as best as she could with a glass of wine in one hand "—for lonely men and women. Mostly men. I'm in the middle of constructing a replica Dimitri because I suspect once you do take off on your voyage, you'll never come back. You'll get lost." A moment of sadness in her eyes.

"But our marriage is a sham." He smiled, showed he wasn't hurt.

"We grew to love each other." She smiled back. Sipped her wine.

Don retrieved the bottle and took a glass from one of the crammed cupboards. "What did you tell her really?"

"The truth."

He looked at her.

Carolyn shrugged. "Not all of it."

He tilted up the wine bottle's bottom, carefully filling their glasses. A look of shame on his face. "Did you tell her I lost my job?"

Carolyn quickly reached for his hand. "It's okay, it really is."

"I'm going to find an even better one."

Squeezing his fingers. "You don't think I know that?"

"Beginning tomorrow. I'll go online, start sending out résumés."

She gave him that special smile of hers. "One door closes, and another door opens."

It was easy to get lost behind the walls.

Each level had square openings in the crawlspace's floor at one or two spots along their narrow lengths, presumably for maintenance, which he could use to squeeze up or down to the house's next level. A bit like climbing up and down trees when he was a boy.

The narrow passages themselves were dimly lit by tiny holes sparkling along the inside wall. Abandoned nail holes

The Space Between

from hung pictures and paintings that had since been moved. At first it was enough to just peer through these holes into the rooms he found. But over the long days of his explorations, it bothered him more and more that he was always on the outside. He wanted to know what it would be like to walk within those rooms.

An apartment on the bottom floor was almost always vacant during the day, both owners presumably at work, or looking for it. One morning, sitting in front of his computer with a cup of coffee, working down the list of companies he'd send his résumé to that day, he decided he'd go to the next step with that apartment. Standing half-up out of his chair to kiss Carolyn goodbye. Listening for the sound of their front door opening. Closing. As if, as soon as he was sure she'd be gone for the day, he was going to masturbate.

He waited a long half-hour, to be certain. Digits turning at a slow, slow, slow rate as he counted down.

At the half-hour, Don rose from his chair. Urinated, so he could stay inside the walls as long as possible.

Crawling the lengths of the spaces, going down through the square openings, he became a little disoriented, as he often did, but eventually he arrived at what he thought was the correct peep hole. Brought his right eye up to its ragged circle. Looked through.

This was it! The refrigerator with the snapshots pressed to its front by different cartoon magnets.

Hunched over, he made his way to the small dwarf door of the apartment.

What if the door was locked?

Anxiety.

But his and Carolyn's door didn't have a lock. Why would you have a lock for a crawlspace door? Reached his hand out, turned the latch.

The latch tilted.

The door swung open.

Beyond, another couple's kitchen.

Stooped over, like some invading troll, he emerged from their crawl space. Stood up.

The oddest feeling, doing something he knew was wrong. It reminded him of one evening when he was quite

| 206

young, walking home from a friend's birthday party. He cut across some backyards, happened to glance up at a silent house, to make sure he hadn't been spotted, saw a lit second story window and, in its black frame, a woman removing her clothes. She wasn't young, and she wasn't slim, but he stayed rooted to that spot on the back lawn, staring. Fascinated. In the years to come he would see a number of women's naked bodies, all of them more beautiful than this body, but the one he always recalled the most was hers. It was like looking into the future, to where women without clothes would be in his life. It was like solving—or at least, starting to solve—one of the world's great mysteries.

He advanced across the kitchen's vinyl floor, intensely aware the front door might open at any moment. He was a burglar. Stealing into someone else's life. The thought thrilled him. And made him realize how dull his adult life had become.

The refrigerator with the cartoon magnets. He looked at the photographs on its white door. For the first time he could actually see what they showed. About a dozen pictures in all. A young man and woman. Early twenties. Together. Big smiles, happy eyes. Her showing some leg. Him, shirt off, flexing. One of those photo booth strips of four square pictures taken seconds apart, their distorted faces too close to the lens. He felt a pang of jealousy. They reminded him of himself and Carolyn, when they were first starting out. Deliriously happy. Dirt poor.

On an impulse, he opened the refrigerator door, the interior light automatically coming on. A package of twin steaks, probably being saved for Friday night, one of the cheaper cuts. Some beers. A tall bottle of inexpensive white wine. Three different kinds of lettuce. Fresh grapes. He realized he was crying.

Reached inside. Plucked from the cluster a single cold, green grape. Put it between his lips. Bit down, feeling within his mouth the mild burst, the sudden release of juice, sweetness. It had been a long, long time since he had eaten a grape. Maybe it just felt that way.

Don slammed the fridge shut when he realized he'd helped himself to several more of them. Opened it again,

The Space Between

broke away the telltale stems that pointed at what was missing. Pocketed them.

One of the photos had been knocked askew on the fridge door. He straightened it, kept his fingers on its edges a moment wondering why he was so struck by the image of husband and wife cutting wedding cake.

In other rooms, more evidence of their happiness. A full vase of flowers, tall and fresh and colourful. One of the caricature portraits tourists buy, her all smiles and cheekbones, him squeezing her fit-to-pop with arms more muscular than any workout could produce. Don looked at the books they'd read, crammed on shelves, books they were reading, left on bedside tables. He went to the bathroom, checked the medicine cabinet. Sprayed her perfume because he loved the clean floral smell of her brand and knew he couldn't afford it for Carolyn anymore.

Don walked a floor plan that was the same as his, only reversed. Opened cupboards. Looked in drawers. The delicious thrill of trespass faded, replaced by a sense of familiarity that went beyond the layout; he'd had this, once. Not the rooms, the walls, the floors—those he had *now*— but everything contained within the space between had once been his and Carolyn's.

He peed in their toilet, flushed, washed his hands... and realized how long he'd lingered. A whole bladderful of time had passed. He said to his reflection, "What are you doing?" and had no answer.

He went to the dwarf door and climbed back home. Shrinking, diminishing, crawling away.

Carolyn came in smelling the air. "Mmm." Saw the wine on the table, said it again; "*Mmm.*"

Don handed her a glass then checked under the broiler releasing more of the delicious aroma that had already filled the apartment.

"Steaks?" Carolyn peeked at the meat, sizzling and spitting its juices.

"I was inspired."

Carolyn beamed a smile at him, bounced a little on the spot. "You got a job!" Saw his smile slip. "Oh, I just thought—"

"I sent out more résumés. Made more enquiries. Couple of places look okay."

"That's good." She sat at the table, picked at the small bunch of grapes Don had set beside the wine bottle. Her eyes were on something far away.

Don prepared a light salad—three different lettuces—and saw that already the leaves were browning, beginning to wilt.

After dinner, after Carolyn's shower ("I miss our bathtub"), they decided to make love.

"What's the matter?" Carolyn asked him eventually.

"Everything," he wanted to say. "Nothing. I don't know."

"Is it me?"

It wasn't. It really wasn't. Carolyn was beautiful. Don still thought so, was still as aroused by her body as he was comforted by its familiarity. He gathered her into his arms so he didn't have to say any of this, and she believed him.

"It's okay," she said. "Really. It's just stress."

He stroked her hair, neither agreeing nor disagreeing, and wondered what everybody else was doing in their own homes.

"You'll find a place again."

Her words followed him into dreams of corridors that turned on him and doors that only closed.

By lunch he'd sent his résumé and portfolio to a dozen other places. Altered copy-and-paste cover letters, "…be grateful if you would consider me for…appreciate the opportunity to work at…happy to negotiate…" Positions he'd held two promotions ago, at companies undergraduates applied to as backups.

The Space Between

"What am I *doing*?" he asked the screen after the final "send". He didn't know. He never knew anymore. What else *could* he do? He had no answer for that either.

The monitor was suddenly filled with the twists and turns of the never-ending pipes of his screensaver.

Don went to the kitchen. He didn't bother with lunch, ignored the "eat me drink me" temptation of the refrigerator, and went straight to the tiny door in the wall.

Climbing around inside the walls reminded him of when he used to commute to work. All by himself, steering, crawling. Then there he'd be, with people again. A part.

A floor somewhere below them housed an elderly couple who seemed to never go out. Peepholes in all their rooms, although out of respect for their privacy he never leaned his eye against the one for their bathroom.

All day long they'd sit in the living room, watching TV. He always knew when his shuffling hands and knees were approaching their apartment by the booming noise of weather reports and commercials, soap operas and old comedies in the dimly-lit wall space. He'd sit behind these walls for hours, watching TV with them. Despite the volume, it was peaceful. Reassuring. They had succeeded. Whatever challenges they had gone through in life, they had survived. Over the long decades; first friends, then lovers, then friends again. Who now needed no conversation, just each other's presence. In the stillness of their rooms she would rise to fix them lunch, a sandwich they would share, one triangular half for each; he would trudge over to get a blanket for her knees as she sat, tilt into his palm her day's regimen of pills. Going to the pantry to get the other an extra paper napkin for a particularly messy meal substituted for hours of late night drunken conversations; a veined hand on a shoulder took the place of a sunny afternoon's rolling around on a bed sheet. They had reached the clearing. They had found the peaceful pond at the end of life.

Would he and Carolyn ever reach that green pond? Ever hold old hands, watching the dragonflies buzz their four wings above the tossed stone's ripples?

He crawled back to his own apartment. Stood outside the dwarf door. Shut it with his foot. Dusted his shoulders, the knees of his pants.

An email was waiting for him.

He used his palms to wipe sweaty hair from his forehead, then reached down to the mouse and double-clicked.

Scanned the reply, ready for disappointment.

Sat up.

Have a need for someone with your background. Impressed by your résumé. A mutually convenient time for you to come in for an interview, to meet with the key members of our team. We want to move quickly on this. A fast-growing company that could use someone with your expertise. We are willing to meet your salary requirements, and offer a generous benefits package.

He sat in front of his computer, stunned.

After all this time.

A projection into the near future. Acting nonchalant when Carolyn came home, then holding out the printed email. Watching her read it, then her blue eyes looking up over the top edge of the white page, at him. With admiration.

Flexed his fingers. Cracked his knuckles.

Fingertips on the keyboard.

Paused.

Typed.

Thank you for your quick response. I do believe I'd be a perfect fit with your company. And in fact I managed the installation of the Fizzsys software you've just purchased, and know how to implement it across systems.

However, something's come up in my personal life. I won't be available for an interview for at least a month. I need to stay here, in my home, to explore my current project, until then. I hope you understand.

Reply to his email, twenty minutes later. Ping. Opened it, heart loud in the walls of his chest.

They didn't understand. The Chief of Operations was polite. Every word was meant to be soothing. They were going to explore other options.

He went back into the walls. Where else did he have to go?

He was so happy in these narrow corridors! A wall away from the world and all of its demands. A space where he could just watch, passively, as life went on. Trying to forget that he had just lost a job opportunity, that money was getting tight. The big blue numbers in their checkbook getting smaller and smaller.

Climbing up and down the storeys, crawling right and left along the passages, he wound up at a peephole he didn't recognize. Stood up in a stoop, bringing his eye to the hole.

Hard white wall tiles, like all the bathrooms he had seen. The mirrored door to the small medicine cabinet ajar. He realized with a start he was looking at a reflection of the wall he was behind.

A noise stopped. He hadn't been conscious of the noise until it stopped. Thought it was just something wrong with his ears, which happened sometimes, crawling around in all this dust. A rushing sound.

A new sound, from the right side of the bathroom, beyond his peephole. A shower curtain sliding on its rings.

Blinked.

A naked body passed across the mirror's reflection.

A woman's body.

Did not blink.

A woman's body, from the undersides of her breasts to the curls of her dark pubic hair.

The soft hourglass abdomen of a woman.

Not the stylized nudity of a model in a magazine, but the real beauty of a woman's body in natural rest, the way a trusted lover would see it. All the more erotic because she didn't know she was seen. No attempt to suck in her stomach, flat though it was. She had a tiny tattoo on one hip. A blue butterfly.

Through the humid air of the peephole he could smell, only an arm's length away, the cleanness of her skin, fresh from the shower. That soapy perfume mixed with the lemon scent of wet hair.

Her reflection turned, reached down. The breathtaking narrowness of her back sliding across the mirror, her abdomen reappearing, hand holding a white towel.

Don's right hand lifted from the side of the peephole. On their own, all five fingers lowered. He was outvoted. Six to one. Below the buttons on his shirt. Below his belt. He remembered the woman he'd seen in the window all those years ago, that glimpse of a future merging with this one as if there'd never been time between them.

He stood away from the hole.

Can't. Not here. Not where she'd hear, maybe call an exterminator.

Crawled quietly away, swollen, aching. Down, up, right, left, getting frustrated. Where was his release? Carolyn would be home soon. Where was his door?

And finally. Following the trail of his knees in the dust. The dwarf door.

Pushed it open, crawled out. Stood and toed the door closed, breathing heavily.

Reached down. Slapped at the dirt on his pants.

"Don?"

He jerked around.

Carolyn, by the refrigerator, staring at him.

"I thought I heard something. Behind the walls. I was investigating."

He showed her his dusty palms, a gesture to keep her gaze up, away from the tallness in his pants.

"Filthy," she agreed.

"Why are you home so early?" Don set the kettle on the stove.

"Early?" She checked her watch, a beautiful bracelet model he'd bought her for the first birthday she'd had with him. How long before they'd have to sell it? Say goodbye to their happy past, one piece at a time. "Don, it's almost seven. Same time I always come home."

Yes, because she worked late now, didn't she. Had to. Just so they could afford even this place.

"Really? It's that late? Sorry, I've been caught up with things." He went to the fridge, started removing items for their dinner.

"Don? Don. Stop that a minute, will you? Don!"

The kettle was whistling. Neither of them went to it, the shrill boiling point prolonged in being ignored.

"It's good you've been busy," Carolyn said. "Did you—"

"I've got to make dinner."

Don went to the fridge again but he didn't open it. Only

The Space Between

looked at the blank face of it, his back to his wife.

He heard her sigh. The kettle went quiet.

"Fine," she said. "I'm going to take a shower."

Don thought of the woman somewhere below him, towelling herself dry, and said, "Fine."

Don watched her silhouette through the shower curtain, admired the way it turned, showed him this curve and that. Her hands went to her hair. Her hands played over her own body.

He undressed, wondering at what he was doing even as he did it and deciding that he liked it. This was good. Steam was filling the room and from within it came the gentle sigh of a woman enjoying her shower. Don dropped his clothes at the sound of another and went to the curtain, pulled it aside, and startled the woman he found there.

"Don!"

"I've got your back," he said.

She seemed embarrassed as she hooked the shower nozzle back up.

"I mean, I'll wash it for you," he said, stepping into the tub.

"Don..."

He lathered his hands with soap—"don't we have something lemon?"—and ran the suds down her body. He kissed her. "You remember that time by the pier?" he said, slipping wet hands over her breasts, under them, kissing her neck. "Remember?" he said. Quietly.

She closed her eyes. He turned her around so her back was pressed to his chest and she leaned against him. He reminded her of their walk, their time in the arcade, all the while soaping her and kissing her, and sometimes she would reach behind for him. The shower was hot and good.

"Remember you talked about getting a tattoo?"

Carolyn chuckled softly and turned to him, still pressed close to his body. "I remember. Something lame, like your name in a heart or 'I love Don' or something."

"You should. Get one, I mean."

She smiled at him. Said, "Silly."

He caressed her hip with his thumb.

"A butterfly," he said. He tried to kneel, to kiss where he imagined it, but this tub was cramped and he slipped. Grabbed the goldfish curtain to stay balanced.

"I'm too old now," she said, taking him in her hands.

The water was losing its heat. Not yet cold, but no longer running as hot as it had been.

"Too old?"

Carolyn tried to raise him back up. He shook her off, did it himself. "All right," she said, "maybe when we can afford it then."

The water beat down on them with its chill.

"Don? What's wrong?"

He said nothing. Stared at her hip.

"Are you crying, Don?"

"Soap," he said. "I've got soap in my eyes." He tried to step out of the tub but the fucking curtain clung to his skin. He tore at the fish, slipped again getting out from under the spray.

"Don?"

"I need a towel."

"What about my back?"

But he was already gone, wiping his face dry. Wet footprints marked his dripping exit.

They ate dinner in silence.

The crawlspace was always warm. There was something reassuring about the closeness of the walls. A swaddling of wood frame and plasterboard, hard edges softened by dust. He traversed them easily now, turned his body sideways, crawled, pulled himself up using crossbeam supports or lowered himself through narrow spaces that embraced him all the way down. One couple down here had a young baby

The Space Between

and it was worth the effort sometimes to share bedtimes. Don listened as the father he never was read stories to a child he and Carolyn talked about having. Once upon a time.

He sidestepped his way through passages that pressed him front and back like armour plating. He hooked his way down, across, up, with elbow and foot, puffed the air from his mouth to clear the dust as he breathed. Walls were shields as he watched those who worked from home. In one of the ground floor apartments, a man negotiated a business deal on his phone. Don muttered encouragement and advice through the walls and when the deal was done he felt like he'd closed it himself.

Some apartments were difficult to get to, but not impossible. Nothing was beyond his reach within the walls. He was learning where to duck his head, which wooden boards carried risks of splinters, and he knew now how to avoid them to see where couples enjoyed dinners and discussions and television. He watched a film with the young couple on the second floor, though he'd seen it with Carolyn some years ago. He'd never liked the way it ended— no happily ever after here—but tonight the couple offered their own epilogue as the credits rolled. As he watched he wondered if he and Carolyn had done that too, but couldn't remember.

He moved against wall and floor with the intimacy of familiarity. Penetrated deeper into the building and the lives of others it contained. He held pipes that were warm in his hands and snaked his grip along cables that guided him around and between. In the apartment directly below his own he watched a couple make love.

"Did you hear that?"

The woman, sitting on top of the man, thighs straddling his hips, was no longer moving. Listened, head half turned so that Don could almost see her profile.

Don stayed silent. Didn't even breathe.

The woman began to move again. Rose, lowered, in his lap.

She leaned back, the man's arm around her waist.

"You have such great tits," the man said. Tried to cover them with his hands.

Don agreed. He's seen them before.

He made his own noise as she did. Hers was a response to the man's compliment, crude as it was. Don knew the sound because he remembered it. Knew what it built to.

His own sound was loud but lacking the same joy. His was anguish.

"There!" Carolyn said, not with encouragement but with, "I heard it again." Pulled the top sheet up under her chin.

Don was falling. Or so it felt. So that's why she was coming home later each night.

Up, left, right, down, sideways through the spaces, hurtling along inside the walls, banging his shoulders, scraping his knees, rushing to get back to their own dwarf door, to learn the truth. To run from it.

Bursting out, stumbling forward across the vinyl floor. Striding to the bedroom, passing through the doorway.

Carolyn in bed, reading. Looking up, startled, at his dramatic entrance.

He raised a finger—wait—while he got his breath. Bent forward, hand to his chest.

Her quiet voice. "Are you okay?"

"I'm fine! Fine. When did you get home?"

She put a postcard to the page she had been reading. Shut her book. "About an hour ago." A wife's pause. "I was surprised you weren't home. "

"I was looking...."

"For a job? At seven o'clock?"

He brushed the dirt from his pants. Caught himself.

"Why are your clothes so dusty, Don?"

"I fell."

"You fell?"

"I scraped my elbows. See?" Held them out to her as proof.

"Were you at an interview?"

"I was walking around, to see if any office windows were lit. And if they were, I was going to ring the front bell and talk to the owner. I thought maybe a face to face, after hours, a

The Space Between

more casual setting, might be a way to bypass all the usual crap. Because just sending résumés out on the Internet, like I've been doing, obviously hasn't been that effective. It's time to think outside the box." He was rambling. Some of it felt true.

Carolyn concerned. "Are you feeling okay?" Put her book on her nightstand. A good sign. "I know this has been a strain…"

"I feel great."

"You look pale. Maybe take a day off, get out, watch the world go by. You know?"

"I'm sorry I wasn't here when you got home. About an hour ago?"

"Pretty much."

Naked, sliding open a drawer in the bureau for his pajamas. "Maybe I *should* get out more. I could ask one of the guys out for lunch, there's one who lives alone in the building."

She sat up in bed. "Maybe he works from home." Sat up even taller. "A lot of people work from home now. Maybe he could give you some tips!"

Tried to keep the bitterness out of his voice. "Oh, I'm sure he could." Buttoned his pajama top.

"Sweetheart, you sure you're okay?"

"I'm fine."

He turned his back on her and tried to sleep.

He was in someone else's apartment, but no longer sure whose apartment it was, or what floor he was on. Didn't really matter, at this point. His wife was preparing to jump ship.

Don sat in the living room like it was his own, watching a daytime quiz show. Got up at one point to see if there were any snacks in the fridge. A bag of pepperoni slices in one of the trays. He took about a third of the dark red circles, sat back down in his chair, nibbling on them. Got up again during a commercial to pee. Zipped back up, wondered, Should he flush? Let the renters figure out what had happened. The people in these other apartments were so stupid. They had no idea there was a king among them, living in the walls, observing everything they did.

He caught a glimpse of his reflection in the medicine cabinet mirror.

Hollow eyes, haggard cheeks. Unshaven jaw. Was that really him?

Walked back to the kitchen. Troubled. Started thinking about what he had been doing. Remembered that first night. The steaks, the peppermint ice cream. The love.

Looked around the kitchen he had no business being in. "I'm lost," he said.

When did it happen? The first time he crawled behind the dwarf door? The fifteenth? The fiftieth?

I just want to find my way back home. Start over.

Three feet away, a key in the front door.

The door knob turning.

He rushed into the crawl space, banging the upwards curve of his spine. Swung the dwarf door shut as the front door of the apartment opened. Scuttled down the length of the space between the walls, frantic. Which way? Which way? Thick, noxious spray surrounded him. Reaching up, he climbed to the next floor. Heard, behind him, a man's voice. "This is the only sure-fire way of getting rid of pests."

The floor he climbed to was also swirling with spray. Even more potent, in such a confined space. His throat tightened. He tapped his Adam's apple, trying to breathe. Arms numb, face desperate, he shuffled on his hands and knees across the dusty floor. Spray billowed down from above.

Coughing. Clamping both hands over his mouth, eyes blinking, so he wouldn't be heard.

He had his favourites. That newlywed couple on one of the lower floors, who didn't have a lot of money. They were both really funny. The hip, sarcastic humor he remembered from his and Carolyn's early days together. He'd stand sometimes

The Space Between

at the foot of their bed while they made love, admiring her leggy sensuality, his athletic ability to keep thrusting deep for a long, long time. Whenever they quarreled, Don would be upset. It really isn't important who should have loaded the dishwasher. But he had a lot of confidence in them.

And of course the elderly couple, tending to each other in their sunset. Such tenderness! He spent many quiet hours sitting at their kitchen counter, watching them enjoy a simple lunch at the table. Did each have their own flaws? Of course. But it seemed, in their old age, those flaws had been accepted by the other. It was no longer about being right. It was about being together.

Don, in their bedroom, fastening his black bowtie, spotted a tiny peephole in their wallpaper. Brought his blue eye up against it, adjusting his focus. Saw a cramped world of slanted boards, shadows, dust. One of the shadows retreating to the side, but that must have been a trick of the light.

Carolyn appeared, little black dress, the string of pearls Don had bought her to celebrate his promotion. And that was the greatest part. Not the incredible way she looked after all these years, but the pride on his wife's face. He had done well. A husband to be proud of.

Behind the walls, he followed them from the bedroom to the kitchen.

Carolyn emerged. But her husband never joined her. All the boxes they had packed up for their move to the new house were missing.

Where was her little black dress? Her string of pearls?

A plain top, cheap slacks.

The microwave beeped. She opened the small door, retrieved a Salisbury steak TV dinner. Set its rising steam down at the sole place setting at their kitchen table.

Her face was lined. Those beautiful blue eyes, once alive with angels, were sad.

He had to get back to her. Let her know everything was going to be okay. Was already okay.

He crawled through the dust to the end of the passageway. To the dwarf door. Pushed against it.

I'm coming!

But the dwarf door wouldn't swing open. The dwarf door was immovable. Carolyn? Carolyn?

He heard nothing back.

He pushed against the door again, this time asking, Don? Though he no longer knew who that was. Did he even live there anymore?

But the dwarf door was unforgiving.

VRANGR
C. M. MULLER

Before the inheritance, Arthur Speth had neither heard of Vrangr, North Dakota, nor of the great-aunt who authored the will. This mysterious relative had, for some inexplicable reason, bequeathed him both her house and a generous parcel of land on the outskirts of said town. Included in the will was a handwritten note detailing how one might locate Vrangr; this would prove beneficial, for upon consulting the internet, Speth found no mention of the place. Even his musty old atlas proved discouraging. If the town did exist, cartographers had thought best not to include it. There was no description of the house, but the fact that it resided on nearly eight hundred acres of land led Speth to envision a sizable and well-furnished abode. Details concerning Aunt Torgren were also absent; indeed, the wraithlike executor who delivered the news claimed to know nothing about her. Upon relaying the essential information, the rain-soaked figure had slithered back to whatever shadowy realm he called home, leaving Speth to wonder if the meeting had even taken place. But here was the will, written as it was in nearly illegible script but legitimate-looking all the same.

Since childhood Speth had been fascinated with history, particularly as it related to his own family, and had long assumed he had a good handle on its major and minor figures; which, of course, made this supposed great-aunt such an enigma. Had she purposefully been excised from the family record? And what of Vrangr itself, what significance did it hold? For all Speth knew, it was the place where his ancestors had first settled after crossing the Atlantic, the place of origin as it were. But why, then, had it never been mentioned in all these years? Desperate for answers, Speth consulted the family albums he had inherited upon his mother's passing and began to systematically remove photos containing individuals he could not properly identify. Most of the images were thoroughly documented on back (in a variety of generational scripts, including his mother's), but none matched the name he sought.

Speth had not looked at the albums in years, but doing so made him remember just how obsessed he had once been with the past. As a teen he had longed for a kind of alchemical absorption into these old black and white photos. Even now, nearing middle age, he still distrusted modernity—but he had come to terms with it, securing employment at the local library, where the past commingled rather nicely with the present. His apartment was littered with books of a mostly historical nature, and he did little else outside of work but read and watch old movies. He would be the first to admit that his life had become directionless since his mother's death the previous year.

The mystery and lure of Vrangr lingered for the remainder of the day, but in the end Speth continued to have reservations about the will's authenticity. This, coupled with the idea of driving such a great distance (nine hours, by his calculation), made the entire proposition seem little more than a fool's errand. Then again, maybe things would become clearer in the days to come.

Before turning in for the night, Speth channel surfed until he arrived upon a delightful period piece that in the end overwhelmed him with joy.

He slept soundly that night, experiencing a dream wherein he glimpsed himself, or at least a past version of himself. While the countenance of this past-Speth was uncannily similar, his manner of dress bespoke a much earlier century. The man even sported infinity-shaped spectacles, on which the modern-day Speth also prided himself. This individual sat in a rocking chair on the porch of a lavish farmhouse; reposing at his side was a stately woman encumbered in a frilly white dress. She read from a palm-sized leather book as her pipe-smoking companion gazed in Speth's direction. While the man indicated no sign of recognition, it was nevertheless an eerie feeling to be stared at like that. In the front yard, a passel of children chased one another across the huge expanse. Speth longed to inch closer, in the hope of touring the interior of the house (or chatting with its owners), but he was locked to this one distant perspective.

The following morning he awoke with an impulse to flee. It was quarter to noon (this surprised Speth, for normally he was an early riser), so he frantically collected a few items and stuffed them into a small duffle bag. He then phoned the library to inform the director that he had taken ill and would therefore not be able to make his one o'clock shift. His voice was groggy, which only helped matters, and he managed to conclude the call in just under twenty seconds.

While spontaneity had never been his strong suit, Speth embraced it now like a newfound book of wonders, and in less than half an hour he was driving by rote through the streets of the city. Once he reached the interstate, he continued on a westerly route until he passed the dividing-line into North Dakota, where the landscape gradually levelled off to a vast and nearly featureless expanse. Speth's only companion, due to the unreliability of his radio antenna, was an '80s cassette tape, the only one in his collection which had not been mangled by the player. While he had high hopes of making the journey in a single day, he decided not to push his luck. His arrival would coincide with nightfall, and he had little interest in experiencing Vrangr (and his inheritance) in the dark. Therefore, with less than 200 miles remaining, Speth began searching for a motel. The one he eventually decided upon was cheap and rundown, but it afforded him the rest and relaxation he required, even if the mattress was uncomfortable and the exterior vending machine expelled one flat soda after another. None of these inconveniences mattered in light of what awaited him.

The remainder of his evening was spent watching an old film on the outdated television in his room, which presented the fictional world not in its intended black and white but a grainy viridescence that pained his eyes and spirit. He left the set on, for the sound worked splendidly, and merely shifted his focus to the papered wall above, attempting to visualize his inheritance and to resurrect the details of his dream.

He awoke to the disorientation invariably encountered while sleeping in new environs, but this time the sensation never fully cleared. Surveying the unknown room, he was struck by its meticulousness and antiquity. There were framed portraits of various individuals on the walls, and he examined each before venturing to the far window. From the opposite side looking in, he felt certain he resembled the images he had just glimpsed; however, none of the children running about on the yard below took notice. He turned from the window to again peruse the portraits, discovering to his delight that they had completely changed—each now featured Speth standing proudly before his inheritance.

The dream had no small effect, for upon awakening the following morning Speth gathered his things and returned to the interstate as though he had never left. The way he saw it, his waking life was mere interlude to the dream; the long road ahead, a stepping stone to seeing its promise fulfilled. He cruised down the interstate well above the posted speed limit, feeling alive for the first time since his mother's passing. He didn't worry about being ticketed, for he had yet to come across a state trooper or any other traveller for that matter. It felt strange being the sole motorist, but he accepted it all without question.

At a little past noon, Speth glimpsed the first sign for Vrangr. It was composed of wood that might very well have been erected a full century ago. Even the letters appeared chiselled. Veering off the interstate, Speth pulled to the side of the road where he could again study his great-aunt's directions. He rolled down the window and felt the purity of the country air fill his lungs. Relieved to be so close to his destination, he continued ahead, and in less than three miles arrived at a familiar crossroads; familiar because Aunt Torgren had written "thresher" near two intersecting lines on the map, and sure enough there was the rusted-out implement in the corner of an empty field. Speth turned left, and within a quarter of a mile entered a tightly meshed corridor of corn. After venturing down several more adjoining roads, he began to feel as though he had become trapped within a maize labyrinth, of the sort which used to fascinate and unnerve him as a child. It was a disorienting feeling, but only in the sense of being unable to successfully retrace his route to the interstate. If he read the map correctly, Vrangr should only be a few miles distant, though he had yet to glimpse any telltale signs of a town: no church steeple rising above a copse of trees, no water tower, no opposing traffic or wandering souls. Nothing but corn and the dust kicked up by his vehicle, and a growing sense that he had been duped, that the entire enterprise was little more than a hoax.

Upon entering the supposedly final stretch of road, Speth came to an idling halt, wondering if he had followed the directions incorrectly. He contemplated retracing his route, and in doing so shifted his attention to the map on the passenger seat. It, however, was gone. Only a thin layering of dust remained, the outline of which suggested a single sheet of paper. Speth had a hard time believing in its disintegration but for the evidence. Without the map, he knew that finding his way back would be challenging. Then again, maybe Vrangr was closer than he imagined. Perhaps all he need do was continue up this final road. Feeling faint,

Speth stepped outside to stretch and get some fresh air. He glanced across the way, shielding his eyes from the sun.

When his vision adjusted to the glare, he saw the structure. At first he thought it a mirage, but the longer he stared the more distinct it became, until at last it materialized into a lavish farmhouse. He closed his eyes, merely to confirm that his mind wasn't playing tricks. Upon opening them, however, he discovered the truth of the matter. Contrary to his dream, the structure was as equally decayed as the Vrangr sign on the interstate.

Speth eventually broke free of his paralysis and approached the overgrown drive that led to the porch. Considering the overall disrepair of the house, the windows remained intact and the front door appeared solid and functional. There was even a rocking chair on the porch, but Speth saw this as just another detail mocking his dream. With each approaching step he longed for it all to vanish, longed to find himself in nothing more than an endless field of corn. Then again, he had not travelled all this way to come up empty-handed. Perhaps the interior would prove more bountiful. Speth stepped onto the porch and, placing a hand on the rocker, recalled the children of his dream. He turned to examine the weedy expanse, displeased to find nothing but his sun-battered vehicle.

Proceeding into the house, Speth tensed as the structure groaned under his shifting weight. For all he knew, the mere opening of the door had started a chain reaction that would end with him being buried. Regardless, he continued forward, wandering from room to room on the first floor, encountering nothing but dust and the usual detritus of a long-abandoned dwelling. The only thing of substance was the fireplace, which still contained three charred logs and an ample layering of ash. As Speth ascended to the second floor, the creaking stairs again put him on edge. By the time he reached the landing, he felt light-headed and wanted nothing more to do with his "inheritance". Nevertheless, he made a thorough search of each room. Entering the last, he felt dismayed but unsurprised by its emptiness. He shambled to the window overlooking the front of the house and gazed out. The infinite plain of Vrangr spread before

Vrangr

him, but his focus shifted to the lone country road and the man who stood before his vehicle, the man shading his eyes from the sun.

Panic swept through Speth, and his only thought was to wonder if the man saw him there in the second-story window. Just as he was about to raise a pale hand in greeting, the man turned and slipped into his vehicle and in no time drove away.

The figure in the window could do little else but watch the rising dust until it dissipated into thin air.

WRITINGS FOUND IN A RED NOTEBOOK
DAVID SURFACE

AUGUST 12

Entered Nebraska today, crossing the Badlands on our way to Wyoming and the Medicine Bow.

Feeling of great distance everywhere. The space from one point to another feels like the space between stars—you can measure it on maps and charts, even see it on the horizon, but it still takes light years to cross.

Annie read what I just wrote. She said I make this place sound like Mars or some kind of alternate dimension, when it's all just sand and rock. So is Mars, I told her.

Annie says my imagination was the first thing that attracted her to me: my stories, songs, and poems that I showed her on the first night we met back in college. She said no one had ever done that on a first date—I told her that should have been her first warning.

I want to show Annie that I can be practical too. I can set up, operate, and strip down the propane stove. The tent is still hard and takes too much time. If it's late and we're tired (like tonight), we sleep in the car. We could sleep out under the sky if we wanted, but somehow it doesn't feel safe.

Annie's mother used to travel with a gun. I saw it once in the glove compartment of her old red pickup when we were on another camping trip years ago. I was looking for a roadmap when my fingers touched something cold and hard. She told me *any woman who travels alone without a gun is a fool.* I remember saying *But you're not alone; you've got me,* partly as a joke. When I saw the look on her face, I was sorry I said it.

When we were packing for this trip, Annie asked if I thought we should bring any protection. I started to make a joke about her choice of words, some lame crack about condoms, but stopped, knowing it probably wouldn't be funny under the circumstances.

Packed two sleeping bags for this trip and we're still using both of them. I don't know why. I thought maybe it would be different for us out here. I think being alone together like this, *really* alone together, makes us more self-conscious and uncomfortable. Maybe it's too soon. Maybe we just need a little more time.

August 13

Decided to try one of those roads that looks like a dotted line on the map. It was Annie's idea. (*The shortest distance between two points.*) Left the main road around dusk to cut across open land. Tires rumbling over nothing but dirt and rocks. Not really a road anymore—more like the memory of a road.

A half-tank of gas left—should be enough to reach Lusk in four hours.

August 13

Thought we were going to die tonight.

We'd been driving in the dark for a while when I saw headlights behind us. No other cars for miles and it spooked me. When I saw how fast they were closing in on us, I got ready to pull over to let them pass. But the headlights pulled up behind us, right on our tail, filling the mirror and blinding me.

Annie started yelling *what's this guy's problem,* but I knew. He wanted to kill us. We'd crossed over into a place where we had no business being; now he was going to run us off the road and kill us.

I took one hand off the wheel and felt for my knife in

my jacket pocket, wrapped my fingers around it and tried to imagine what I'd do, whether a three-inch blade could stop a man. Our wheels were banging over rocks and rough terrain at seventy miles per hour with this guy right on our bumper, Annie yelling at me to pull over and let him pass, but I kept my foot down on the gas pedal—I knew if I stopped or slowed down, we'd be dead.

When I heard the truck's engine roaring louder behind us, saw the lights leaving the rear-view mirror and swelling past us on the right, I gripped the knife in my pocket and turned to face him.

There, just a few inches outside my window I saw two stick-thin, talon-like hands clinging to the steering wheel, two dead eyes like black stones, a withered, hollow-cheeked face and a toothless gaping mouth that looked like the desert wind was howling through it. I watched this shrunken, ancient vision rattle past us, red taillights fading out like two sparks far ahead.

Took my foot off the gas pedal, we rolled to a stop and sat there, not saying anything. Then a star fell right in front of us. I saw it cross from left to right across the sky right in front of our windshield. It felt like it meant something. Even though I couldn't say what it was, I knew it meant *something*.

Decided to sleep in the car again. Locked all the doors before going to sleep, my knife still here in my pocket where I can reach it.

August 14

Can't find the road. Woke up this morning and realized we're on open range. A few faint lines or indentations visible on the landscape—can't tell if they're old cattle trails or something else, like those canal-markings on the surface of Mars.

Tried looking at the map to find the nearest road, the closest town. All I could see was the jumble of names, the spider-scrawl of highways and roads that go everywhere and nowhere at once; like paint spilled on a flat surface, my mind wanted to run in all directions at once, and I could feel it freezing to keep from coming apart.

Annie asked, *What are we going to do?* I should know the

answer to this question, but I don't. Whatever gene other men possess that allows them to see into the future and figure things out, I don't have. I want to tell Annie this. I want to tell her she'd be better off without me.

Annie says we should keep driving west. I tell her we should turn around and go back where we came from and try to find the main road. She says that's crazy, that if we just keep driving we'll be sure to find a road or a town or something. I'm too tired to argue.

Last night when I thought we were going to die, I started to forgive Annie. The things we do to each other that seem so big and terrible at the time don't really matter that much in the end. Not sure if that's supposed to be a comforting thought or something else.

The earth is changing, like everything is falling away, receding farther and farther into the distance. That's how it looks, but the truth is, nothing is moving away from us— we're the ones who are moving away from everything.

Should have reached Lusk by now. I haven't said anything but I'm guessing Annie must know. I can tell by the sound of her voice, *This doesn't make sense...* The only thing she's said for miles.

The surface of the earth here is cracked, millions of cracks as far as the eye can see, spreading outward in all directions like a spider web or a bullet hole in a sheet of glass. The horizon is a flat line. Not a single telephone pole or power line, not a single tree or bush. Nothing but a flat line all around us in every direction, nothing for the eye to hold onto. Hard to tell the difference between the earth and the sky. Maybe there is no difference.

That's stupid, of course. Everyone knows the earth is the earth and the sky is the sky. Though sometimes, things change places. Like a long time ago, millions of years ago, maybe billions, this whole area used to be covered by an ocean. Miles of saltwater over our heads, vast and terrible creatures moving all around us through the cold and dark.

The fucking car has died. We're stuck here. We should have just kept going. We should have never stopped.

It all started when we spotted something on the horizon four hours ago, some kind of outcropping of rock, miles away. It looked small, like one of those plastic mountains at the bottom of a fishbowl. The closer we got, the bigger it grew, until we saw how big it really was.

It looked like a giant had broken off a piece of mountain range from the surface of the moon and dropped it right at the center of all this flatness. Scalloped ridges and peaks rising into the sky, strange lunar shapes blasted by wind and sand.

Annie and I got out of the car to explore. Strange faded reddish-colored rock, coarse and grainy underfoot. Tried to climb high enough to look around but the rock was too steep, so came back down and got in the car to leave. Turned the key, a few clicks, then nothing.

I should have learned how to fix a car. I should have brought food and water. I should have brought a gun. I should have stayed on the main road. There are hundreds of things I should have done. And I haven't done any of them.

AUGUST 15

Slept in the car last night. Rough sleep full of strange dreams I can't remember now. Annie and I ate some crackers we had in the car and talked about what we should do. Annie thinks we should start walking. Walk where? In what direction?

Tried to climb the rock again this morning to get a better view of what's around us, maybe a building or a fencepost or some sign of people. Climbed as far as we could, but it was too steep; our feet kept slipping out from under us and there was nothing to hold onto.

On a ridge about twenty feet up, found names and dates carved on the rock. *BILLY AND THELMA 1970. MARK AND REBECCA 1968. JOHN AND LINDA, 1962.*

Argued with Annie about trying to walk out of here, but something about all those names carved on the rock made me change my mind.

Writings Found in a Red Notebook

How the fuck could this happen? I don't understand.

Started walking around 10 o'clock, trying to keep the sun at our backs. Annie said that if we kept walking west we'd find something. Annie walking five feet ahead of me, just like the first time we went hiking in the woods. After three hours the sky above was a white blur and I couldn't find the sun. Annie said just keep moving. So I did, scanning the horizon for any kind of object. Three hours later I saw something, a dark blur against the sky that I thought was a storm cloud, but turned solid as we got closer. Another mountainous outcropping of rock, a smaller object on the ground near it. When we got closer we saw it was a car and started running toward it. We stopped running when we saw it was our car.

Don't know how long Annie and I stood there shouting at each other. Annie wanted to blame me. How could she blame me when she was the one leading the way? That was my fault too, according to her. If I'd just stepped up and led the way first, she wouldn't have to.

After a while, Annie stopped shouting and looked like she wanted to cry. I should have tried to hold her and comfort her, but for some reason I couldn't and we went to sleep in the car again without touching.

Strange dreams again. The same one I've been having since I was a little kid. I'm in a big group of people, hundreds of us, men, women, and children camping on the ground, huddled around fires, wrapped in blankets. Some kind of mass migration or evacuation; we're trying to get away from something that's coming—we can't see it but it's very close. There are soldiers with swords and helmets telling us we have to get up and get our things and keep moving if we want to stay alive. I never see the thing that's coming for us, but I know it's there, right behind us, maybe just over the next hill, and I know we have to keep moving.

AUGUST 17

Not many crackers left, not much water either. Hard to tell

what time it is—my watch stopped working today.

AUGUST 18

Found something strange. A small building made of sod, about ten by twelve feet, near the base of the rock. We found it circling around the rock, looking for a better way to climb up to the top. A rectangular opening where a door used to be, no windows, dark and empty, cool inside. Very old and crudely made; must have been built by settlers, though why any human beings would ever want to live here, I can't imagine.

Annie says we should sleep inside this thing tonight, but I don't want to. There's something about it. It doesn't feel safe. How can I tell her that?

Annie says she's sick of sleeping in the car and waking up cramped and stiff. *At least we can stretch out here,* she says. I can't explain to her how much I don't want to do this. I think it's the door. Maybe I'd feel better if there was a door we could close. Or maybe not. Maybe that would make it worse.

AUGUST 18

Slept in the sod house last night. Strange dreams again, the old one about trying to get away from some approaching army. In the dream we need to move fast but there are so many of us and we're weighted down with so many things, clothes, pots and pans, food, small children. Some of us have started leaving these things behind so we can move faster. We leave them on the ground where the enemy will find them tomorrow, like offerings, but even as we do, we know these things will not slow them down. They are gaining and we can't get away from them fast enough.

Woke up from this dream before dawn, light coming from the night sky outside the door, a perfect rectangle of sky and stars.

No more food left, and only a little water. If we tried to walk out of here now we'd die. Our only choice is to wait here till someone finds us.

Writings Found in a Red Notebook

It's not too late. I really believe that. It's not too late for us.

AUGUST 19

Found more carvings on the rock today, higher up, older than the last ones. *JAMES AND NORA GREEN, 1945. NATE AND KELLY JACKSON, 1939. ZACHARY AND BEULAH CARTER, 1898.* What brought these people here? What happened to them?

Heard Annie cry out, a short, muffled sound like the ones she makes in her sleep. Found her staring at something on the side of the cliff. Two words carved in the rock among all the dates and names. *HELP US.*

AUGUST 20

Two days without food. The hunger pains are getting worse—I can only imagine how bad they are for Annie.

I think about what a small thing it takes to throw us off-course. Choosing one line on a map instead of another. Deciding to stop the car instead of keeping going. One wrong move. One wrong word.

Now I think I know what that falling star meant.

AUGUST 21

Three days without food. Looked around for some kind of grass or weeds to eat but the ground is nothing but hard-baked dirt. Remembered seeing dried grass in the walls of the sod house, broke off a piece with a rock and found dried grass running through the baked clay like veins and arteries. Rubbed the chunk of dirt between my hands till most of it crumbled away, then put the grass in my mouth and spit out the mud when it got wet. Tough and hard to chew but stopped the hunger for a while.

The whole time I felt eyes watching us, like we were doing something we were not supposed to do.

Annie and I sat tearing off pieces of the house and crumbling the dirt away between our hands. I looked at Annie and saw the whole lower-half of her face black with mud, hard to look at—saw her staring back at me and realized I must look the same to her.

August 22

Annie refused to eat the grass from the walls of the house today. When I asked her why, she whispered, *Because. They won't like it.*

August ?

Woke up before dawn again from another dream and looked out the door at the stars. They looked different, like some were missing. Then I saw a few stars go out, one after another, from left to right across the sky. Then I realized. Something was moving across the doorway. Something huge, as big as a mountain, was blocking out the stars. Frozen with terror, I closed my eyes and waited. When nothing happened, I opened my eyes and all the stars were back again.

I think I know why we're still here. We're not ready yet. Whatever is going to happen is waiting for us to be ready.

August ?

The car is gone. I went looking for it this morning to see if there might be anything left inside that we can use and it wasn't there. No tire-tracks, no oil stains, no marks on the ground at all.

When I told Annie that the car was gone, she looked me right in the eye and said, *What car?*

August ?

Last night Annie lay down on the ground looking up at the stars, and told me everything. The secrets I was afraid to hear and the ones she was afraid to tell. She told them all until there was nothing left.

When we were through we both lay there on our backs,

not looking at each other, not touching. I heard Annie say, *I'm ready now.*

AUGUST ?

Couldn't find Annie this morning. Thought about the car vanishing and started to panic. Heard a scraping sound and followed it till I found her high on a ledge with a rock in her hand, scratching something into the cliff. I saw the first four letters of my name and tore the rock out of her hand, screaming at her like a crazy man until she ran away crying. I didn't care. I had to stop her before she finished, because I knew what would happen if she did.

Found the rock she'd been using and started scraping away what she'd begun. I scraped and scraped until there was nothing left.

AUGUST ?

My name is James Thomas Franklin. I was born on January 12, 1962 in Frankfort, Kentucky. My mother was Sarah Johnson from Paducah and my father was Mitchell Franklin from Virginia Beach. I have a younger sister named Katherine who grew up to be a social worker in Washington. I met Annie Robbins in college, married her and moved to New York City when I was twenty-four. I worked as a dishwasher, office temp, bookstore clerk, and part-time teacher and I have written and published five short stories and seven poems. I have tried to be a good husband, a good son, and a good brother. All those things will still be true when I am gone. They will not vanish with me, because that is not how things happen. Things do not simply vanish, even though they may appear to. Just because something looks like it's gone doesn't mean it really is. Nothing is ever really gone. Nothing.

Climbed to the ledge right before sunset and used my knife to carve our names into the rock, adding them to all the others, weeping as I did it because I know what it means, even though I still can't say it out loud.

They are coming. I have seen them.

Climbed to the top of the rock this morning for one last look, for one single sign of humanity that might tell us where to go, and I saw them. Annie is waiting for me below but I don't want to go down and face her. She's going to ask me what I saw and what's going to happen to us. What am I going to say? What am I going to tell her now?

I can see them. Coming from far away. They are running toward us on all fours. They fill the horizon like a swarm. Some of them are riding and the creatures they are riding on have human faces.

Please. Help us.

CONTRIBUTORS

Tara Isabella Burton's fiction has appeared or is forthcoming in *Arc, Shimmer, PANK,* and more. Her nonfiction writing on French decadence and the "weird tale" can be found at *Strange Horizons* and *Wormwood* (Tartarus Press), and *Los Angeles Review of Books,* among other places. She also writes for *The Atlantic, National Geographic Traveler, Salon, Guernica* and more. In 2012 she received the Shiva Naipaul Memorial Prize for travel writing. An earlier draft of her first novel, now on submission, was long listed for the 2013 Mslexia Novel Competition.

S. M. Beiko is the author of the YA novel *The Lake and the Library.* When not writing, she attempts to stay warm in the Winnipeg winters, and does editorial and design work.

Based in Buenos Aries, **Santiago Caruso's** surrealist-gothic art has graced many book and CD covers. Visit him at: www. santiagocaruso.com.ar

This is **Ray Cluley's** third appearance in *Shadows & Tall Trees.* He has also been published in *Black Static, Interzone* and *Crimewave* from TTA Press, and there is a story forthcoming in *Icarus* from Lethe Press. His work has featured in a variety of anthologies, including as reprints for Ellen Datlow's *Best Horror of the Year* and Steve Berman's *Wilde Stories 2013: The Year's Best Gay Speculative Fiction.* His story 'Shark! Shark!' recently won the British Fantasy Award for Best Short Story. 'Within the Wind, Beneath the Snow', a limited edition novelette, will appear later this year from Spectral Press, while a collection, *Probably Monsters,* is due from ChiZine Press in 2015. Ray also writes non-fiction but generally he prefers to make stuff up. You can find out more at probablymonsters.wordpress.com

F. Brett Cox's fiction, poetry, essays, and reviews have appeared in numerous publications, most recently in *Eclipse*

Online, New Haven Review, and the anthology *Manifest West: Even Cowboys Carry Cell Phones.* With Andy Duncan, he co-edited the anthology *Crossroads: Tales of the Southern Literary Fantastic* (Tor, 2004). He currently serves as Vice-President of the Board of Directors of the Shirley Jackson Award. A native of North Carolina, Brett is Associate Professor of English at Norwich University and lives with his wife, playwright Jeanne Beckwith, in Roxbury, Vermont, where cell phone service remains unavailable.

Myriam Frey is a Swiss writer, translator and occasional illustrator. A trained architect, she recently rolled up the tracing paper and abandoned the profession in favour of her old love, language. She's currently preparing to go back to university to study Applied Linguistics. Her short stories have appeared in Ambit Magazine, on Paraxis.org and in *Still,* an anthology by Negative Press, London. Myriam lives in Olten, Switzerland, with her husband and two children. You can find some of her work on www.myriamfrey.ch.

Christopher Harman lives in Preston in the UK and is a librarian.

Since his first story in 1992, his work has appeared in magazines such as *Ghosts and Scholars, Supernatural Tales, Dark Horizons, New Genre, All Hallows* and *Postscripts,* and also in books such *as Acquainted with the Night, Shades of Darkness, Strange Tales from Tartarus, Unfit for Eden, The Ghosts and Scholars Book of Shadows, Rustblind and Silverbright: A Slipstream Anthology of Railway Stories* and three volumes of the *Terror Tales* series ("Cotswolds", "East Anglia" and "the Seaside").

The Heaven Tree and Other Stories is a collection of his work that has recently been published by Sarob Press.

Michael Kelly is an anthologist, publisher, and writer based near Toronto, Canada. His fiction has appeared in a number of journals, magazines and anthologies, including *Black Static, The Mammoth Book of Best New Horror,* and *Weird Fiction Review.* As editor, he's been a finalist for the Shirley Jackson Award, and the British Fantasy Society Award. He runs

Undertow Publications, an imprint of ChiZine Publications.

This is **V.H. Leslie's** second appearance for fiction in *Shadows & Tall Trees*. Her other stories have appeared in *Black Static, Interzone, Weird Fiction Review* and recently in *Strange Tales IV*. Her story 'Namesake' has also just been selected for *Best British Horror*. She also writes non-fiction for a range of literary publications and is a columnist for *This is Horror*. She was recently awarded a Hawthornden Fellowship and the Lightship First Chapter Prize. For more details on her work please visit:
www.vhleslie.wordpress.com

Robert Levy is a screenwriter and playwright whose work has been seen Off-Broadway. His dark fantasy/horror novel, *The Glittering World*, is set in Cape Breton and will be published in 2015 by Gallery/Simon & Schuster. Shorter work has recently appeared in *Icarus: The Magazine of Gay Speculative Fiction* and Harper Perennial's anthology *The Moment: Wild, Poignant, Life-Changing Stories from 125 Writers and Authors Famous and Obscure*.

Alison Moore's first novel, *The Lighthouse*, was shortlisted for the Man Booker Prize 2012 and the National Book Awards 2012 (New Writer of the Year) before winning the McKitterick Prize 2013. Her second novel, *He Wants,* will be published in August 2014. Her shorter fiction has been published in *Best British Short Stories* anthologies and in her debut collection *The Pre-War House and Other Stories*, whose title story won first prize in the novella category of The New Writer Prose and Poetry Prizes. Born in Manchester in 1971, she lives near Nottingham and is an honorary lecturer in the School of English at Nottingham University.
www.alison-moore.com

Ralph Robert Moore's fiction has been published in America, Canada, England, Ireland, India and Australia in a wide variety of genre and literary magazines and anthologies, including *Black Static, Shadows & Tall Trees, Midnight Street, ChiZine,* and others. His short story 'The

Machine of a Religious Man' was included in Ellen Datlow's nineteenth edition of *The Year's Best Horror and Fantasy*; 'Our Island' was one of four stories nominated for Best Story of 2012 by The British Fantasy Society. SENTENCE at www. ralphrobertmoore.com contains a wide selection of his writings, both fiction and non-fiction. Moore lives with his wife Mary in Texas.

C. M. Muller lives in St. Paul, Minnesota with his wife and two sons—and, of course, all those quaint and curious volumes of forgotten lore. He is distantly related to the Norwegian writer Jonas Lie, and draws much inspiration from that scrivener of old. In addition to writing, he enjoys the fine art of bookmaking, and has produced three volumes in just that manner. This is his first published story. More information can be found online at: chthonicmatter.wordpress.com

John Oakey is a U. K.-based graphic designer. Some of his work can be seen at www.johnoakeydesign.co.uk

R.B. Russell is an English publisher who runs Tartarus Press with his partner, Rosalie Parker. He has had three collections of his own short stories published, *Putting the Pieces in Place* (2009), *Literary Remains* (2010) and *Leave Your Sleep* (2012), a novella, *Bloody Baudelaire* (2009), and a collected edition, *Ghosts* (2012). He is also, occasionally, an illustrator and songwriter, and enjoys making videos. Two new novellas by Russell have been accepted for publication in 2014/15.

Eric Schaller's fiction has appeared in such magazines as *Sci Fiction*, *Postscripts*, *Shadows & Tall Trees*, and *Lady Churchill's Rosebud Wristlet*, and been reprinted in *The Year's Best Fantasy and Horror*, *Best of the Rest*, *Fantasy: Best of the Year*, and *The Time Traveller's Almanac*. His illustrations can be found in Jeff VanderMeer's *City of Saints and Madmen* and Hal Duncan's *An A to Z of the Fantastic City*. He is co-editor of *The Revelator* www.revelatormagazine.com

Robert Shearman has written four short story collections, and between them they have won the World Fantasy Award, the Shirley Jackson Award, the Edge Hill Readers Prize and three British Fantasy Awards. A fifth collection, *They Do The Same Things Different There*, is to be published by ChiZine later this year.

He writes regularly in the UK for theatre and BBC Radio, winning the *Sunday Times* Playwriting Award and the Guinness Award in association with the Royal National Theatre.

He's probably best known for reintroducing the Daleks to the twenty-first century revival of *Doctor Who*, in an episode that was a finalist for the Hugo Award.

David Surface lives and writes in Sleepy Hollow, NY. His stories have appeared in *Supernatural Tales*, *Shadows & Tall Trees Volume 4*, *The Six-Fingered Hand*, and *The Tenth Black Book of Horror*. He writes a blog on the many sides of horror in writing, film, and life, *Poe's Doorknob* at dsurface.wordpress. com. He is thrilled to be appearing along with so many fine writers in *Shadows & Tall Trees Volume 6*.

Shirley Jackson Award winner **Kaaron Warren** has lived in Melbourne, Sydney, Canberra and Fiji, She's sold many short stories, three novels (the multi-award-winning *Slights*, *Walking the Tree* and *Mistification*) and four short story collections. Her most recent collection, *Through Splintered Walls*, won a Canberra Critic's Circle Award for Fiction, two Ditmar Awards, two Australian Shadows Awards and a Shirley Jackson Award. Her stories have appeared in Australia, the US, the UK and elsewhere in Europe, and have been selected for both Ellen Datlow's and Paula Guran's Year's Best Anthologies.

You can find her at kaaronwarren.wordpress.com and she Tweets @KaaronWarren

Michael Wehunt's fiction has appeared or is forthcoming in such publications as *Cemetery Dance*, *Shock Totem*, and *One Buck Horror*, among others. He spends his time in the lost city of Atlanta. Please visit him at www.michaelwehunt.com

Charles Wilkinson's publications include *The Snowman and Other Poems* (Iron Press, 1978) and *The Pain Tree and Other Stories* (London Magazine Editions, 2000). His stories have appeared in *Best Short Stories 1990* (Heinemann), *Best English Short Stories 2* (Norton), *Midwinter Mysteries* (Little, Brown), *Unthology* (Unthank Books), *London Magazine, Able Muse* (U.S.A.) and in genre magazines/ anthologies such as *Supernatural Tales, Horror Without Victims* (Megazanthus Press), *The Sea in Birmingham* (TSFG), *Sacrum Regnum, Rustblind and Silverbright* (Eibonvale Press) and *Theaker's Quarterly Fiction*. *Ag & Au*, a pamphlet of his poems, has come out from Flarestack. He lives in Powys, Wales.

Conrad Williams is the author of seven novels: *Head Injuries, London Revenant, The Unblemished, One, Decay Inevitable, Loss of Separation* and *Blonde on a Stick*. He has also written four novellas and over 100 short stories, some of which are collected in Use Once Then Destroy and Born With Teeth.

In addition to his International Horror Guild Award for his novel The Unblemished, he is a three-time recipient of the British Fantasy Award, including Best Novel for *One*. His debut anthology, *Gutshot*, was shortlisted at both the British Fantasy and World Fantasy Awards. He has also been a finalist for the Shirley Jackson award on two occasions. He lives with his wife, three sons and a big Maine Coon in Manchester.

Undertow Publications (UP), an independent publisher based near Toronto, Canada. UP is an imprint of ChiZine Publications.

Enquiries can be made by regular post or e-mail, and should be addressed to the editor at:

Shadows & Tall Trees
c/o Michael Kelly, Editor
1905 Faylee Crescent
Pickering, ON
L1V 2T3
Canada

undertowbooks@gmail.com

www.undertowbooks.com